ROSE AND THORN

Black Rose Sorceress Series, Book 2

Connie Suttle

SubtleDemon Publishing, LLC

Copyright © 2017, by Connie Suttle

All Rights Reserved

ISBN: 1634780086

ISBN-13: 9781634780087

This book is a work of fiction. Names, characters and incidents portrayed within its pages are purely fictitious and a product of the author's imagination. Any resemblance to actual persons, living or dead, is purely coincidental.

This book, whole or in part, MAY NOT be copied or reproduced by electronic or mechanical means (including photocopying or the implementation of any type of storage or retrieval system) without the express written permission of the author, except where permitted by law.

Published by: SubtleDemon Publishing, LLC
PO Box 95696
Oklahoma City, OK 73143

Cover art by Renee Barratt @ The Cover Counts

To Walter, Joe, Larry, Lee, Dianne, Sarah and Mark.
Thank you.

Acknowledgements

As always, this book is the result of collaboration. If it weren't for the support of my editor, my cover artist and my beta readers, it would be less than it is. All mistakes, as usual, are mine and no other's.

About the Author:

Connie Suttle lives in Oklahoma with her husband and a conglomerate of cats. They have finally banded together to make their demands, which has proven disconcerting to all humans involved.

You may find Connie in the following ways:
Facebook: Connie Suttle Author
Twitter: @subtledemon
Website and Blog: subtledemon.com

Other books by Connie Suttle:

Blood Destiny Series:
Blood Wager
Blood Passage
Blood Sense
Blood Domination
Blood Royal
Blood Queen
Blood Rebellion
Blood War
Blood Redemption

Blood Reunion
* * *

Legend of the Ir'Indicti Series:
Bumble
Shadowed
Target
Vendetta
Destroyer
* * *

High Demon Series:
Demon Lost
Demon Revealed
Demon's King
Demon's Quest
Demon's Revenge
Demon's Dream
* * *

God Wars Series:
Blood Double
Blood Trouble
Blood Revolution
Blood Love
Blood Finale
* * *

Saa Thalarr Series:
Hope and Vengeance
Wyvern and Company
Observe and Protect*
* * *

Chapter 1

*K*aakos
Sovereign Leader of the Free Nation of Ny-nes

"It is as you said," Venge, my top General, reported. "None of our troops survived the counterattack."

"I see. How wise it was of us to reserve some of our best troops, and to begin training others before the last ones made the journey to enemy lands."

"Very wise," Venge agreed. "The new trainees will be ready soon, my lord. The weapons have been improved, too, or so our designers claim."

"I look forward to the next battle," I responded. "We will eliminate our enemy and live in bliss after, as it is written."

"A most auspicious day," Venge bowed and left my office.

Rose and Thorn

I turned to the window behind me, to gaze into the distance at Ny, the great city beyond my palace. As on most days, a thick, brown haze gathered above it, but that did not concern me.

The inconsequential lives of those dwelling there? They also did not concern me. The enemy's destruction was my ultimate goal; nothing else compared to that.

"I will have your death," I promised the land of Az-ca. "As it should have been at the beginning."

* * *

Past
King's City
Kerok

"Look at this." Hunter set a large book on my desk, atop the paperwork I'd been bent over for the past hour, attempting to work out expenses for the army—what was left of it, anyway.

A first glance at the open pages made me frown at Hunter. "It's blacked out," I attempted to shove the book toward him. I worked on expenses to take my mind off our inability to find Merrin and his sycophantic deserters. They'd disappeared, as if they'd never been. I wasn't naïve enough to believe them dead, though.

"This is *The Book of the Rose*, from your father's library," Hunter's statement drew me away from my thoughts and made me go still. In the past, I'd only read the first chapter. I found it boring and filled with information I'd already learned. I'd forgotten about it immediately, turning to more important studies of war and providing for an army.

"Why would anyone cover the pages with blocks of ink?" I blinked at Hunter.

Chapter 1

"No idea, but every page past this one is the same—blacked out. Solid pages of ink fill the last fourth of the entire book."

"What do you think this means?" I asked my next question.

"Once, *The Rose Mark* wasn't a forbidden book. Do you think that manual was written on these pages, too?"

"I suppose that's possible," I drew in a breath and held it before allowing it to escape. "You know I have the copy that Drenn found in the catacombs," I said.

"I know. I'm glad you finally locked it away—we don't need the Council breathing down our necks and starting rumors we can't quell."

Hunter's words reminded me that we'd only sent half a dozen Council members packing—those Barth said were most dangerous and held the closest ties to Merrin. Aside from aiding a known criminal, they hadn't committed overt crimes. Father had stripped them of their titles and sent them away after they admitted—following Barth's divination—that they'd had contact with Merrin after his supposed demise.

We had eyes on them, now—after they'd returned to their homes. If Merrin appeared to any of them, their lives would be forfeit. Father hadn't told them that; I did. I meant it, too. They'd get a visit from Garkus or Kage—perhaps both. Neither would waste time dealing with traitors.

"Any word from our—ephemeral friend?" Hunter asked cautiously.

"I haven't heard from Kyri. I'm beginning to think she was only a phantom."

Hunter went still this time. "What did you call her?"

I jerked my chin up, my eyes meeting Hunter's. "By the first warrior," I breathed before dropping my eyes to the ink-blackened book before me. "Do you think?"

"It's possible," Hunter shrugged. "You said she told you to send mindspeak. Maybe you should ask."

"I hesitate," I began.

"Ah. The old adage. If you don't, then Sherra could be alive. If you do, she could be as dead as everyone believes she is."

"It's been seven weeks, Hunter, and no word from her. The only good to come out of those weeks is that the enemy hasn't returned to attack us. I think it's only a matter of time, and now that we know they have flying machines, we have to watch the skies constantly."

"I know." Hunter chose one of my guest chairs and sat, allowing his body to sag in weariness. "I think they're working to replace what was lost, and they'll come back even stronger—with more flying machines."

Flying machines. When that information was given to the Council, they were all afraid. The enemy could now fly over the poisoned lands or across water, to drop their bombs directly on the domes protecting the King's City and the farms surrounding it. They were no longer limited to the narrow land bridge as their vehicles were.

If an attack came at night by air, we only had our sense of hearing to alert us to the danger. A terrifying prospect at the very least, and all my loyal officers were discussing ways to deal with the situation.

"At least the enemy camp was obliterated by their own devices," Hunter said.

"Because Sherra saw to it." My words were bitter. "I was busy holding off our own traitorous troops, when the enemy

Chapter 1

sent an infernal weapon against us." I clenched a fist in anger—this was Merrin's fault. He'd interfered and turned many of my troops against me—and the Crown.

He was responsible for Sherra's death—if she were dead. I wanted Merrin's throat in my hands, so I could squeeze the air from his body.

"He will die on sight," Hunter soothed. "Immediately, once he's found. A swift death, my Prince."

"You're right." I felt defeated. Helpless. If Sherra were alive, why didn't she mindspeak to tell me so?

Every day, I floundered against that notion—that if she were truly alive, she'd let me know herself.

If she were alive, there was nothing to prevent it.

"Don't give up, Thorn," Hunter said softly. "We don't know everything there is to know."

"Hunter, every day I'm reminded of how little we do know."

* * *

Present
Sherra

West Cana. That's what they called this land, where Kyri's City lay. Pottles—Doret—said there were a few other settlements farther north, but that they were intentionally remote and well-hidden, so the enemy would never guess at their existence.

It had taken three long months to recover from the poison my body had been exposed to, and another four months to find my strength again. Until that happened, the lessons Kyri taught me taxed my strength. This morning, she'd declared me completely healed and ready for more complicated training.

"Everything is now warmer than it once was," Kyri interrupted my thoughts. She sat on the other end of the stone bench I occupied, while in the distance, below the high cliff where we were, waters of an ocean glittered in an unusually clear afternoon.

"Doret says the same," I sighed. "At least it's cooler here than in Az-ca."

"One of the reasons I chose it," Kyri dipped her chin in a nod. "Without desalinated seawater for the King's City, it would have fallen long ago."

"Who built the King's City?" I asked.

"Someone with vision," she shrugged. "But that's a difficult lesson for another day. Today, we'll travel to one of the northern villages. I want you to meet the people there. Are you ready?"

"Yes," I agreed and stood.

Kyri rose beside me before *stepping* us to another place.

* * *

The village we visited was far different from the one Kyri created. Here, nothing was made of stone or concrete—all was constructed of wood, which was more bountiful where we were than in any place I'd ever been.

In fact, the high hillside behind the tiers of homes was covered in evergreens. The trunks of some were so thick two men couldn't wrap their arms about them.

A man approached as Kyri led me down a dirt-and-cobble street, set amid houses and a small community market, where vegetables and meats were being traded.

Most of the other people barely glanced in our direction before going on with their everyday lives.

Chapter 1

The village could have been Merthis, except the houses and buildings were in better repair—what I could see of them, anyway.

"Kyri," the man smiled at my companion. "I haven't met this one, have I?"

His accent was strange and one I'd never heard before.

"Cole, this is Sherra, a trainee," Kyri smiled at the man. "Already, she is very talented."

"Would you like tea?" Cole asked, motioning us forward. "I just made a fresh pot."

"Of course," Kyri said.

My curiosity threatened to burst into questions; I doubted this man—or any of his fellow villagers—had come from any place I recognized.

We walked onto a sanded and varnished porch, before Cole led us into the small home. Inside, we found a small sitting room and next to that, a kitchen with a table and chairs.

Cole poured three cups of tea while Kyri and I sat on carefully carved chairs at the table. I had the idea that Cole had been expecting two visitors and made the appropriate amount of tea.

"Cole is considered the head man, or leader, of Ketchi," Kyri explained as Cole set our cups before us and took a seat across the table.

"Not bad for someone who was once an enemy of your people," Cole lifted his cup of tea in a salute before drinking.

"He came here when he was seven," Kyri answered my unspoken question. "He, like many others from that country, was born with power. You can imagine what happens to most of those children born there who hold such abilities."

My indrawn breath at what my imagination presented was audible. "They murder children?" I whispered.

"Hmmph," Cole responded.

"Most are tortured," Kyri gave a short answer. "Before they are killed. Their own parents believe they have been spelled or affected by the demons of Az-ca, when nothing is further from the truth."

"Or that their child was secretly taken by the enemy, leaving one of their devil children behind to infiltrate their numbers."

"That's—that's outrageous." I couldn't believe what I was hearing. "How many?" My voice quavered as I asked the question.

"Numbers are growing as is expected, given the circumstances," Kyri shrugged and drank her tea. Following her example, I, too, lifted my cup to drink.

"They think that if they obliterate you, then the possession of their children will stop. That won't happen, of course, but you won't convince them otherwise. The recent attack was only the beginning," Cole observed. "They've recovered ancient technology, and they won't stop until you're all dead."

"How do you feel about this?" I asked after getting my rapid heartbeats to slow.

"If they had any sense, they'd recognize it for what it is— the evolution of the race into beings better able to deal with the climate and poisonous air, which was caused by those who came before us."

"How do you know all these things?" I turned to Kyri. If I touched Cole, I'm sure I'd find power there, although it could be different and feel alien to what I'd already experienced from those in Az-ca.

Chapter 1

"Some of us can still read the old records," Kyri sighed. "I've given Cole access to those. You must understand, too, that I cannot save every child with power from Ny-nes. Only a few are brought here."

"Only a few will react properly to the teaching," Cole said, although he sounded regretful.

I sipped tea while I digested that information. "Does this mean that you've traveled to Ny-nes?" I asked Kyri.

"Yes, but not for the reasons you think, and not in recent history. That is a lesson for a future training session. You have the talent of divination, Sherra. I am going to teach you how to use it to see into other places and people. Once you accomplish that, you won't need to worry where you put your feet when you *step*."

"I will teach you what I—and others from this village— know of the people of Ny-nes," Cole said. "You'll need it when you travel to Ny-nes with Kyri to take down the manufacturing plants."

"But," I argued.

"They'll only send more planes armed with bombs if they aren't dealt with," Kyri snapped. "I know the King forbids it. If he understood what you saved them from seven months ago, he'd be begging someone to go."

"You're calling the flying machine a plane?"

"Short for airplane. It's an ancient term. It seems the population of Ny-nes has learned once again how to traverse the skies, although the flying range of the planes may be limited at the moment, because they've lost the technology to create better solar batteries. Still, what they have spells doom for Az-ca if something isn't done about it."

"They sent the first of the airplanes and the special bombs they'd successfully manufactured against you," Cole went on. "They believe that the one who destroyed those things was also destroyed. They will build more, and improvements will be made, I can assure you."

"We use the term barbarian for them, when normally that term is employed for a group that isn't technologically advanced," Kyri said. "I call them barbarians, because of their backward penchant for murdering their talented children and anyone else that doesn't follow their beliefs."

"This is frightening." I studied the small amount of brown liquid remaining in my cup. "Az-ca's army only knows the enemy wants to kill all of us. These explanations make that notion so much worse."

"Centuries have passed since anyone from Az-ca learned anything about the mindset of the enemy," Kyri breathed. "So much has been lost due to foolishness, anger and jealousy."

"Does it bother you that I killed the barbarian army?" I lifted my eyes to Cole's.

"They are my enemy, too," he replied, his eyes never leaving mine. "Do you think they'd let me live if they knew where I was? It is their desire to attack us, and never the other way around. We don't seek them out, but that has to change if we are to survive."

"I'd ask you to touch him, but I worry the memories he carries of abuse and torture will upset you," Kyri said softly. "They are terrible, and everyone in this village carries something similar. They lean on one another for strength and support."

"If Kyri hadn't found me," Cole shrugged and turned his face away to contemplate his past.

"They also torture and kill those who are like Armon and Levi," Kyri explained. "Same sex partnerships are considered an abomination."

"Are some of those here, too?" I was mentally begging her to say yes—that she'd rescued as many as she could.

"Yes. There are many here who were persecuted and marked for death," she said. "Someday, you will help me in this."

"I may have to change all of Az-ca," I snorted.

"A daunting task," Kyri nodded. "But you must try. You have powerful allies," she added.

"Who may not remain allies, once I tell them what I want," I began.

"It will require a great deal of work, certainly. And there is the issue of the rogue warrior, who still lives."

"Did you see his handiwork?" I blinked at Kyri. "I saw burned and tortured bodies—of those who disagreed with his plans."

"I was aware."

My shoulders sagged at her admission. *You can't save all of them,* Kyri's mindspeak was gentle. *It affects too many things going forward. Had those bodies not been there, Barth would have had nothing to divine to learn of Merrin's continued existence. If you hadn't been there to assist Barth, he would have seen only half of it. Merrin's developed new talents, thanks to Drenn's interference.*

I saw terrible things when I saw Drenn and Merrin, I said.

Wait, you saw Drenn in all that?

Yes.

That's—I didn't expect that. It shouldn't be possible, using divination to jump from one to another like that.

I thought it was from Barth, I confessed.

He should be able to block that from you, even if he knew all of it, Kyri replied. *I think you saw things Barth didn't, and some things Barth may not have wanted you to see. How long were you in contact with the Chief Diviner?*

Moments at best—I pulled my hand away quickly.

"I'm sorry, Cole," Kyri apologized to our host. "I just learned something I hadn't known before—from Sherra."

"You have nothing to apologize for," he waved away her concern. "Want more tea?"

"I would appreciate that," she said.

* * *

Merrin

Some of my allies were beginning to see me in a different light. I didn't care—they were just as dead as I'd be if Wulf or Kerok found us.

We'd stayed in or near the caves I'd used after escaping judgment the first time. The stored rations Drenn had sent to those caves had finally run out after seven months. This forced us to search for other sources of food and necessities. That's why we'd come to an isolated farm—to take what we needed.

"They're villagers," I waved a hand to quell protests from three former warriors, who'd come to help me take food back to the others.

A family of four lay dead outside the pitiful cabin we'd come to pilfer, when they should have been out mucking in the dirt to raise more vegetables. This way, we wouldn't have to worry about the two goats and a scattering of chickens they'd kept for milk and eggs—we could kill those things here and cook them if we wanted, and sleep off the gluttony inside the house afterward, before moving on. In all likelihood,

Chapter 1

nobody would look for the missing family for days, their location was so remote from the nearest village.

"One of you step back to the caves and bring the others. We'll have our feast here," I ordered. One of the three disappeared quickly.

I had fourteen disciples, six of those with their escorts, for a total of twenty to help me wage war against the new Crown Prince and take over the palace—and the kingship. I was an heir, too, after Thorn and my traitorous uncle, Hunter.

King Wulf was dying; Barth could be disposed of along with the others, and I'd have a clear path to rule Az-ca.

I wasn't discounting the army—but I'd already had plenty of success in that area. Many were willing to follow me, especially if they believed the lies and misdirection I was ready to spread among them.

Much of it was information they already knew—that the enemy had developed flying machines. Once I was in charge, I only had to tell them that the solution was to go on the offensive and destroy the enemy, down to the last child.

I doubted the enemy was capable of creating more such weapons—they'd leveled everything they'd had against us and lost, thanks to Thorn's escort and her willingness to sacrifice herself for him and the rest of the army.

I'd visited the enemy camp afterward—there was nothing left, man or machine, in that gaping hole. In my estimation, it would take years for Ny-nes to recover from what happened on the battlefield seven months ago.

Once I was in charge of Az-ca, I'd send the army on a secret mission, one that involved their absence for a few days. When they returned, I'd start the new rumor that the enemy was defeated and Az-ca was now safe.

After that, I intended to see that my friends and allies profited by my leadership. Anyone who thought to oppose me would be outcast or killed, depending on their level of treason.

All it would take was a few well-placed rumors among the population, regarding recent events involving the enemy. That would bring all of them in line and convince them to support me. Wulf shouldn't have allowed Drenn's favorites on the Council to live after stripping them of their titles.

Even if I allowed Thorn to survive the takeover, he'd have no sympathy and nowhere to go, because the army and the population would be mine to command.

"I think goat for supper; keep the chickens until we have eggs for breakfast and then kill them for the midday meal," Querl, my most trusted sycophant, suggested.

"Sounds good," I agreed. "Begin the preparations; we'll eat very well tonight."

* * *

King's City
Kerok
"We're still not sure how many Merrin took with him, or whether they're still alive," Armon handed me a copy of his and Levi's most recent muster roll. "We have as many unattached warriors as we can spare hunting for Merrin, but as usual, there's nothing to find. Querl is one of Merrin's fools, you can count on that, though. Eventually, I think we'll find solid evidence of that."

"We have that testimony from a few who turned themselves in," I agreed and took the papers from Armon's hands. "Father's physician is now treating Linel, too. Says the outlook for both is—grim."

Chapter 1

"Not good news for even your worst enemy," Armon shook his head. "I'm sorry to hear it about both."

"Father's losing his will to live," I admitted, my words bitter. "Drenn's attempt on our lives and subsequent death, followed by the enemy attack while we're fighting our own, made things much worse."

"And the loss of," Armon breathed a heavy sigh.

"Yes."

"We'd all be dead, my Prince," Armon said softly.

"I know."

"We all miss her."

I hadn't told Armon or anyone else in the army about Kyri's mysterious appearance; more and more, I considered it a hallucination. Hunter and Barth were the only ones I'd told, because Hunter had been locked out of my office during the strange event.

We suspected Sherra was dead, and life stretched out before us with an empty, cavernous hole in it to plague our existence.

This time, there were no ashes to bury; no place to stand, reflect and remember. *My rose*, I sent mindspeak. *I miss you.*

As expected, there was no reply.

"Thorn?" Hunter knocked on my study door.

"Come in, Hunt," I called out. He walked in, wearing a frown. "Bad news," he announced. "Merrin and his horde have finally made their presence known. They attacked a remote farm, killed what they thought was the entire family and then feasted on their animals. Two older sons saw them from a distance. Rather than approaching, they ran back to the nearest village and alerted the messenger we placed there. The information just came to us."

"Armon, get troops together and go after them," I stood quickly. "Hunter, tell Armon where to *step*." I clenched my fists—I wanted to go with them. The fucking law forbade it.

"Are you familiar with the village of Pa-sen?" Hunter asked Armon.

"Well enough. We'll get there, my Prince." Armon nodded to me and left my study at a run.

Chapter 2

*A*rmon

Strongest shield, Caral, I sent mindspeak as we dropped low onto a patch of dry grass not far from the cabin.

It's up, Colonel.

It was probably up the moment we'd landed—Caral was no fool and more than dependable. My words were spoken out of habit, I think. "Good. Stay down," I whispered the order. "They can't see us from here." It was true—there was no window on this side of the cabin and Merrin, foolishly, hadn't posted guards outside the small shack.

Levi, Misten, Wend, Marc and six unattached warriors were with us. The scent of cooking meat floated past on the breeze—Merrin and his deserters were having a meal after killing four of the cabin's inhabitants.

Rose and Thorn

Those bodies, two of them small children, lay in the yard—they hadn't bothered to burn them, yet. I could have told Merrin that Querl was as lazy as they came, but neglecting that chore had alerted absent family members to their presence.

"Prepare to level blasts," I spoke softly.

The warriors readied themselves.

"Now," I shouted. I and seven others rose and fired our strongest blasts at the cabin, only to be met halfway by fierce blasts from the cabin itself.

The resulting fireball exploded in between with a terrible roar, almost deafening us and shaking the ground so hard it leveled the cabin and knocked several of my men off their feet. If Caral's shield hadn't held, we'd have died where we stood—on remote ground outside the tiny village of Pasen.

When the smoke cleared, burning remnants of the cabin lay everywhere, while three scorched bodies burned with them. Merrin and the others had escaped, leaving three warriors behind to cover for him and the others while they fled.

* * *

Kerok

"He knew we were there," Armon shrugged. "I don't know how, but he did, and they were ready for us. I'm grateful Caral's shield held, or we'd be dead."

Armon carried the report to me himself, rather than going through Hunter first. Hunter occupied a second chair in my study, as I worked to quell my anger. *How did Merrin know?* This illustrated blatantly what concerned me most—that Merrin had developed hidden talents, which enabled him to stay one or two steps ahead of our best troops and their efforts to find and destroy him.

"There were no windows on that side, or guards placed outside the cabin," Armon explained. "He left three behind to sacrifice themselves, while he ran like the coward he is."

"I worry we'll see more incidents like this one," Hunter interjected. "They have to eat, and it's now evident that they'll kill to do it, rather than settling for theft only."

"I'll entertain any and all suggestions on how to combat this new twist in Merrin's plans, whatever those may be," I growled.

"He wants your place, that's simple enough," Armon said. "His eye is on Az-ca, now, since Drenn eliminated himself from the equation. Instead of being second-in-command as he'd hoped, he now wants everything."

"Merrin probably blames us for Drenn's death, when he put that blasted weapon in his hands to begin with," Hunter snapped. "It's the same as placing something dangerous within reach of an infant, who doesn't realize the thing is dangerous to him, too."

"You knew him better than I, but I agree with your assessment," Armon nodded at Hunter. "You don't start trainees on fireblasts the first day. They have to work up to it."

"Weren says the same thing," I sighed.

"Has he made the decision to take Linel's place?" Armon turned back to me. "I like Weren, so I hope you've been able to convince him."

"I think he'll do it—he has to tie up loose ends and convince his wife that you and the others will keep him protected at the front—when the enemy returns."

Weren, as a warrior instructor, was allowed to marry, once he'd moved permanently into that position. Father had granted permission himself. Weren's worries weren't only for himself, but for the woman he loved, too. Sadly, they'd never had children, as Weren's talents on the battlefield were formidable in the past. A child with Weren's talents would be a welcome addition to the warriors or escorts.

"It's a shame that, well," Armon shrugged.

"That Sherra isn't still here to allay Marta's fears?" I finished Armon's thought. "Every day, I feel the bite of that absence more."

"We've offered Weren a promotion to General, and the option of taking Marta with him, if she wants to go," Hunter said. "I'm not sure about her response, however, because living in a tent after having a permanent, comfortable home in the King's City could be a deciding factor."

"It's certainly not the most comfortable," Armon agreed. "Living in a tent, that is. Even with spare conditions at training camps, having a bed surrounded by walls that don't move with the wind feels like a luxury."

"Noted, Colonel," I said. "Weren promised to let me know tomorrow, and I'll pass the information to you when I hear from him."

"I'd like permission to place a warrior and escort trained in the new method in the larger villages—for protection," Armon said.

"That's a good idea," I said. "Hunter, do you have those village lists from the last census?"

"Yes, but you know how old that information is," Hunter began.

"It's about to be updated," I said. "Armon, I'd like two or three warriors and their escorts for the most-populated areas. Send two to the lesser populated—if we have sufficient troops. I expect new counts from them while they protect the King's citizens."

"I'll put a list of warriors and escorts together, and have it ready for you tomorrow."

"Good. Be here for the midday meal, then—that's when Weren will meet with us."

"I'll have my information ready, too," Hunter confirmed. "Thank you, my Prince. It's far past time that we had new counts taken."

* * *

Sherra

"We call it a mirror shield," Kyri nodded approval as she walked around the shield I'd built. "I can't see you at all."

She'd just taught me how to project the garden where I stood onto the outside of a bubble shield, which surrounded me. "You can let others walk through it, as long as you don't allow them to bump into you. They'll never realize you're there, spying on them."

"I'm more concerned about a group of them walking through at the same time," I responded. "Wait. I have an idea."

"What idea is that?"

"Come inside the shield," I invited. She walked through, so she could see as well as hear me.

"What are you thinking?" Kyri had a small glint of mischief in her eyes.

"What if I form a smaller mirror shield around myself, and attach it to the wall of the first one?"

I demonstrated as I spoke, making the shield and connecting it to the back side of the bubble shield.

"Then what?"

"Well, I roll the shield, of course." I had a swift, giddy feeling as I was lifted up by my own shield and rotated, until I hung suspended over Kyri's head. "You can walk through all you want, now, and you'll never see me or run into me."

"That's amazing—I see only sky above me," Kyri laughed. "It's perfect."

"You're the one who wants to spy on people," I said and rolled myself down again before releasing the second shield.

"Trust me, you'll want to as well, to discover what their plans are," Kyri became serious in a blink. Shoving long, dark hair over a shoulder, her forehead wrinkled as she considered my new talents.

"Perhaps we should plan a trip to Ny-nes," she said after a few moments. "Just to look around. I want to know how extensive their manufacturing facilities are, and what they plan to build in the future. We'll ask Cole for images of a safe place to *step*."

"But I thought you'd been there already—to take the children away," I floundered.

"I didn't go to collect children—not after a while, anyway," Kyri confessed. "The last time I was there, I went to observe the enemy," her voice had gone soft. "The ones I choose now are invited, but they must transport themselves. Cole was the youngest to make the trip. They *step* to the tiled red rose Doret and I showed you. All of them made that journey."

"I barely have that memory—of stepping here after the bomb exploded," I confessed, while allowing the mirror shield to dissipate about us.

"We are grateful you had enough energy left to do it," Kyri admitted. "Doret and I thought you were dead."

Chapter 2

"I thought I was dead, too. The blast destroyed everything else."

"And caused earthquakes and some of the land mass to drop into the sea to the west," Kyri said, a thoughtful expression on her face. "Come, let's go inside—Doret informs me that our evening meal is ready."

Inside consisted of a rounded, concrete structure with only half the top portion peeking above ground; the rest was underground, and even the top was covered mostly with soil and flowering plants.

Half-moon shaped windows were spaced regularly around the top level, to allow natural light into Kyri's home. Nearby, other buildings stood, but all of them were squarely-built and above ground, or mostly so.

One of those buildings, with many windows, held a library. Most of the books there I couldn't read, because in Kyri's words, the written language had evolved and my reading skills couldn't adjust to the differences.

"Letters were reduced to only a line or two, and words to only a few letters, rather than their original, longer forms," Kyri explained to me on my first visit to the library months earlier.

She'd lifted an ancient, leather-bound volume from a table and opened it for me. An image on one page accompanied text covering the opposite page, but the image presented was also of writing—on a document even more complicated than the other.

"What does this say?" I'd pointed at the larger writing at the top of the image, which I had no hope of deciphering.

"I'll tell you sometime—it involves ancient history, after all."

Kyri cleared her throat to draw me back from my memory. "I believe we have fish and fresh vegetables waiting," she said.

Fish. I'd seldom eaten that rare delicacy while living in Az-ca. Fish were scarce in lakes and streams, and what was caught would be sold quickly to those with more money than most villagers would ever see.

This fish came from a large lake nearby, which also supplied some of the water for Kyri's small city.

Within the city, a system was set up to collect rainwater and purify it, using wind or solar power, before pumping it to each building. Kyri said there was no sense throwing away what was given by nature.

"We have a new trick to add to the mirror shield," Kyri told Pottles the moment we walked into the kitchen after washing our hands.

Yes, she was still Pottles to me, and always would be. Doret was just something other people called her.

"Sounds intriguing; tell me," Pottles grinned before motioning for us to sit at the table.

"The food smells wonderful," I told Pottles, before explaining the mirror shield trick I'd developed.

Soon enough, Pottles set plates of fish, carrots and green vegetables down. Kyri and I waited until Pottles was seated before lifting our forks.

"I have information that Merrin escaped by the hair of his ears," Pottles said while we ate. "He and his band of deserters killed a family living in a remote cabin outside Pa-sen."

"Filth," Kyri mumbled. I persuaded chunks of flaky, moist fish to stay on my fork as I raised the food to my

Chapter 2

mouth. I didn't have to speak—Kyri knew how I felt about Merrin.

I'd seen Merrin's handiwork already.

What I wanted to know was how Kerok was dealing with Merrin's threat. The biggest drawback to living in Kyri's City, albeit temporarily, was that nobody could send or receive mindspeak while there, or in Kyri's presence. So far, I'd been in one or the other situation constantly.

I missed Kerok. I had no idea whether he missed me, or was eventually grateful that I'd disappeared and was likely dead. As he was now the Crown Prince of Az-ca, he wouldn't be forced to look for another escort.

He could, though, if he wanted, look for a wife.

"Who almost took Merrin?" I asked. "Before he escaped?"

"Your friends," Pottles said. "Armon, Levi, Caral and several others. They almost had him, but Merrin put his new-found talents to use and managed to get away. Three of Merrin's decoys died when he left them behind to cover his ass."

"Were any of ours hurt?" I now held my fork in nerveless fingers.

"No. Caral's shield held," Pottles said. "They're all fine, just rattled, that's all."

"Thank goodness," I breathed. I worried about all my friends. Worried that Merrin would bring harm to them. That Merrin would attempt to take the throne. That he still had hidden allies in the King's City.

"We're working on all that," Kyri reached out to pat my arm. "Stop worrying so much, all right? This is your time to learn and practice. There is so much to do, once this time is over. Enjoy your rest in the peace of my city."

"Are they taking Merrin's threat seriously enough?" I asked.

"Yes, daughter. They are," Pottles assured me. "There's something that Kyri and I know that they don't, however, and it involves a second forbidden book."

"What book is that?" I asked, hesitating slightly over the word *book*.

"This is Drenn's fault," Kyri snorted. "When you dig through the catacombs, you have no idea what you may find. He found the worst thing down there."

"It's called *Thorn's Book of Advanced Divination Techniques*," Pottles said. "It was held back from everyone and outlawed for a reason."

"Thorn's Book?" My words sounded just as confused as I was.

"The King the current Crown Prince is named after. A many, many times great-grandfather," Kyri explained. "He wrote the book and practiced the art of it. Others, with less than legal intentions, could pervert it to their own uses. It allows one who is suitable, who possesses the slightest talent for divination, to render his deeds invisible to even the best diviners. I believe it's why Barth could only see so far into those two who were murdered at the front. Once you connected with him, you enhanced his power and enabled the both of you to see what Merrin did."

"Does Kerok know about this?"

"Not yet," Pottles hedged. "We should let him know soon, I think. Finish your dinner—it's your turn to clean the kitchen."

* * *

As I put clean dishes away after washing and drying, I considered Kerok, the forbidden book Merrin held, and how much danger Az-ca could face as a result. As I had no idea what, exactly, the book contained, I had no idea how to warn Kerok, even if I could.

It made me wonder if Kyri had a copy of that book somewhere. Was it so dangerous that she wouldn't allow someone she trusted to read it?

Carefully bending to set the metal skillet in its place inside a lower cabinet, I rose with a sigh. When Kyri spoke behind me, I jumped with a yelp of surprise.

"I didn't mean to startle you," she held out a hand. "I've placed a copy of the forbidden book in your room—read it at your leisure. Just remember that passing the information to another is akin to leaving the entire planet open to attack, and placing every living thing in the direst danger."

"You mean it's a secret meant to be kept?" I searched her dark eyes for an answer. They were a deep well of knowledge, but provided no answer for my question.

"That's what I mean," she agreed. "No matter what, never let any part of it escape your mouth or your mind."

"I'm not sure I want to read it, then. Take it back, Kyri. If it's that dangerous, I don't need or want it."

Until that moment, I didn't realize she'd been holding her breath. She let it out slowly, before smiling and pulling me into a hug.

"I just passed a test, didn't I?" I asked.

"With flying colors."

"What does that mean?" I pulled away to ask. "Flying colors?"

"It's an ancient saying," she shrugged. "It means you passed with great success."

"That's all right, then."

She laughed. "I don't actually have a copy of that book, and I only know parts of it myself—spells that could be adapted in some way for others to use. Come on, I can give you the few things I know—those could be enough to deal with Merrin, I think."

"Good. Thank you. That's what worried me the most," I confessed.

* * *

"Adahi and I believe this is what Merrin used to alert himself to someone approaching the cabin," Kyri said.

She'd placed four divination lines around her living space, while coaching me with mind-images.

What I saw through her was a square of light. Anyone breaking the plane she'd constructed about her would alert her to their presence. "If you place it correctly, even someone *stepping* into the space will send a signal to the one who placed the perimeter divination."

"So Merrin knew the moment they set down, and while Armon was instructing Caral to place a shield and the others to fire blasts on his command, Merrin escaped, leaving three of his deserters behind to fight back."

"That's what I think, too," Kyri affirmed. "It's likely he used it to hide from those searching for him these past months, and he'll continue to use it, until he's caught or killed. It won't keep anyone out as your shield will, but he'll know every time that someone has breached his perimeter."

"Do you think there's a way to get past it without his knowledge?"

"I don't know. Have any ideas?"

"Not yet, but I'll consider it."

Chapter 2

"Good. Let me know if you come up with something. Now, it's time for bed. Sleep well; we'll consider other things in the morning."

* * *

King's Palace
Kerok

My dreams were of Sherra, when I finally slept.

In my dream, she stood on one side of a line, surrounded by trees and plants I'd never seen. It looked as if it had been raining where she was.

I, on the other hand, stood at the edge of the boundary between Az-ca and enemy territory. Two unlikely spaces had been joined, it appeared, leaving the enemy lands out. *He's using a perimeter shield*, Sherra told me.

Who? I was just as confused by her words as by our surroundings.

Merrin. A perimeter shield. In Thorn's Book.

My book?

No. An ancestor.

I practically leapt out of bed when a guard pounded on my door, waking me from my dreams.

Barth and Hunter swept into my suite, announcing that three former Council members had disappeared from their homes hours earlier.

Merrin was suspected in the kidnappings, because food and supplies were also missing from every home.

* * *

"I can see Merrin, until the images are abruptly cut off," Barth rubbed his forehead in aggravation.

He, Hunter, several guards and I stood inside Gram Plicton's home, where the disgraced former Council member lived—*until Merrin arrived to remove him.*

"It hasn't gone past me that Merrin chose three, when that's the number of sycophants he lost recently," Hunter remarked.

"I doubt they'll like the new accommodations he'll offer, or lack of beds," Barth muttered.

"Why does he want them?" I asked. "They have no power—how can they protect him?"

"I have no idea—I wish my visions didn't stop short," Barth said. "It's similar to what he did, I suppose, to those two victims at the front. I only saw past the block when Sherra touched me."

"Then I wish she were here, now," Hunter breathed. "This—defies logic."

"Hmmm-hmmm," Barth cleared his throat and cast a glance in my direction.

"Sorry, my Prince," Hunter held up a hand.

"Stop worrying about it," I said. "If there's nothing else to find here, let's go back to the palace. I need tea—or something stronger. Ask Garkus and Kage to meet with me at breakfast."

* * *

"Barth, you once told me you knew of no other book to be banned in Az-ca, other than *The Rose Mark*. Have you ever heard of Thorn's Book?" I toyed with my wineglass while sitting behind my desk.

"There's a biography he wrote in your father's library," Hunter answered first.

"Bring it to me—when you have a moment," I said.

"Why would you want it?" Barth asked.

"No reason. Have you read it?"

"No," Barth shook his head. "I had enough trouble getting through more recent—ah—monarch's information."

Chapter 2

"Want more wine?" Hunter held up the bottle we were sharing.

"No, I want to sit here and think until time for breakfast," I said. "If Merrin can kidnap former Council members, he can kidnap anyone who can't put up a shield to keep him away."

"I'll have Thorn's biography on your desk in the morning," Hunter said.

* * *

"I want every trainee and every warrior taught how to make a shield," I told Armon, Levi, Garkus and Kage at breakfast. I'd ordered Armon and Levi to join me earlier than planned, and they'd brought their escorts with them.

"I suppose we have to learn, too," Garkus' forehead wrinkled as he considered my order. "So I can pass it on to the others."

"Merrin kidnapped three former Council members last night. If you can't shield yourself, he could attack you—admit it."

"He's right," Kage inclined his head toward Garkus.

"Levi and I can show you how," Armon said. "I wish, well, the one who taught us made it so much easier, just by touching the ones she taught."

"I know who you're talking about, and I'm grateful I'm still here to discuss those things with you," Garkus admitted. "The Prince tried to tell me before, but it was only after the last attack by the enemy that I really understood."

"I want warriors trained before they're sent to protect villages," I turned to Armon. "Do you think you can get that done in a few weeks?"

"We can try, but it'll take every warrior and escort with those talents to do it," Armon said.

Rose and Thorn

"Do it. Keep me advised on the progress made. If any show reluctance, let me know. I'll deal with it personally."

"We'll do it for you, Prince Thorn," Caral said quietly. "And for Sherra."

Misten, sitting beside Caral, nodded her agreement. It reminded me that I wasn't the only one suffering in Sherra's absence. There'd never been a memorial—not since I'd had the vision of Kyri in my study.

Was my hope gone, now, that she'd return to us?

Thorn's biography lay on a corner of my desk, waiting for me to open it and read. I'd do that on the weight of a message in my dream.

I still have hope, I sent to Caral. *I don't want to abandon that hope it until a year has passed. If she hasn't returned to us, then we will mourn for her.*

Caral lowered her head, but not before I caught the sadness in her eyes. She and those around her had no hope. They knew nothing of my vision of Kyri. Just thinking of telling them brought home how foolish it would sound.

"Go to work," I handed the census papers Hunter had given me to Armon. "Choose carefully and teach well. Garkus, Kage, accompany Armon to Secondary Camp. Learn whatever you can about shielding and report to me afterward."

"It will be done, my Prince," Garkus rose and bowed. I watched as all of them left my study. They'd go to the garden outside to *step* away; Father's rule concerning *stepping* inside the palace still held.

* * *

Secondary Camp
Armon

Chapter 2

"Yes, that's it," Caral said. Kage was learning how to shield faster than Garkus, and Garkus looked as if he might explode with frustration over it.

Levi had to turn away more than once to hide a smile.

Rain had fallen the night before, so the ground wasn't dusty as Caral and I taught the King's assassins how to shield, while Levi and Misten watched and offered advice.

"Your shield should recognize your blasts, so you can fire through it while still protecting yourself," Levi told Garkus. "Go ahead, fire a weak blast—just enough to get past the perimeter of your shield."

Levi and I knew Garkus' shield was weak. It made me wish for Sherra's presence. I'd probably had that same wish at least three times every day since her death.

We'd lost so much on that terrible day.

"That's fine, but you need to build a stronger shield," Misten strode toward Garkus. "Imagine it is made from the hardest material you can think of. Don't worry, it will still be invisible," she said.

"Do you think Garkus' personal views on women are holding him back?" Levi whispered beside me as Misten worked with Garkus to improve his shield. "He always said shielding was an escort's work."

I considered Levi's words—he could be right. Garkus hadn't taken his defeat at Sherra's hands very well. Rumors said that Garkus voiced them aloud to Thorn afterward, trying to shame the Prince regarding his concern for her.

Only after she died while destroying the enemy's army did Garkus concede that Sherra's talents were formidable.

I could only imagine how things would have gone had Garkus taken on the enemy single-handed.

Az-ca's total obliteration came to mind.

"I hope the rest of our training doesn't go this slowly," Levi mumbled. I had to turn away to hide a smile this time.

* * *

Ketchi

Sherra

"You must understand that the last time I saw any of this was fifty-three years ago," Cole said. Kyri had taken me back to Ketchi the following morning, to learn about the enemy from Cole.

He'd drawn a map on paper Kyri brought to him; it now contained images dredged from his memories as a child of seven. That meant he was now sixty.

"I imagine these facilities are much larger at present," Kyri sighed as she studied the oblong buildings outside what Cole described as a large city, covered in dust and dirty air.

"The farms are much farther out," Cole said. "In my memory, you understand. "Away from the dirty air. The plants don't get enough sunlight otherwise, I think."

"What makes the air dirty?" I asked. The thought brought images of what dust storms looked like in Az-ca.

"They burn coal and some wood. They used to have a liquid fuel, and it's my guess they've found more of it, to partially power the airplane they sent to Az-ca," Kyri said. "I doubt solar power would get the heavy thing off the ground without some sort of help."

"They may have found a way to make the liquid fuel," Cole offered.

"That's possible," Kyri agreed. "What matters is that they may have it, and can fuel more airplanes to attack."

"Where does the coal come from?"

"They're digging up their entire country, looking for more of it," Kyri sighed. "Large, open pits are everywhere.

Chapter 2

Prisoners are sent to some of the poisoned lands to extract coal from there. As you can guess, they don't live very long."

"They must have children more often than those in Az-ca," I ventured.

"Yes. The birth and death rates are high, and often occur within a matter of days, one from the other," Cole explained. "There were seven children in my family still living, after four had died in infancy. Women have no rights, especially in choosing how many children they birth. The laws prevent it."

"Women have no rights at all," Kyri huffed. "As bad as it was for Cole being born with power, it is much, much worse for a female."

"They're tortured publicly, and the screams," Cole shuddered.

"Some of them as young as three." Kyri rose from Cole's table and walked toward the front door. It was open, so she stood there, looking out at the street beyond.

I sat there, frozen in horror.

Children. Little more than babies. What sort of monsters were they?

"You're right to call them barbarians," Cole said softly. "I don't feel I'm a part of them. I never really did. I was born outcast; I just didn't know it until I was six and accidentally made fire when I couldn't get the fire started in the cooking stove. My own parents handed me to the authorities, who placed me in the lockup immediately."

What I considered betrayal by my father—for ignoring me after I was tattooed, couldn't compare to Cole's experiences. If Kyri hadn't invited him to come to her, he'd have died at age seven. All for something he'd been born with and had no choice in the matter.

Rose and Thorn

"Kyri says we can't save them all. It still makes me angry that someone could be so cruel." Cole rose from the table this time, carrying his empty tea mug to the sink. I watched as his shoulders sagged afterward—these were difficult memories for him to recall.

"I'm going to teach you how to make blasts—and other powerful weapons," Kyri was back and placing a hand on my shoulder. "Then, we'll travel to Ny-nes, spy on their facilities, and make a report to your Prince Thorn—not only concerning their movements, but what we've learned about Merrin and a certain, forbidden book, too."

Chapter 3

Sherra

"Go ahead—there's nothing inside it and it's falling down, anyway," Pottles grinned as I studied the structure before us.

Kyri stood yards away, deep in thought while Pottles urged me to destroy the abandoned building.

Closing my eyes, I practiced divination as Kyri taught me, going from empty room to empty room inside the wood-and-brick building.

As Pottles said, there wasn't anything there, and the roof was slowly caving in. I even checked for an underground room and found nothing.

Gathering the knowledge I'd gained from contact with Kerok, Levi, Armon and other warriors, I built my inner fire. Opening my eyes, I released it.

Rose and Thorn

If I hadn't held a shield around the three of us, we could have been fried by the explosion and subsequent blowback; it pounded against my shield, mixed with fire and detritus from the massive blast.

When I could see and hear again, I found Kyri standing before me, unsure whether to laugh or frown.

"You may want to gauge your fireballs better," Pottles walked up to join Kyri, although her expression was firmly on the frowning side. "That one would have leveled all of Kyri's City, I believe."

Kyri turned to look at the leveled area around us—and it was leveled. Any unevenness in the ground was now forced flat and devoid of any plants, grass or weeds. "If we need ground cleared for building, we know who to call," she said dryly, planting fists firmly on her hips.

"You learned that from watching the warriors?" Pottles asked, her frown slipping away.

"I learned it by touching them and reading their fire and ability," I admitted.

"The same way she showed them how to shield themselves," Kyri shrugged. "We'll work on tempering your blasts to the job at hand," she said. "Let's go home. I need tea."

"I think the blast sent dust a mile away," Pottles said before we left the site. "Dust was all that remained, you know. There's not a single splinter or chunk larger than a grain of sand left."

"That's rather unnerving," I said as Kyri *stepped* us away.

* * *

Kerok

Chapter 3

"We have reports that two sheep and several baskets of fresh vegetables disappeared last night, roughly the same time that three former Council members disappeared," Weren sat heavily on an empty chair at the small table in my suite.

"From the southern-most domes?" I asked. It was something I'd do if I were Merrin—send a few to take food from the best-known quality source, after the failure at a recent remote cabin. That, combined with what they'd taken from the Council members' homes, would last for a few days, at least.

"Yes. I heard it on my way in," Weren explained. "I believe Hunter is speaking with the messenger now."

"Then I'll have a written report soon enough." I wanted to curse, but what good would that do?

"I've decided to take the position, if you still want to give it to me," Weren said. "I only ask that you allow my wife to stay with me whenever I'm at Secondary Camp, or any other place with four walls and a real bed."

"I'll grant that, General. You'll do my army proud."

"I'd like to begin working on the problem of stolen food and disappearing former Council members who will probably convert to Merrin's cause," Weren said. "With your permission, of course. And more than anything, I'd like to learn how to shield myself, since I won't have an escort assigned."

"I'll see to it. At the moment, Armon, Levi and their escorts are training Garkus and Kage to do that very thing. You can go today or tomorrow, learn what they can teach you and have a meeting with both to determine how to proceed in combatting the Merrin conundrum."

"I'll leave tomorrow morning, after I learn what the official report is from Hunter, if you don't mind."

"Of course. I'll have Hunter include you in all written records pertinent to your position. Have your staff here transport anything you need to Secondary Camp—either *stepping* it or by vehicle."

"I'll get it done," Weren nodded.

Two servants arrived with food, so we began to eat while we discussed current events and what the enemy could be planning before making their return.

* * *

Sherra

"I have a question," I said while having tea and honey cakes with Kyri and Pottles.

"What's that?" Kyri lifted a dark eyebrow as she studied me across the table.

"Which one of you is the phantom?"

Kyri and Pottles turned to blink at one another. That's when I knew it was neither of them.

I can't explain why, but the fine hair on my arms rose, and a tingling of fear chased down my spine.

"I've only seen him a few times," Pottles lowered her eyes. "The last time, he brought Veri to me. I was so angry at what I saw in her, I slapped her. He ah, seemed satisfied with that and took her away."

"She was found dead," I breathed.

"As they all are," Kyri admitted. "It is not our doing, Doret's or mine," she added. "Adahi goes his own way and follows his own counsel. He is always right, though, when he brings death to someone."

Chapter 3

He scares the hell out of me, Pottles informed me in mindspeak. *Always covered in a dark cloak, with only his mouth visible when I see him, most of the time.*

"I've never heard that name before," I said aloud. "Adahi?"

"It's a variation on an ancient word from a race nearly extinct. The word, in its original form, means poison," Kyri said. "Adahi seldom speaks at length when he comes; at times, he brings me the ones he's marked for death, as if asking for my approval. They are the worst he carries to me, for various reasons, and I always agree with his sentences. I record the names and deeds of each in a book of records for my library."

"So Veri's name—and the Bulldog's—are in your records?"

"They are."

I shivered at her words. I'd imagined all along, since I'd wakened in Kyri's City, that she or Pottles had to be that silent enforcer. To learn it was someone nobody really knew—that was frightening.

"We believe he is held back from tracking Merrin by the very things that prevent us from finding the bastard," Pottles grumbled. "I think we'd have seen Merrin dead by now, if that weren't the case."

"At least Drenn is dead." I still felt anger that he'd participated in Ura's downfall, and may have done the same thing on other occasions.

"I believe Drenn was marked by Adahi, but, like me, believed the Crown Prince needed to stay in that position and leave Thorn with the army. You see how Drenn's meddling destroyed that plan," Kyri didn't sound pleased. "When Adahi took down the assassins who acted as Drenn's conspirators, that act was designed to keep Drenn on the right side of the laws—at least for a while."

"And it would have worked, except for Merrin's meddling—again," Pottles huffed. "Drenn was scared of his own shadow by that time—as he should be, lying, scheming prick that he was."

I didn't argue with her assessment—I felt the same, although I wouldn't use those exact words, perhaps.

"Have you had time to think about how to get around Merrin's perimeter divinations?" Kyri asked, changing the subject.

"I've been thinking about it, but so far, a workable solution hasn't come to me."

"Keep working on it, then. Whatever you devise, we'll put to a test."

"You won't mind if I erect my own perimeter divination?" I asked. "Just to study it?"

"No. I wouldn't have shown it to you, otherwise."

"Good. I'll set one up outside the garden walls, then. One more thing—how difficult would it be to find something Merrin has touched or—blocked from divination?"

"Not impossible," Pottles considered my request. "Difficult, perhaps."

"Do you have something in mind?" Kyri expressed interest.

"Just that when I figured out how to allow someone or something through my shield, I had to convince my shield that those things were a part of it. If I study Merrin's power in an object, since I can't touch him and have no desire to ever do so, maybe I can duplicate his power well enough that his perimeter divination will let me through."

Chapter 3

"Now there's the brilliance I was hoping for," Kyri laughed. "We'll find something for you—but it may take time and deviousness to do it."

"I'll go try my hand at a perimeter divination, then," I dusted honey cake crumbs from my fingers and stood.

"I'll take care of the dishes," Pottles waved me away as I reached for my plate and cup. "Go do whatever it is you need to. That's more important, I think."

"Then give me something of yours—something you don't care about, that holds enough of your power signature in it," I said. "For experimentation, you understand."

"Go put up your thing, girl. I'll be out in a while after I've had time to look." Pottles shooed me toward the back door.

* * *

Merrin

"You have your own army, you just don't realize it, yet," Gram Plicton informed me. He'd been one of Drenn's closest advisors—in secret, of course. His decision to keep that secret was the only reason he wasn't sitting in the lockup with several others.

"What army is that?" I asked. I had a few sympathizers left in the army, but not many; Thorn had burned power out of most of them already.

"I'm not talking about the King's army," Plicton scoffed at my question. "I'm talking about every man, woman and child who lives outside the King's City. Or have you not bothered to realize the vast difference between those who live inside and outside the domes? It may as well be another country, out there. A really poor one, too. Promise them wealth or a better life, and they'll flock to you. Those bleeding hearts in the palace won't kill them if they attack—

because they're too soft and won't recognize the immediate threat."

"That's fine, but it sounds like an extended war if we go that route. Thorn will figure it out eventually—he has messengers and informants in many villages, who'll send word if we attempt what you suggest."

"Oh, I have a plan for that," Plicton said. "Is there any more tea?" He looked around at the others.

We'd taken an abandoned shack roughly thirty miles from Secondary Camp—weather farther south was becoming unbearably hot, and here it was cooler, at least.

"Bring tea," I barked at one of the six escorts. She turned to do my bidding—as she should. One of the others was busy holding a shield over our heads; clouds were coming in and rain could fall through multiple holes in the roof.

Outside, I'd placed another perimeter divination—that trick had saved lives last time, and kept us away from those who'd sought us in the past. "What's your plan?" I asked as Plicton's cup was refilled.

"There are two medical outposts between the battlefield and the King's City. I say we take both—you have enough warriors with you to take down anybody there with power. The others will be washouts and drudges, who'll do what we say or die for their resistance. We then fill both camps with hostages from one village or two, and challenge the King to take them back. While he and Thorn are working on that problem, we sneak around, village to village, tell them Thorn is holding the people against their will in these army outposts, and start a revolt."

"How will we convince them of that?" I snorted in disbelief.

Chapter 3

"Leave that to me. Who do you think they'll believe—a Council member who has first-hand knowledge of Crown Prince Drenn's murder at the hands of his brother, or the new Crown Prince, who is only waiting for his father to die so he can rule? If we add that Thorn intends to demand more taxes from Az-ca's citizens, you'll have them begging to follow you. If Thorn turns the army loose on rioting citizens, it'll only prove our point in their eyes."

"And we won't give a damn if the citizens are slaughtered," Blane Grove, another of Drenn's cronies, spoke up. "Less for you to worry about, when you take over the King's City."

"Not bad for somebody who only had dreams of taking over the army," Derk Beadl chuckled as he handed me a bottle of wine. "Something to celebrate your new position—it's as good as done."

* * *

Sherra

A catalpa leaf sailed past me as I sat on the rock wall surrounding Kyri's garden. The wind had lifted it up and sent it flying along, before depositing it on the grass outside the perimeter divination I'd constructed.

Pottles said the leaves were heart-shaped, but they didn't resemble any heart I'd ever seen. This one, buoyed by the wind, had sailed quite a distance from the tree it had grown from.

It made me think of the airplanes of the enemy, and what kept them aloft. Sliding off the rock wall, I walked toward the leaf and lifted it from the ground. If I dropped it, without the cooperation of the wind, it would fall straight down or nearly so.

Rose and Thorn

If I made a shield the proper size and thickness, would it sail on the wind?

If I sealed a bubble shield, would it float on water?

Merrin and Kyri had built their perimeter divinations to alert them to anyone passing through. I'd modified that design, making it possible to destroy anyone or anything my perimeter divination didn't recognize as friendly. Not only was it an alarm system, it was also a protection system.

Making my way back to the wall, I set the catalpa leaf down and lifted Pottles' small, pale-yellow shell—one of two things she'd brought me for my experiments.

Things like this may no longer exist, Pottles told me as she placed it in my hand. It fit in my palm and felt thin—delicate. I worried I'd destroy it. *It's called a miracle shell,* she added. *I've had it for a very long time.*

A miracle could be needed to keep it intact. It was the best of the two things, perhaps, that held enough of her power signature for me to use. She was quite careful with most other things, and hadn't formed attachments as she had with this.

One day soon, I'd ask her again about the red rose on her left wrist. She'd put me off when I first asked after my waking in Kyri's City. The idea that the red rose belonged to a murky and forgotten past hadn't left me; it had grown stronger, instead.

All the time I'd known her when I was younger, she'd hidden the rose from me with power. Perhaps when she told me about the red rose, she'd tell me more about her sister, too—the one who'd died serving Az-ca's army; the one whose death made Pottles angrier than anything else I'd ever seen.

You're wasting time, I informed myself. Settling into a comfortable position, I closed my eyes and delved into

Chapter 3

Pottles' power and visions in the shell, hoping to learn enough to pass it through my perimeter divination without setting it off.

Had I wanted to know about Pottles' sister?

Here was that memory, in full.

* * *

If I'd known I'd become a silent, invisible observer in a tragedy, I'd have backed away immediately. At least I only saw Pottles' memories, and not those of her sister, Daria.

Daria was beautiful and powerful, and I felt guilty for my intrusion into Pottles' recollections. I found myself in the King's palace far in the past, when these sisters were young.

"Who will you choose?" Doret, already a Queen, asked Daria.

"Marra has my heart," Daria replied.

Marra? That was a woman's name. My breath caught. *How? Was it possible?*

"She'll be the luckiest warrior in the King's army, then," Doret smiled at her sister.

The images shifted then—to the King's Council, where a new crop of trainees, Daria included, were making choices. Standing beside the King was another man. Straight and tall, he'd be handsome except for the cruel twist to his mouth.

The King's son.

Doret wasn't old enough to have birthed this one.

The King had been married before. Perhaps his first wife was dead and he'd remarried. Regardless, Doret stood on the King's other side, smiling at the trainees and her sister in particular.

"Father, I wish to claim Prince's Privilege," the King's son stepped forward.

Somehow, I understood that he was Prince Commander of the Army. He was also the King's eldest child, as well as holding the title of Crown Prince.

When had things changed?

Turning toward Doret, the Prince's smile turned vicious. "Which trainee do you choose, my son?" The King asked.

"I choose Daria," he said.

The weight of Pottles' grief at that moment threw me out of her memory, and I found myself gasping for breath atop Kyri's garden wall.

* * *

King's Palace
Kerok

"How goes the search for Merrin?" Father asked. The physician had coaxed him into rising from his bed to sit outside in his garden.

He hadn't been outside in a month.

Cursing the disease that robbed him of his strength and made his body frailer every day would be useless—but I did it silently anyway.

"We're catching up to him," I said. I still hadn't told Father about three former Council members who were now missing and likely entrenched in Merrin's camp. Father would see that as a failure on his part to deal appropriately with the situation earlier, and it could bring further harm to his fragile health.

"Good. You know what to do when you find him," Father rasped.

"How's your tea? Do you need it warmed?" I could do that easily, with the power I held. In freezing weather, a warrior was never cold. I could melt snow with my bare footsteps if I chose to do so.

Chapter 3

"I could use a warmup."

I rose from my chair and placed heated hands around Father's cup. "There. That should do it," I smiled at him.

"Drenn always envied you—far too much."

"I know the Crown Prince is never allowed on the battlefield, but I believe just one visit during a battle would have convinced him he was much better off where he was."

"I never went," Father shook his head. "Perhaps you should rethink some of the laws when you, ah," he didn't finish.

"Father, you are still the King and we won't discuss those things until later."

"Thorn, I won't recover," he told me dryly. "We both know that."

"I know." I bowed my head as grief threatened to overwhelm me. Father was always there, secure in his palace and his position, while I'd fought the enemy for years. Life without his constant presence would be more difficult than any battle I'd ever fought, except, perhaps, for the one in which Grae was lost.

And the one where Sherra was lost.

She'd been so far away when she fought her last battle. There wasn't a body to carry off the battlefield; no ashes to bury. Had I lost all my hope that she'd return? Had she died without anyone to stand beside her?

You're thinking morbid thoughts, aren't you? Hunter arrived and bowed to Father while sending mindspeak to me.

"Have a seat, Hunt. I'll pour tea," I motioned him toward an empty chair at Father's outdoor table.

Have you had time to read the book? Hunter asked as I poured a cup of tea for him.

It's next on my agenda, I replied.

Still don't want to tell me why you're interested in it suddenly?

No.

Why?

You'll think I'm an idiot. I think that already; I don't need a second opinion.

Hunter drank tea to hide his smile.

All right, it was a dream, I snapped in mindspeak. *Sherra told me about Thorn's book. It's nothing other than wishful thinking.*

That's an odd dream to have, Hunter responded.

And that's why I asked you about the fucking thing.

"Touchy," Hunter waved a hand as he spoke aloud.

"What are you two discussing?" Father asked.

"Reading material," Hunter answered. "An old, dry biography on his namesake, King Thorn."

"Is that all?" Father snorted. "You probably should have read it long ago. I know Drenn did. He was likely searching for something your namesake did wrong, so he could hold it over your head."

"When did he read it?" Hunter was suddenly interested.

"Probably a year before he died. Maybe more—I don't remember exactly when it was. I found him at this very table, reading it. I was surprised, because he seldom read anything, including new laws and the changes to old ones."

"I can have Barth send someone to get it for you," Hunter offered.

"Go. Read." Father waved a hand. "Hunter and I can talk, now."

"All right." I rose from my seat and walked away from them.

* * *

Chapter 3

Sherra

I'd covered Pottles' power with my own, in an attempt to get the shell through. My thought was that if I could convert the shell in that way, it would pass through the perimeter divination field without any harm.

Still, I worried I'd destroy it, and I wanted to delve further into the information it carried.

When I was past the fright and upset my first visit generated.

"Here goes," I whispered to the shell in my hand, tossing it lightly toward the nearest perimeter divination wall.

It sailed through without a hitch, landing on the soft spot I'd carefully laid out for it, so as not to harm it in any way.

Releasing a pent-up breath, I worked to calm my nerves. *Now, to try it with something I hadn't spelled to exude my own power.*

I took the second object Pottles gave me—a small stone she said she cared nothing about. I hadn't handled it as I had the shell.

I had no idea what memories it carried, and had no desire to learn.

Retrieving the shell first, I laid it gently on the wall before tossing the stone through. An alarm screamed through my mind, making my head hurt and blasting the stone to dust.

* * *

Kerok

Trust Drenn to dog-ear the pages instead of using a book mark. The third page was dog-eared, as was every other page in the entire book, until those creases ended with the last dog-ear he'd placed, roughly three-quarters of the way through.

Curious and annoyed at the same time, I flipped the book open to that page and unfolded the crease, wishing I could remove evidence of the folds in all the pages.

"Fuck."

Drenn had taken a pen and underlined a sentence or two near the bottom of that page. He knew better than to mark up any book from Father's library.

The words he'd underlined caught my eye while I considered Drenn's misdeeds.

My book of Advanced Divination Techniques will go with me when I die, King Thorn had written. *I have ruled it forbidden; it shall never be used by another, except that he be of royal blood and name.*

Kyri's visit, imagined or not, came roaring back to me then. Drenn had gone looking in the catacombs. He'd found *The Rose Mark* that way.

Had he found Thorn's Book, too? The one he wrote concerning advanced divination? I never knew it existed. Thorn himself, in the passage Drenn underlined, said it shall never be used by another, *except that he be of royal blood and name.*

Drenn.

Drenn, having no power or ability to use the book himself, had handed it to the one who *could* use it.

Merrin.

I lifted my eyes from the book, expecting to find empty space between my desk and the door.

A hooded figure sat there instead. I hadn't bothered to put up more than a small, personal shield around me, and

Chapter 3

whoever this was had *stepped* straight to the perimeter of that shield.

"Who the fuck are you?" I snapped, standing in anger and preparing to level a blast if he threatened me or anyone else inside the palace.

"Do not fear." His voice was deep. Commanding. He lifted a hand, palm outward, attempting to show he meant no harm.

Slowly, carefully, he lifted the other hand and lowered the hood.

Dark eyes met mine. Dark hair—long and braided, fell over one shoulder. "I am called Adahi," he said. "You call me the phantom, for lack of a better term," he added.

"It's too bad you're only now piecing this together," he nodded toward the book on my desk. "Your brother was far ahead of you in this, and now a dangerous book is in the hands of someone who should never have touched it. He, too, has royal blood, as you well know, but the temperament to rule is far beyond him. All of this, of course, is because of one missing word."

"A missing word?"

"In the spell," Adahi shrugged. "King Thorn should have written *except he be of* my *royal blood and name.*"

"Why would that make a difference?" I demanded. I sent mindspeak to Hunter, to send guards to my study.

Those unspoken words rattled inside my skull and stayed there, as if caught in a vortex.

"My royal blood and name?" Adahi repeated Thorn's words. *My* royal blood. *My* name.

"Fucking hell." I covered my face with both hands.

Chapter 4

*K*erok

"His name is Adahi? What kind of name is that?" Barth asked.

"He didn't stay long enough to explain it," I snapped. Barth and Hunter had come running the moment I could get mindspeak to them, which was the moment Adahi disappeared from my study.

"At least we know who the phantom is," Hunter pointed out. "It doesn't make me feel safer," he raised a hand to halt my protests.

"He could have shown up months ago, to tell me Merrin has a forbidden book," I growled. "Although it wouldn't have helped us much, since we have no idea what the book contains or how Merrin is using it."

I still hadn't told them that somehow, the book had been meant for me. I felt obligated to read all of Thorn's biography, now, to search for other clues regarding the missing divination book.

"Fuck," I said aloud, when I realized I should have shouted a question at the phantom—Adahi. He could know whether Sherra was alive.

He'd rattled me so much, appearing as he did, that my reasoning had deserted me. What I'd learned, though, *aligned directly with my dream of Sherra.*

My ancestor—Thorn's Book.

The book meant for me. Sherra warned me in my dream that Merrin had the blasted thing. "When's the last time we had a diviner with dream-visions?" I asked Barth.

"At least forty years," Barth answered. "I met him before he died. He said he dreamed of your birth. At the time, you were preparing to take over the army. He said he saw that, too, in his dream."

"Did he say anything else? About my birth?"

"He said you'd be strong. That's all."

I studied Barth for a moment. "You felt as though he were holding something back, didn't you?"

"At the time, I ignored it," Barth shrugged. "Perhaps he saw that you'd be Crown Prince one day, and that is something that should never have been repeated, as you well know."

"You're right," I agreed after considering his words for a moment. Neither Father nor Drenn—*especially Drenn*—needed to hear anything of the sort. Drenn may have sought my death sooner and more diligently, if that information were given by a reliable source.

"I find myself wishing he were still alive," Hunter observed. "I think I'd like to speak with him about recent events."

Chapter 4

"Hunter, where in the catacombs is King Thorn buried?" I asked, changing the topic.

"I'll find the map in your father's library and bring it to you."

"That map is in Drenn's suite—with his other things," Barth interrupted. "I found it when I went through everything, and left it there, in case your father wanted to go in there, sometime. I've had Drenn's suite shut and locked since I went through it."

"Shall we go get it, then?" I asked. "I find myself wondering more and more about my namesake, and I'm concerned by the damage that may have been done to the catacombs by my departed brother."

"Certainly. It's time, perhaps, that you went into Drenn's suite," Barth said. "Your brother had many things that belonged in the library, or in the treasury, or in your father's suite."

* * *

"The box of gold coins is missing," Barth hissed as we took in the ransacked mess that now remained of Drenn's suite. Merrin had been here, no doubt, and that angered me more than anything.

"How much?" Hunter asked, pulling his usual scrap of paper from a pocket to write on.

"At least a thousand coins," Barth replied. Across Drenn's bedroom, drawers had been pulled out and upturned, clothing scattered and personal items were missing. Even the mattress had been flipped off the bed, to search beneath it, I was sure.

The map to the catacombs, however—Merrin had no real use for it, and so he'd left it behind. It lay on the floor near Drenn's bed, half-covered by a shirt Merrin didn't want, because he never thought he looked good in red.

"Send for Armon and Caral," I turned to Hunter. "She can place a shield about this room and keep anyone from *stepping* inside it. We'll have her place similar shields around the library and the treasury. Merrin needs to learn that we can block him if we want."

"I'll send mindspeak now," Hunter nodded and scribbled more on his scrap of paper.

Less than half an hour later, Armon and Caral arrived and were ushered into Drenn's suite by Garkus.

"What happened here?" Garkus looked around in surprise.

"Merrin," I said. "Caral, I'd like you to place shields around this suite, the treasury and the library, please, that nobody can *step* into."

"I can do that," she agreed. "I assume it will only be you, Hunter or Barth allowed to go into any of them?"

"Yes. If that changes, I'll let you know. Set it up this way for now, and we'll shut the door again on this mess." I swept out a hand to indicate my brother's quarters. I should have guessed Merrin wouldn't be finished with Drenn—or the rest of us in the palace.

"I'll take you to the other locations, once you're done here," Hunter nodded to Caral.

"Thank you for coming—both of you," I told Armon and his escort. "I didn't know who else to call."

"We are always at your command," Armon said. Silently he added, *Will you be safe enough? This is frightening.*

I keep a shield around me at all times, I replied. *And for this and other things, I'll see to it that Caral gets a promotion.*

Chapter 4

Thank you—it is deserved.

"Weren should arrive tomorrow morning for training. Caral, make sure he learns everything you can teach him."

"I will," Caral said, her tone serious, although a smile threatened to appear. I understood then that Garkus' training wasn't going as well as I'd hoped.

Keep trying—Garkus is thick-headed, I sent mindspeak to Caral.

We have to make it about him, somehow, she responded. *So he'll have a successful story to tell later.*

No doubt. Now *I* wanted to smile and couldn't.

"I'll check the inventory list I made when I went through this suite after Drenn's death," Barth said, "and compare it to what's left. We'll see if Merrin got away with anything else, my Prince."

"Thank you," I told him. "I'll be in my study, if needed." I walked toward the door, catacomb map in hand, while Hunter followed close behind.

* * *

Sherra

"I see it's still intact," Pottles grinned as I set the shell at her elbow on the kitchen table.

"I had some success," I admitted. "The stone is dust, though, which, oddly enough, was also a success."

"Pfff, I didn't care about it anyway," Pottles waved a hand. "Are you well enough along to show Kyri and me?"

"I think I will be in a day or two. This was only one such pass. I need Merrin's objects to make a full determination."

"I see you had other ideas while you were experimenting," Pottles said.

"I have ideas, yes," I poured a cup of tea for myself and pulled out a chair to sit with her. "A catalpa leaf floated past

59

me on the breeze while I was thinking. It made me wonder if a shield could be shaped to also float on the breeze."

Pottles' hand stopped halfway as she reached for her teacup. "That's—an unusual idea," she hesitated. "The other ideas?"

"Just one other—for now. I also wondered if a bubble shield, sealed tightly enough, would float and roll on water."

"I'm not the one to comment on either of those ideas," Pottles admitted. "I'm afraid of heights and I never learned to swim."

"I saw Adahi," Kyri walked into the kitchen, a rough shoulder-sack thrown over one arm. "He gave me these things—said they'd been used by Merrin, and blocked from divination, also by Merrin."

"Where did Adahi get them?" Pottles asked, taking the sack from Kyri.

"He says Merrin ransacked Drenn's suite. Adahi took the few things that Merrin used to hone his new skills."

"What were they?" I asked.

"The most important thing inside that bag is an empty, rosewood box," Kyri sighed. "Taken from the treasury, emptied, and then left in Drenn's old suite. That box held the Crown Prince's coronet. Merrin certainly has his sights set on the throne of Az-ca."

"What's the other thing?"

"I'll show you." Kyri drew out the rosewood box, first—it was beautifully carved, with silver hinges and clasp. Kerok should have had that box, not Merrin.

"And this." Kyri drew out an empty dagger sheath.

"The King's ceremonial dagger," Pottles breathed. I realized she'd seen the dagger herself—long ago, when she was Queen of Az-ca.

Chapter 4

"Merrin has both those things in his possession, now," Kyri fumed. "Adahi, as you may guess, was more than incensed."

"Does Kerok know?" I asked.

"I'm sure he'll learn soon enough," Kyri breathed.

* * *

Kerok

When I returned to my desk, I found a handwritten note waiting, with my name on it.

"Who was in here?" I lifted the note and waved it at Hunter.

"I don't know." Hunter turned and walked straight out the door to question the guards outside.

"Nobody," he said when he walked back in.

"Fucking hell," I snapped before lifting the flap to read.

The Crown Prince's Coronet and King's ceremonial dagger have been stolen by your cousin. Watch your back carefully, Prince Thorn.

Adahi.

"Search the treasury. Immediately," I barked at Hunter. "Find the Prince's coronet and the King's dagger—if you can."

* * *

"I've gone through everything, and there's minor evidence that Merrin was in the treasury, but like before, the information is blocked past the initial divination of his presence," Barth settled on a chair in my study with a weary sigh. "It is as you say—the coronet and ceremonial dagger are gone. There may be more gold coins missing; I can't testify to how much, because of Merrin's divination block."

"Caral erected her shields? So he can't *step* in again?" I asked.

"Yes. I asked her to do the same around your father's suite and yours, too. You should be doubly protected."

He knew I carried a shield around me at all times, and that Father now was shielded day and night by someone with the talent.

"Good. Thank you for thinking of that," I told him. "It angers me that nobody is safe from his—predations."

"I never thought we'd be fighting an enemy from within our own borders," Barth complained.

"He probably thinks the enemy is gone for good," I said. "So he won't have to worry about them while he takes Az-ca for himself."

"After seeing the hole where the enemy army once was, it could be a logical conclusion—to Merrin, anyway. I have my doubts," Barth observed.

"As do I. Merrin never felt the anger and hate focused on Az-ca, as I did. He has no idea how devoted they are to the idea of crushing us. When they return, they may be angrier and more determined than ever."

"Merrin was never one to think very far ahead," Hunter walked in to join us. "I asked for tea to be brought," he said and settled on the chair beside Barth's.

"Merrin was never one to think of anyone except himself," I added my opinion to Hunter's.

"True enough," Hunter agreed.

* * *

Sherra

"Kyri, if I can get a feel for Merrin through the things you brought me, will you grant a favor?" I asked.

"What favor is that?"

Our evening meal was over; we sat in Kyri's small sitting room while she read and Pottles mended a pair of trousers.

Chapter 4

"I'd like to, ah, place a shield around the King's City, to keep Merrin from ever *stepping* inside it again, in every way possible."

"Worried about Thorn, eh?" Pottles chuckled.

"And others. I'd like to also place the same sort of protection around Secondary Camp, and any other place Merrin could cause trouble."

"Show me that you can successfully get through another's perimeter divination, and I'll allow it," Kyri looked up from her book. It was one of the volumes I couldn't read—I had no idea what she was studying with such intensity.

"I'll work on that," I assured her. I'd do anything to make sure those I loved were protected. I wished my mindspeak would reach Kerok from where I was; I'd tell him help was coming as soon as I could bring it.

Besides, I missed him and all the others I'd come to love. I'd been away from them for more than seven months, and it had worn me down.

I know, Kyri sent mindspeak. *We'll get to that, I promise.*

* * *

Secondary Camp
Caral

"Weren is coming tomorrow morning," I told Misten. "I think he'll be easy to teach—maybe easier than Kage, even."

"Garkus held Kage back," Misten grumped. "We both know that."

"Yeah. We do."

She and I shared a cabin next to the one Armon and Levi shared. Ours had two bedrooms; theirs held one.

"Kerok told me in mindspeak that he was holding out hope until a full year passed," I said. "He said we'll have a memorial for Sherra then."

"There are days I have hope, too," she told me. "But those aren't every day, or even every other day. Most days I realize she's really gone, Caral, and that's unsettling."

"She bought this time for us," I said. "From fighting the enemy, so we can concentrate on the enemy inside our borders. Kerok never came out and said it while I was there, but I think Merrin has plenty of followers, and he could pull in others."

"He certainly found a way to turn the army against itself."

"He could have gotten all of us killed, if Sherra hadn't been watching the enemy at the same time."

"Caral, do you think things will change for us when Kerok becomes King? I mean as far as relationships go?"

"I don't know." I turned away from Misten, then, fighting off the urge to pull her against me and comfort her. "If Sherra were still with us, I think she might convince him. Without her, well, things will likely continue as they always have."

"I think we were both in love with her."

"I think so, too." My laugh was humorless. Lifting a stack of clean sheets off the kitchen table where a drudge had left them, I gave a half-wave to Misten and stalked toward my bedroom.

Things will go as they've gone, not as they should, my older sister, Derissa, always said when I was growing up.

She'd been born without power, and was the one in my family to take care of me after the diviner discovered my talent. I'll never forget how she'd watched over me, once a

Chapter 4

rose was tattooed on my wrist. I had no hope of seeing her again, either, as much as I wanted to.

* * *

Kerok

I wondered if sleep would come if I bothered to lie down. The day had been long and filled with events ranging from aggravating to infuriating.

Merrin lay at the root of all of it, too.

I sat heavily on the edge of my bed and considered whether to spend the energy to remove my boots.

That's when the knock came on the outer door. Rising, I strode out of my bedroom and through the sitting area to answer, expecting Barth or Hunter to be on the other side, with perhaps more bad news.

I staggered backward after pulling the door open; Adahi stood there, a frown on his face.

"The escort's shield is quite strong," he snapped and pushed past me into the room. The doorknob pulled away from my nerveless fingers, while the door closed and locked on its own.

Whirling, I stared at Adahi.

He'd done that. How?

"It's time you learned what I am, and have been for centuries," he shrugged.

"What's that?" Unconsciously, I strengthened the shield about me.

"Something the enemy is truly afraid of," his grin shocked me. "I'm a sorcerer," he added. "Your Sherra is a sorceress. You have sufficient talent; therefore, I will attempt to teach you as best I can. You're going to need everything I can give you in the coming days."

"Sherra?" I'd locked onto what I considered the most important word.

"Relax, dear Prince," he held up a hand. "Kyri is teaching her. If I read things correctly, she may return to you soon. Let's hope Az-ca doesn't go to hell between now and then."

* * *

North Camp
Instructor Falia

Ana set her mug of tea on the table across from me at breakfast, before sitting down with a sigh.

"Not hungry?" I asked. She hadn't picked up a plate from the drudges.

"I'll eat in a bit," she waved a hand. "I just—had a strange dream last night. About Sherra."

"She's dead," I pointed out.

"I know. I need to tell you anyway," Ana said.

"All right."

"I saw her clearly," Ana began. "But she was standing on the other side of a line. I knew we couldn't touch each other, even though we were close enough. Then, she said really strange things."

"What strange things?" I sipped my tea.

"She said that I could mindspeak, and that she wanted to bring my power back, so I could send a message to Colonel Armon."

"Wishful thinking, Ana," I said. "As much as we want things to be different, the power was burned out of us long ago. That's all this dream was—a wish."

"I'm not finished," Ana snapped. "This morning, after I dreamed of Sherra and what she told me to do, I did this." Ana held out her right hand, palm up.

Chapter 4

My gasp when Ana made fire was heard by Miri, who'd just walked through the door.

* * *

Secondary Camp

Armon

Armon, this is Ana, from North Camp.

The mindspeak made me drop the razor I held into the pan of water.

Ana? There was no doubt of it, however—I recognized her voice. *How?* I sent a second question.

I dreamed of Sherra last night, she told me. *Sherra told me to contact you. To tell you that all personnel at all training camps and outposts should be gathered to Secondary Camp—to save their lives. She also said that if anybody could, that the power should be wakened in all who wished it, and that they should be trained quickly.*

I, I floundered. I didn't know how to respond to this. *Let me get back to you,* I said before shouting for Levi.

Kerok

Ana had a dream about Sherra? The day before, I'd have called it only a dream and dismissed it.

Here we were, the morning after Adahi told me Sherra was alive, and Ana, the last person I thought capable of mindspeak, had done just that.

Yes, Armon responded. *Ana says she can make fire and mindspeak as of this morning. I'm inclined to err on the side of caution, my Prince.*

Pass the message to Weren when he arrives. Tell him I want warriors sent to all training camps and outposts, to transport all personnel to Secondary Camp. It won't hurt to leave the camps and outposts empty for a while.

It will be done, Armon agreed.

Rose and Thorn

I'll have Barth send diviners capable of restoring power, I added. *We'll see what can be done with all of them.*

I'll hand those orders to Weren, so he may take command and issue them formally.

Thank you, Armon.

* * *

Merrin

"We'll take Central Outpost tonight," I drew a rough map on paper I'd filched from Drenn's suite. The outpost in question was halfway between the battlefield and the King's City, which held at best two or three older warriors to protect it. It was the one that was used as a waypoint for vehicles stolen from the enemy.

If we were lucky, we'd find a few vehicles parked there, for the army's use. Most others were sent to the farms—to transport fruit, vegetables and animals. A waste of resources, in my mind.

I surmised, too, that most of the remaining army was at Secondary Camp, and wouldn't give the targeted outpost a second thought. It could be days or weeks, even, before anyone thought to check on the outpost, and we'd not only have its store of food, supplies and beds, but we could begin filling it with villagers wishing to join our uprising.

"How would you like to get the word to Thorn, when we turn the country against him while he's not looking?" Gram laughed.

"I *stepped* right into the palace," I shrugged. I'd taken the gold from Drenn's suite, and then two more small chests from the treasury, in addition to the coronet and the King's dagger. All those things lay on the rough floor nearby; evidence that we could do whatever we wanted in the King's City and nobody could stop us.

Chapter 4

"The gold I took can be used to entice reluctant villages. Couple that with the promise of plenty of food and we'll have as many willing bodies as we want."

They'd have no idea we'd use them as living shields if it came down to it.

"What do we do with the girls in the villages—the ones with the rose marks?" Derk asked.

I took a moment to study Derk. He had an immoral preference for young girls. It was one of the things Drenn liked about him.

"You know the law," I said. "They have to be virgin when they're tested again, or they're dead."

A slow smile spread across Derk's thin mouth.

* * *

Sherra

"Sherra? Daughter?" Pottles patted my cheek until I came back to myself. I'd taken the dagger sheath into my hand at the breakfast table, thinking I'd attempt to get past the blocking spell Merrin had placed upon it.

I'd gotten past it. Far past it, and looked straight into Merrin's evils.

"It was a spell that Merrin did, Pottles," I blinked at her to bring her face into focus. "Merrin is planning something awful. I mean, I had a dream last night about Ana, and I was warning her about something, but this is—horrible."

"What happened?" Kyri strode quickly into the kitchen.

"She saw something that Merrin's up to," Pottles snorted.

"What is it?" Kyri sat at the table and took my hand in hers.

"I can show you," I breathed, and sent the images I'd received to Kyri.

Rose and Thorn

* * *

"The youngest is six," Kyri paced the kitchen floor. "The King's Diviner may be the only other one to know that a black rose girl hasn't been born in six years."

I'd never seen Kyri this upset before. I felt helpless in the face of this new threat. How could we save them? *Pottles,* I sent mindspeak, *what about the young boys selected for warrior training?*

They didn't have a tattoo readily marking them as a target, but if Merrin wanted to harm them, or pervert their talents to his ways, he could do that easily by threatening parents or friends.

Pottles transferred my message to Kyri, who stopped pacing and turned toward me. "Also in danger, but not as much as the girls," Kyri replied.

She looked pale to me, her mouth tight and brow wrinkled with thought and worry.

"Sherra, I need your help," she said.

"I'll do anything," I said immediately.

"It will require that I *pull* from your energy," she responded. "Something I never thought I'd have to do again."

Her last words were spoken in a whisper.

"I'll do anything," I repeated.

"The older ones—sixteen or more, will be invited," Pottles began moving chairs back from the table. "They'll be informed of the danger and the choice will be theirs. Those younger ones Kyri will pull away, but that will take a great deal of energy. I'll alert the others in the city that we'll be bringing in children who need our help."

"There aren't that many," Kyri sighed. "Less than sixty, of all ages, between six and twenty. We'll be taking those as old as fifteen, and there are thirty-four of them. Sherra, drink

70 "

Chapter 4

plenty of water and remain seated. I'll need a great deal of your energy to do this."

Table legs scraped across kitchen tiles as Pottles moved it out of the way. *Kyri needs room,* she informed me before walking toward the back door to deliver Kyri's message.

With hands shaking, I took the glass of water Kyri handed me and drank it dry.

* * *

King's City
Kerok

Hunter smothered a shout when Adahi appeared inside my study, shortly after I'd held a mindspoken conversation with Armon.

Warriors would be dispatched quickly, to empty training camps and outposts. I still didn't understand the danger, but, as Armon said, we'd err on the side of caution.

"Calm yourself, Advisor," Adahi lowered his hood and nodded at Hunter.

"Hunter, this is Adahi, who is also the phantom." My introduction lacked finesse, but it was the best I could do for someone who insisted on *stepping* inside the palace rather than going through the front door.

"I came to warn you, and to give needed information," Adahi growled. That's when I knew he withheld a seething anger. Something had enraged the phantom, and I had no idea—*it's Merrin. Isn't it?*

"The black rose girls aged fifteen and under will disappear from the villages," Adahi said. "Merrin has targeted them for his and his followers' lasciviousness, to render them useless to the army later."

Hunter's gasp sounded through my now-silent study. "Kyri is taking the younger ones, to keep them safe. An invitation will be issued to those sixteen and older, to go to her. It will be their choice." Adahi's words were flat, to hide his inner fury.

"How many?" I asked.

"The numbers are worse than you've imagined," Adahi informed me. "Kyri will pull away thirty-four girls, leaving twenty-three older ones behind. A black rose girl hasn't been marked in the past six years."

"May the first warrior save us," Hunter breathed.

Chapter 5

K*ing's City*
Kerok

Barth had joined Hunter and me inside my study shortly after Adahi's departure. "Weren and Armon are clearing out the outposts and training camps," I said after Hunter informed Barth of Adahi's messages. "Barth, were you aware of the low number of black rose girls?"

"I guessed. The itinerant diviners your father employs always sends those records straight to him, you understand, but for the past six years, no records have arrived. Only brief messages came to him."

"What about the warrior boys?"

"Better than the girls, but not overly so," Barth shrugged. "Those numbers stopped coming roughly three years ago."

"Do you think Drenn was made aware—that numbers were dwindling like that?" I asked.

"No idea. If he had that information, he hid it well," Barth observed.

"He would have been terrified if he knew there wouldn't be an adequate army under his rule," Hunter shook his head.

"So Merrin wouldn't have that information, either," I mused. "He has no idea."

"Neither does the Council," Barth said. "And it's just as well. Most of them are bloated with their own self-importance, and have forgotten the villages they are supposed to represent."

"Father should have examined each of them years ago," I fumed. "To determine whether their *service* was still needed by Az-ca."

"We agree," Hunter said. "But we will never criticize your father's rule—he has been steadfast in most things, you understand."

"I know. Barth, bring me the records—all of them—on the remaining Council members."

"It will be done, my Prince."

* * *

Doret

We'd never brought children from Az-ca before—not more than thirty at once, anyway. People from Kyri's City had shown up by the dozens, to offer their help as one by one, children appeared in her kitchen.

The youngest were weeping, which was understandable. The oldest, at fifteen, looked terrified.

The girl's power was sufficient to tell her something was amiss in Az-ca, but she didn't have the experience to determine what it was.

Chapter 5

Kyri would explain things to her, and to the others twelve and over. They'd be told that many of those in Kyri's City had been rescued from faraway lands—across oceans, even.

They'd been rendered childless by the poison still present in their homelands; poison released in wars centuries ago. These children would be more than welcome in their homes.

"That's the last of them," Kyri announced as Nguyen-Mei lifted the seven-year-old in her arms and held her close, comforting and soothing away her tears.

Sherra, who'd sat still while Kyri's hands were on her shoulders, opened her eyes. "Done?" she asked.

"We're done. That's—some talent you have, granddaughter."

I saw Nguyen-Mei out the back door, promising to check with her later, then turned back to Sherra and Kyri.

Sherra didn't even stagger when she stood.

"I'd suggest food and rest for today," Kyri advised. "I'm going to do the same."

Sherra's a dreamwalker, I informed Kyri, as I filled glasses of water for her and Sherra. I'd find something for both to eat, too, while they drank.

I guessed that when she connected with me, Kyri admitted. *It's—next to impossible. The dreamer knows more than the conscious one*, she added. *There hasn't been one since before the End-War.*

I knew, as did Kyri, that the dreamwalker then had ensured that the race survived, in one way or another. It had been on his advice that the domes and infrastructures of Az-ca had been built—well enough to last for many centuries.

* * *

Rose and Thorn

Sherra

After eating, I'd napped on Pottles' advice. When I woke, I found the rosewood box and the dagger sheath on the small table beside my bed.

Merrin would tell me more secrets through those things; I was sure of it. Just not today—I still felt tired from helping Kyri pull young roses away from Az-ca.

Perhaps some families would miss their children. Some would miss the King's gold more.

I found myself hoping that Kyri's invitations to the older ones would bear fruit and soon—any delay would increase their danger at Merrin's hands.

Closing my eyes, I considered another nap.

* * *

Secondary Camp
Caral

"There are messages—from Thorn and Hunter," Armon joined me in the mess hall. "There's quite a crowd coming in, if I understand things properly. I also have this, relayed by a messenger."

Armon handed a sealed note to me. My indrawn breath told Armon I recognized the handwriting.

Derissa.

Derissa had sent a message to me. With nerveless fingers, I broke the seal to read what she'd written.

Dear sister, Romma's daughter has disappeared, she wrote. *We are terrified. Mari is only seven,* she added. *Please, if you know anything about this disappearance, let us know—Derissa.*

Armon read the message over my shoulder, and he and I exchanged a glance after finishing it.

Chapter 5

"Armon, I need Kerok's permission to visit my sister," I begged. Mari was a black rose girl. If Romma didn't care about her, my sister surely did.

"I'll get it," Armon gruffed. "I'll send you, Misten and Levi," he added. "Give me a moment to alert Thorn."

Ten minutes later, I had permission, a bag of gold from a messenger and terrifying news.

Merrin had somehow threatened all the black rose girls. Someone, Armon didn't explain who, had pulled the youngest girls away. The rest of the message was murky at best, and involved an invitation for the older girls to go elsewhere.

I didn't ask where elsewhere could be; my concern was for Derissa.

"Bring her back with you, if she's willing," Armon said after consulting Kerok again in mindspeak. "Her family, too, if she has one."

"She didn't when I left," I said. "I'll ask her."

"Then go, and return soon," Armon said. "Thorn says we can hire your sister to help with the new arrivals in camp, if she so desires."

"Thank you." I hugged Armon hard. He chuckled when I let him go. The moment Levi and Misten joined us, I handed the gold to Levi, told him where to set his feet and he *stepped* us away.

* * *

"Caral," Derissa shouted my name and came running the moment she realized we'd arrived. Levi had set down right outside my family home, although only Derissa lived there, now. Mother was dead and Father had remarried, then moved into his new wife's home, leaving Derissa and me behind.

I didn't miss him.

Derissa threw herself into my arms; she was shorter than I and had been since I was twelve. After an embrace that lasted forever and not long enough, she pulled away. "You got my message," she wiped tears away.

"I did," I told her. "I came to tell you that Mari is safe; the Crown Prince says so. He also says that we can offer you paid work if you want it, at a training camp."

"Wh-what?" She blinked at me in confusion.

"Captain Caral knows what she's talking about," Levi came to my assistance. "Mari is indeed safe elsewhere, and you may come back with us, if that is your wish."

"I can see Caral? Every day?"

"Unless she's on the battlefield or on assignment for the Prince or General Weren," Levi confirmed.

"Caral?" Romma, Mari's mother, approached us warily.

"Mari's safe. The Crown Prince says so," Derissa turned toward Romma.

"Where is she?" Romma demanded.

It was easy to see that she was more concerned for the King's gold instead of her daughter.

"Levi," I turned toward him.

He drew the money pouch from his pocket. Thorn had been concerned, too; that's why he'd sent a messenger with ten gold pieces if it were needed. Romma snatched the pouch from Levi's outstretched hand.

"Romma," Derissa hissed.

"It won't do any good to mourn," Romma sniffed and stalked away with the money pouch. "Mari was dead the moment they tattooed her."

Chapter 5

"Damnation," Levi breathed the curse as he watched Romma walk down the street and slam her front door behind her.

"I think I'm ready to go back with you—if you'll wait while I gather some clothes," Derissa said, wiping more tears away. Romma's reaction had made up Derissa's mind for her.

"We'll help," Misten offered. The four of us walked into my former home, to assist Derissa in any way we could.

* * *

"You have your choice of working in the kitchen, laundry, cabin service, or serving as a camp messenger," Armon listed the jobs available. "I think we may have plenty of openings in all those places, once the drudges and washouts are given the choice to complete their training."

"I'm comfortable in a kitchen," Derissa said right away. "I know how to cook and clean up."

"Then you can start there," Armon agreed. "Caral will show you to the barracks where the other kitchen workers stay, and you can start tomorrow morning. Caral and I have training to do this afternoon, if you'd like to watch."

"I—would love to know what my sister does," Derissa smiled at me.

"Then she'll take you to drop off your things, and you can meet me on the training field afterward."

"What kind of training?" Derissa asked as we walked toward the kitchen workers' barracks.

"We're training warriors how to shield this afternoon," I slipped an arm around my sister's shoulders. "I can't tell you how happy I am to see you."

"I worried things wouldn't work out for you," she sighed. "They never tell us what happens to any of you after you leave—unless it's a death notice."

"Maybe I can ask for that to be changed," I said. "It's only fair that the roses and warriors be able to contact their families, if they want to."

"You act as if you know Crown Prince Drenn personally."

"You haven't heard?" I stopped in my tracks, causing Derissa to stop, too.

"Heard what?"

"Drenn killed himself—accidentally. Prince Thorn is now the Crown Prince."

"The Prince Commander?" Derissa bit her lip in concern.

"That's the one, and I do know him pretty well, actually. I knew his rose better, but we still don't know for sure whether she survived the last battle or not."

"I see I'm behind on news from the King's City," Derissa breathed.

"We'll catch you up," I promised. "You're welcome to come to our cabin anytime, when Misten and I are off duty."

"I'd like that," Derissa said. "So much."

* * *

Doret

"What will we do—if she decides to leave us?" I asked.

"It may not be her that leaves us, as you put it, but dreamwalking Sherra," Kyri shoved dark hair away from her face. "We can't hold onto her now, she's so strong."

"My question is this—will the dreamwalker be able to *step* Sherra away from here? Or send and receive mindspeak?"

Chapter 5

"I don't know." Kyri turned away from me.

"You don't know for sure," I amended her statement.

"That's correct. I don't know for sure. When I sent you to watch over her after her mother died, I knew we had to ensure that she was raised with the proper guidance, and given a formidable sense of what was right and fair. If we'd left her with her father only, Az-ca could be under siege by a black rose sorceress gone berserk."

"I don't think that would have happened," I countered. "You weren't there with her through those years. I was."

"Doret, she's said herself that you were her only friend. Be honest, that village turned their backs on her. With the power she holds, what do you think the results might be?"

"I still think you're selling her short," I hissed. "Sherra may turn into Adahi one day, but the assassinations will be just and fair."

"And if the opposite happens? We don't have the power to stop her. She's young and still relatively inexperienced. She can either save everything, or destroy it."

"That's only if the power goes to her head," I replied. "I don't think it will."

"You know she's just as unseeable as Merrin ever was—perhaps more so. Without your connection to her, and knowing where she'd be throughout her training and such, we'd never have found her after she turned twelve."

"Kyri, I know you've had bad experiences in the past. I don't think this will turn out like the others."

"I didn't either, until I felt the massive power in her, and learned she could dreamwalk."

"Can we set this aside for now?" I begged. "You're tired after what you did today."

Rose and Thorn

"You're probably right, and I'm seeing things that aren't there," Kyri admitted. "I just feel—old."

I didn't tease and tell her she *was* old—we both were, but she was far older than I. Now wasn't the time to bring age into this. Sherra—Kyri had hopes that she'd take over the work she'd done so long. Kyri also held hope that Sherra was the key to other things, too.

I wasn't sure that's what Sherra's ultimate purpose was, but I didn't say it. I'd seen a stubborn determination in Sherra from the moment she'd first made fire at age ten. All I'd done was tell her the truth—about what the black rose on her wrist meant.

I still hadn't told her about the red rose on my wrist. That was a tale to be told carefully, because it involved a terrible injustice and the subjugation of many.

* * *

Merrin

"We need two mindspeakers," I told Gram. "One who can remain hidden and transmit information to us from the King's City, and one here to receive it."

"I don't know any," Gram frowned. "I'd like to get regular information, however. If I approach former colleagues, there's a good chance they'd call the King's assassins immediately, before I have time to offer a deal or extra gold."

"What about blackmail?" I asked. "Surely you have information on one or two of them?"

"Barth has already done divination," Gram argued. "If there was anything useful, he'd have found it already."

"True enough." I considered the conundrum for a moment. "What about retired warriors?"

"There are a few I'm sure, but I don't have their names."

Chapter 5

"Who would have that information?"

"Messengers, perhaps? There may be logs in the Prince Commander's records at North Camp, since he spent so much time there recently."

"Then I'll make a trip to North Camp, before we take the outpost tonight."

"Sounds reasonable. Those instructors won't be able to stop you, even if they learn you've infiltrated."

"I'd like to see them try," I flexed my fingers before folding hands into fists. I hadn't made fireblasts in days. Perhaps I needed a few targets to work off frustrations.

"I'll go now," I made up my mind quickly. "Plicton, you're in charge while I'm gone."

* * *

Caral

When Ana, Miri and Falia walked up to stand beside Derissa at the training field perimeter, I was overjoyed. We'd have a chance to instruct our instructors, and I looked forward to it. Not out of malice or anything close, but out of respect for them and the ones they'd train in the future.

Armon turned and grinned at me, before nodding to our newest onlookers. *We cleared out everything important before we left*, Ana sent mindspeak to me. I almost laughed aloud at her new talent.

I can't tell you how happy I am to see you, I replied. *You're going to be what you should have always been.*

We're scared—and excited at the same time, she told me.

Don't worry—you'll be amazing at this.

* * *

Merrin

Rose and Thorn

The desk drawer hit the wall with a crash, the wood splintering with the impact and bursting apart. The drawer was empty. Thorn's whole damn desk was empty. He always left files here.

Always.

Where the fuck were they?

The instructors had to know, or the drudges, who cleaned and mopped. A trip to the mess hall was next, to find someone who could tell me where the information had gone, before I blasted them to ash and dust.

Stepping to the mess hall, I found it empty. More than furious, I stalked through the kitchen. Everything was clean and put away, as if waiting for drudges to prepare the next meal.

It should have been bustling with activity, while they cooked the evening meal. At least thirty lived here year-round, including the instructors.

Ana. I'd find her first and demand answers, before I killed the bitch. I *stepped* to her quarters, which were at the back of her trainee barracks.

Like the kitchen, her small living space was also vacant.

Somebody had emptied North Camp.

If anyone had been left at the camp, they'd have heard my shout of anger and come running.

Only silence prevailed once I ran out of breath.

Thorn. He had to be behind this.

Well, it was time I taught him a few lessons—the prick. Deliberately, I *stepped* to the center training field, before releasing blasts in every direction. The camp would burn, with nothing to stop it.

My next stop nobody would guess, until it was nothing more than cinders, too. There wasn't a way to harm the

Chapter 5

already-dead, but those they'd left behind, well, they'd just become targets.

The village of Merthis was as good as gone.

* * *

Kyri

"Thank you for the help," I nodded at Adahi.

I worried about Sherra *stepping* away without telling me, so I'd asked Adahi to place additional shielding around her bedroom while she slept.

"I fear this may be ill-advised interference," he cautioned. "If I determine that it is so, the shields will be removed."

"I'm concerned that we'll lose her," I confessed.

"Kyri, you can't let your past rule your future—or the girl's," he said. "She has her own life. You have yours."

"You know why I worry," I dropped my gaze. "You know what her power may be able to accomplish."

"I know why you worry. That's the reason I answered your call. Don't hold her back or place restraints on her abilities—that will be a mistake, I think."

"We've been careful so far," I said, meeting his dark gaze again. "At your suggestion. We just—can't lose her. She has to develop her talent, so she can," my words trailed off. Adahi knew what was at stake as well as I did.

"Then continue to be careful." Adahi walked toward the door and let himself out.

* * *

Sherra

I slept deeper and longer than I'd intended, and woke feeling fearful and disoriented. It took several minutes to get my bearings and recall where I was and why.

85

Rose and Thorn

In my dreams, I'd been trapped in a room with no way out, and it had frightened me terribly.

Sitting up on the edge of my bed, I worked to draw deep breaths to steady myself. An unsettling feeling refused to go away, however.

Determined to work past it, I rose, ignored my rumpled clothing and headed for the door. Pottles could help, perhaps, or at least share a cup of tea with me.

The hall leading to the kitchen was a long one, and I walked it as steadily as I could, while a sudden, encroaching headache went from annoying to debilitating. By the time I heard Pottles' voice, saying that Merthis had been destroyed, the pain had become agonizing.

* * *

Kerok

"Burned to the ground—both of them," Hunter placed notes on my desk. "No living witnesses to either incident, but there's evidence, according to Bray, that a warrior's blasts cause the fires."

"What about the residents of Merthis?"

"All dead, as far as we can tell. Charred bodies everywhere."

"Merrin did this. Merthis is almost a hundred miles from North Camp, and there are at least three villages in between. He has something to settle with me, and this is his way of doing it."

"At least we pulled the personnel away from North Camp in time," Hunter said softly. "Ana retrieved the contents of your desk and files at North Camp; those are at Secondary Camp in General Weren's hands, now."

"You think Merrin wanted those?" I looked up at Hunter. "Never mind, I know he did. We just don't know why he wanted them."

"What sort of records did you keep there?"

"Things I didn't want Drenn pilfering through—military records, mostly, concerning unusual talents, warrior-escort pairs, promotions, disciplinary actions—that sort of thing."

"Unusual talents?"

"Such as being able to *step* others, mindspeak, you know." I waved a hand.

"How much would it benefit Merrin to have mindspeakers?" Hunter demanded. "Even if he had to kidnap them or offer them a pile of gold to get them?"

"People of an entire village died because he wanted that?"

"Thorn, listen carefully to me. Barth described the torture of those poor souls at the front. Merrin will stop at nothing to get what he wants, and what he wants is your father's throne and us out of the way."

"Fuck." I massaged my forehead to stave off a headache. "And we were so close to having enough people trained to send out to the villages—for their protection."

"Then we need to step up those efforts," Hunter snapped. "Or we'll see more destroyed villages."

"Or villages perverted to his cause," I said. "Word came from Armon—he says Caral's sister had no idea Drenn was dead, and thought he was still the Crown Prince."

"That doesn't sound good," Hunter observed. "What have those lazy Council members been up to, if they haven't bothered to take news to those they represent? We have plenty of messengers, and the King pays for their trips to villages to deliver updates on recent events."

Rose and Thorn

"Get Barth. We'll find out what's going on," I said. "If I have to relieve every one of them of their duties, I'll do it. Find out which one is responsible for Dar-den," I named Caral's village. "Bring the one responsible for Merthis, too."

"It will be done right away." Hunter turned and left my study abruptly.

* * *

Doret

Sherra's back was turned toward me as she hunched her body atop the garden wall behind Kyri's house. With arms hugging her knees, she stared into the trees and wild ferns beyond, without seeing any of them.

Kyri told me what she'd asked Adahi to do—after it was done and Merthis was obliterated by Merrin—*the bastard.* He'd burned down North Camp, too, but nobody was there at the time.

Merrin had too much of a particular ancestor in him. He'd inherited a full measure of volatile temper, combined with a talent for vengeance—and that didn't bode well for any of us. If Sherra were to discover what Kyri had done, well, she could disappear and we might never find her again.

Adahi's shields had been strong enough to thwart a dreamwalker—at least for now. Sherra had a tendency—and a knack—for solving problems. To her, this could be a huge problem, and one in which her dreamwalker would search for a solution.

Granted, Sherra didn't have friends in Merthis, but one of them had been her father, and she'd known the others. Merthis was filled with innocents for the most part, even if they'd ignored Sherra. She wouldn't forgive their deaths quickly—if ever.

Chapter 5

As for me, I felt guilty, although I hadn't been consulted in the shielding matter. I understood both sides of this, and that only served to make it worse. Kyri needed to trust Sherra, but she'd been betrayed in the past. I couldn't repair that damage, and hoped it wouldn't end up driving Sherra away.

We need her too much, I reminded myself.

* * *

Sherra

I'd been asleep when Merthis died in smoke and flames. None were spared to my knowledge, and this was before Merrin learned we'd taken the young roses away. I'd been the only black rose in Merthis when I left, I knew that much.

What would Merrin do when he learned we'd circumvented most of his plan to ruin those girls?

Yes, the older ones were still there, but I held hope that some would answer Kyri's call and come of their own accord.

The rest—I shuddered to think what could happen to them.

I sat on the wide, garden wall behind the house, hugging myself and wiping tears away—tears for Merthis and for the young roses still in Az-ca.

* * *

King's Palace
Kerok

The moment they took their seats in my study, they looked guilty. Barth and Hunter, who'd shown them in, were both frowning.

"Would you like to tell me, or let Barth do it?" I asked as pleasantly as I could.

"Everybody else does it," Jacob, who represented Darden and six other villages, whined.

Lewus, who represented Merthis and five more, didn't bother to speak or make excuses. He sat with his eyes down, his fingers gripping the chair arms tightly.

"Do what?" I turned back to Jacob.

"Take the messenger money and use it for ah, other things, sometimes."

"You're telling me that taking the news to the villages about Drenn's death wasn't important enough for you to do what is required of you?" I lifted a pen from my desk and turned it in my fingers—mostly to keep from climbing across the desk and strangling both Council members.

Lewus hunched farther down in his chair, as if he hoped he could collapse into nothing and escape my glare.

"When you say *everybody does it*, that means all of you? That not a single Council member has bothered to send the news of the Crown Prince's death?"

"A few may have done it, I didn't ask," Jacob sounded rattled.

As he should.

"Stand up, both of you," I snapped. Jacob stood right away. Lewus' movement was slower.

"What are you going to do with us?" Jacob warbled.

"I'm going to take you to Merthis, first, so you can view the damage. Then we're going to come back, and you and every piece of lazy, money-grubbing filth who calls himself a Council member will dispatch the news, beginning with the word that Merrin, former Captain in the King's Army, is a deserter, a murderer and has been convicted of treason against the King."

"Why not tell them of your brother's death, first?" Lewus spoke for the first time.

Chapter 5

"Because Merrin just killed every man, woman and child in Merthis with fireblasts, and probably enjoyed it," I shouted.

Chapter 6

_K_erok

The short visit to Merthis hadn't gone well. Lewus vomited on his shoes at the stench and sight of it. Jacob's mouth tightened, but he remained silent.

They were ordered to take this news back to the Council, and then prepare statements to deliver to the rest of the villages. I told them I wanted copies of everything sent to me afterward, to ensure that the word was being distributed properly.

Once I was back in my study, still seething over the day's events, Barth tapped on the door before entering. He looked weary.

"I've pulled in every available diviner, to do a deep divination on all of the Council," he sighed before taking a chair and blinking tiredly at me. "We'll find out where the messenger money went," Barth shifted heavily into a more comfortable position. "Your father knows something is happening, but he didn't ask."

"How much money?" I could answer financial questions about the army in my sleep. Monies paid to the Council hadn't crossed my mind often.

"It's two gold pieces a month for the messengers, who have several villages to visit, and they should be going out at least twice a month. I suppose the messengers have been living off what the villages pay them, because the Council hasn't been using their services."

"And the villages can't pay much, so they're barely subsisting, unless I miss my guess."

"We'll find out how far back this goes, and who the genius was who first thought of it," Barth sighed.

"Drenn," I shrugged. "He probably knew all about it, because he was in charge of that seething mass of idiocy."

"It's possible." Barth nodded absently.

"I'd call it likely, if he were in charge of messenger payments."

"Hunter will know."

"What's the matter?" I asked. Barth was behaving in a distracted manner.

"I just spoke with your father's physician—he met me on my way here."

I went still. "Tell me," I whispered.

"He says things are getting worse. Perhaps a few months are left to him. Wulf is failing quickly, now."

"I'm sure the current state of Az-ca isn't helping," I said. "Even if we don't tell him, he can surely feel that something's wrong."

Chapter 6

"I think everyone in the King's City is on edge, and the moment the news is delivered to the villages, they'll be on their guard, too."

"As they should be, with Merrin still on the loose. I should have killed him the moment I set him down in the poisoned lands."

"Hindsight," Barth said softly. "We have plenty of that. It's foresight—the kind that can see through the fog around Merrin, which we truly need."

"Who can do that?" I asked. "Do you know of anyone?"

"I do not, my Prince, and that is indeed a pity."

* * *

Sherra

Breakfast was done; the dishes washed and put away when I walked past the wall surrounding Kyri's garden. I held a necklace in my hand—something of Kyri's she'd given to me before constructing her own perimeter divination.

I had to force my mind away from events in Az-ca to concentrate on the task at hand; things could go wrong if bad memories lurked in the necklace, as they had in Pottles' shell.

The information gained from the shell I hadn't told anyone about—it was a secret I felt I had to keep. Finding something terrible in Kyri's past could cause me to collapse, as I was grieving in my heart for Merthis and the lives lost, there.

She stood outside the invisible lines of her perimeter divination, waiting for me to delve into the object I held, and then walk past the lines she'd constructed as if I were her.

The stone pendant dangling from the gold chain was blue—a blue I'd never seen in any stone before. It looked similar to turquoise, but it wasn't turquoise. I'm not sure how I knew that; I did, just by handling it.

Closing my eyes, I slipped into Kyri's power—and one of her memories.

A boy stood before her; dark-haired and blue-eyed. He'd done something she'd told him not to do.

He has power, whispered through my mind. Kyri was teaching him. "I told you to place a shield around the hens," she lectured angrily. "You know they need air. You made the shield too small and sealed it too tightly. The hens are dead of suffocation."

"I'm sorry. It won't happen again," he said, ducking his head.

Whether she knew or not, I did.

He'd done it deliberately, and was only apologizing after his goal was accomplished.

Who was this boy, that Kyri thought to teach?

What was his name? I couldn't find it, and I'd spent far too much time in the memory already. Kyri would be waiting, and could grow suspicious if I didn't withdraw soon. The name would have to wait—I didn't have time to work through the memory to discover it.

I released an audible sigh the moment I opened my eyes. "I think I have it," I turned toward Kyri, who nodded and smiled. Handing the necklace to her, I prepared myself and walked through her perimeter shield as if I'd constructed it myself.

* * *

Doret

"We'll get to Merrin," Kyri's words held hope and determination. "Sherra walked right through my divination

Chapter 6

lines without raising the alarm. If I weren't so pleased, it would be frightening."

"I'm not frightened. I'm firmly in the very pleased camp on this."

Kyri pulled the pan of snap beans toward her at the table, and began breaking them into bite-sized pieces for cooking. "I'm wondering when I should take her to Ny-nes," Kyri whispered.

I went still. Kyri could no longer go to Ny-nes. She'd told Sherra she'd take her before, when that wasn't exactly true.

Kyri could get her as far as the eastern edges of the great salt river, before sending the girl farther into that mess alone.

Unless.

"You think this will get you back into Ny-nes—this new talent she's developed." I watched as Kyri's mouth tightened at my words, but she didn't say anything.

Kyri wouldn't explain the why of any of this to Sherra, and she'd made me promise not to tell, either. In this case, I thought Sherra needed the information and Kyri was withholding it.

The extra shield around Sherra's room irked me, too, and Kyri knew it. Without it, Sherra may have known through her dreamwalking that Merthis was in danger. There was also a remote possibility that she may have managed to help the people living there, before Merrin fried all of them.

Sherra was still in the garden behind the house, handling the dagger sheath. The rosewood box lay on the wall beside her—she'd chosen the wall's broad top as a favorite place to sit.

I considered sending mindspeak, but didn't. Like her, I wanted Merrin dead. I hoped she'd be able to hand that death to him and his followers without feeling guilt later.

Until now, she'd concentrated on saving lives. I knew, as did Kyri, that at least six escorts had followed Merrin, with their warriors.

How were they faring, now? I couldn't imagine that their lot in life had improved by following that piece of filth. Would Sherra be able to destroy them, too, if it came down to it?

Drenn had placed his trust in Merrin, accepting an enemy weapon to use against his own family. He had no idea what to do with it, other than point and shoot. He'd died from his trust and ignorance—of the man and the pistol.

"You're frowning." Sherra walked in and poured a glass of water for herself. "Want tea? I'll make some."

"I'd take tea," I agreed with a sigh. Kyri nodded her acceptance as well.

* * *

King's Palace
Kerok
Hunter's mindspeak let me know something had gone terribly wrong the moment he'd contacted me.

I met him, Barth and a messenger at the table in the gardens, where they waited. Hunter had the foresight and manners to offer the messenger food and drink, and the poor man acted as if he were starved. I recognized him, as he'd served under me in the army in years past. Acting as a messenger was his chosen occupation after retiring.

"What happened?" I asked, nodding at the man to keep his seat.

"Two villages emptied," he said. "Both near Central Outpost. I went there afterward, to ask the commander if he knew anything. I barely got out of there alive—it's been taken over by the missing villagers and a few—well, deserters, I suppose."

My eyes locked with Barth's for a moment. "Did you see Captain Merrin there?" I asked.

"No. I saw two warriors, their escorts and Gram Plicton. I used to deliver for him, so I knew his name. I didn't recognize the others. One of the warriors fired a blast at me, while Plicton shouted at him to stop. I *stepped* away, Prince Thorn. I didn't wait to see what their purpose in all this was."

"You did the wise thing, Oren—it is Oren, isn't it?"

"Yes, my Prince."

"Oren, I think I'd like to add you to my staff," I added. "As a messenger to the Crown Prince. You can begin work now by telling Hunter everything you can recall about your ah, brief visit to Central Outpost, while he writes it down for the records."

"I'll be honored to serve," Oren dipped his head to me.

"Good. Hunter, get started on that. Barth, come with me. We have a personal message to deliver to General Weren."

* * *

"I have your records from North Camp," Weren said, and led us to the back bedroom in his cabin. "I had a desk brought in, and they've all been put away. If you need privacy to search," he offered.

"No," I held up a hand. "I should be able to find the records of inventory for Central Outpost easily enough. If you'll send for the post commander, I'd like to speak with him, too."

"His cabin is in the northwestern corner. I'll send for him right away."

* * *

Sherra

"I keep having the same dreams," I told Pottles as we drank our tea at the kitchen table.

"What dreams?"

"That I'm trapped somewhere, and can't get out."

"How long has this been happening?"

"The past two nights. It's—terrifying. I'm afraid to go to sleep, now."

"What's this?" Kyri walked into the kitchen and went straight for the cupboard to find a teacup.

"She's been having nightmares—the same one, actually, two nights in a row," Pottles snorted. "That she's trapped and can't escape."

"Nobody is trapped. Tell yourself that before you sleep," Kyri's voice sounded indifferent to my fears.

Pottles snorted again, but she didn't say anything.

I didn't tell Kyri that I'd struggled to convince my dreaming self that it was only a dream. That had only ramped up my terror and I'd awakened, gasping for breath.

As the chickens surely had gasped and struggled to breathe in that boy's shield—*before they died of suffocation.*

That was Kyri's memory, and has nothing to do with your nightmares, I attempted to convince myself.

Perhaps.

* * *

Secondary Camp
Kerok

"Two trucks, jarred food, uniforms, kitchen supplies and staples," Garth, the outpost commander, confirmed what I'd

Chapter 6

already guessed. "Welton says that there are medical supplies left there; he didn't know how long we'd be gone, and left the bulk of those things stored in the post hospital."

"They can't eat those," I waved a hand. "Destroy, yes, but there'd be no purpose in that. What I'm interested in is camp records, Commander. Did you have a list of personnel, which mentioned their talents?"

"I did," Garth nodded.

"Which ones were mindspeakers?"

"We had only one," Garth shrugged.

"Bring him. Weren, I need the list of all mindspeakers," I barked at the General. "I think they'll become targets—we believe Merrin wants mindspeakers to further his treasonous plans."

* * *

"There's more bad news, I'm afraid," Hunter set a glass of whiskey on my desk moments after Barth and I returned to the palace.

"What now?" I barked at him. "Sorry—that's wasn't directed at you." I lifted the glass of whiskey and downed it in a single swallow.

"Northeast Outpost has been taken, too. At least the messenger landed outside the walls before attempting to go through the gate. When he was nearly fireblasted to death, he fled to report the incident to us."

"Do we know if villagers are inside—with Merrin's deserters?"

"He didn't get a look at anyone; he was fired on the moment he set down."

"Merrin's new tricks at work, no doubt. At least he can't prevent anyone from *stepping* inside his boundaries. Not yet, anyway."

"If my guess is correct, Merrin's spreading his allies thin between two outposts. That means he'll either stick with those two, or go looking to recruit others to his cause."

"What do you suggest we do?" I pushed my empty glass toward Hunter.

"We don't have sufficient troops to properly guard all villages and outposts—not fully trained ones," Hunter said and poured more whiskey for me.

"Tell me about it." I emptied the glass a second time.

"If we can get the washouts and instructors trained—but that will take time," Hunter added before I could voice my protest.

"You know Merrin doesn't give a damn about any of those villagers. He'll kill them in front of us to get something he wants," I rumbled. "He may be telling them otherwise—at least for now, but they're nothing more than hostages at this point."

"You're sure we can't *step* in to do a rescue?"

"You saw what happened when Armon and his crew *stepped* to that cabin," I said. "Merrin knew immediately and got away before they had time to do anything useful, other than shield themselves from the repercussions and fallout of opposing blasts."

"According to the last census, those villages together held close to two hundred," Hunter informed me. "Those numbers could be up or down from that count, as you well know."

"I do." I considered asking for a third shot of whiskey, but held back. "Were there any black rose girls, sixteen and older there?"

"I'll consult your father's records and let you know."

Chapter 6

"I want the number and age of the boys scheduled for warrior training, too," I said as Hunter turned to leave my study.

"I'll see to it."

* * *

Kaakos

Sovereign Leader of the Free Nation of Ny-nes

"High Cleric Ruarke is here, Sovereign Leader." A guard bowed to me after making his announcement.

"Ah. Show him in."

I nodded my dismissal of the guard the moment Ruarke strode inside my office, black robes swinging about him as walked.

He must have seen something important, to come unannounced like this. He and I—we were very much alike. I waved him toward a chair before my desk.

"I have word from my spies," Ruarke said after accepting the offered seat.

"What do they have?" I asked.

"A rift has occurred in Az-ca." His smile was slow, indicating devious thoughts—much like the smile he wore while torturing adults and children.

"Tell me," I touched fingertips together and focused attention on my guest.

"I don't have the full tale. I only know this; a member of the King's army escaped his death sentence, and is now pulling allies to him. He wants to take the King's City—and the throne—for himself. He has developed a taste for blood, Lord Kaakos."

"How do we exploit this?" If Az-ca were on the verge of a civil war, how much easier would it be to destroy?

"I doubt he will be concerned as to where suitable allies come from," Ruarke offered.

"You're suggesting that we infiltrate?"

"It's why I'm here," Ruarke chuckled. "With our combined efforts, I believe it will be simple to provide ah, extra followers for the opposition."

"How do you propose getting them across the border?"

"I recently had an idea," Ruarke said.

"What idea is that?"

"Mechanical power, instead of demon power." Ruarke withdrew a square, metal contraption from his robes.

Setting the device on my desk, he leaned back while I examined the thing. In the center, it held one button, with a dial.

"What does it do?" I asked.

"Nothing. But it will convince your troops that we've found a way to make a machine do what the devils of Az-ca can, without offending any laws."

"Truly?" This had definite possibilities, and I wondered why we didn't think of it before.

"Yes. The dial's first position will be to transport us. The second dial position will serve to send fireblasts. The third will protect us with a shield."

"But only you and I are allowed to operate it," I guessed.

"Yes. In the hands of a lesser being, it could be employed to commit crimes against Ny-nes and make the bearer like our enemies. I believe I can convince the troops that only the worthy will be able to operate it."

"Then make another and have it delivered to me soon. Select your clerics and brief them on their mission. I'll send the rest of the army in vehicles to follow you."

Chapter 6

"I'm hoping Az-ca will fall quickly, once the regular troops arrive."

"Infiltrate the opposition carefully, Ruarke. I dislike the idea of ruling Ny-nes without your steadfast support. Once we destroy those with power, the rest will be sheep to do with as we please."

"It will be as you say, my lord."

* * *

Central Outpost
Merrin

"There are only two." Gram shoved two boys before me. I sat behind the post commander's desk, considering how to go about testing these young warriors.

One was sixteen, perhaps; the other, twelve at most.

I didn't care if they could make fire yet—that's not what I needed. I needed mindspeakers, and hoped at least one of these could achieve it.

I wouldn't know, however, unless someone else with the talent confirmed it. As for the black rose girl, I'd test her, too. If the seventeen-year-old had mindspeaking talent, I could be persuaded to leave her intact, if only for her cooperation.

Barring that, I'd hand her to Gram as a gift for his support.

"Bring the girl, too," I nodded to Gram. We'd see if luck were with us in this. If not, there were two young men at the other outpost we'd taken.

Gram frowned at my last command—he didn't want anything to stand between him and the girl, as he'd already marked her as his. I could disabuse him of that notion easily, and he knew it.

Rose and Thorn

"We need a mindspeaker from inside the King's City," Gram pointed out. I didn't fail to notice the angry sarcasm in his voice.

"I am well aware," I snapped at him. "I especially need someone from within the army, or connected in some way. I'm working on that. For now, we need to find a mindspeaker here. If one of these will serve, then we're halfway to our goal. Stop worrying, Plicton, the talent is rare and our chances aren't good with only three candidates."

I watched as he deflated—he'd drawn in a breath to argue, and I wasn't in the mood to trade words. We had enough food and supplies to feed the villagers for perhaps three weeks. We'd have to kill some of them or steal to feed ourselves after that.

By that time, Thorn would send his army, and I had plans for that event, too. I just needed mindspeakers to inform me of Thorn's and the army's movements, so we'd be prepared for our guests' arrival.

"How is it going with our villagers?" I asked, determined to distract Gram from the girl.

"I've separated the skeptics from the believers," Gram was more than proud of his political prowess at convincing any halfwit that night was day.

"Good. It'll make things easier for us when the army arrives."

"What if they attack both outposts at once?" he asked.

"I've already placed a special perimeter around both. I'll know, and depending upon the forces arriving, we'll deal with that when it occurs. Tossing a few burned and dismembered bodies over the walls should convince them to stand down—long enough for us to get away if necessary," I

Chapter 6

shrugged. "I already have my eye on Secondary Camp, if the army is split and sent against the outposts."

"A much better location, food and accommodations-wise," Gram agreed.

"Most certainly. Bring the girl, Plicton. What did you say her name was, again?"

"Anari."

"Good. We'll tend to our young men, here," I nodded to the boys, who'd been present during the entire conversation and now gazed fearfully at one another.

If they weren't terrified enough to cooperate now, they would be soon.

* * *

Anari

I knew them by the black roses on their wrists—the roses that matched the one tattooed on my own wrist.

Had I discounted the invitation in my dream the night before? Perhaps I shouldn't have. The voice had shown me the tiled rose. Had given instructions on how to reach it, too, after warning me of the danger I was surely in.

"Come," a black rose escort jerked her head toward the door.

I had questions for her. Questions she wasn't inclined to answer, because the head man who'd ordered us gathered and taken to this outpost wouldn't allow questions from any of us.

The Council member, who'd worked at convincing us that we were safer here, hadn't convinced me.

My parents, perhaps, believed, and I'd followed them when we were separated from perhaps a fourth of the villagers—those who'd asked questions and refused to accept what Council member Plicton claimed.

Rose and Thorn

Surely if the Crown Prince had been murdered by his own brother, we'd have heard of that by now. There was enough trade going back and forth that news would filter into the villages eventually.

According to Plicton, this had occurred months ago.

Why had we heard nothing?

"Don't dawdle," the escort snapped at me.

I rose from a cross-legged position against the wall and followed her toward the door, while my parents, standing nearby, offered no question or resistance.

Sheep to be driven. That's all we'd been our entire lives.

Keeping my questions to myself, I followed the escort as she led me toward the head man's office. When I arrived, I found the warrior boys, Laren and Kyal, there already.

They looked terrified, while Plicton grinned as I walked in. That grin—it frightened me all on its own.

As for the head man, he sat behind a desk, thinking it surely made him important to do so.

Laren, what's going on?

He and I—we'd formed some sort of bond; one neither of us could explain, it just was. Both of us were ignored most of the time, so we'd developed a friendship of sorts. Poor Kyal, who'd just turned eleven, looked bewildered as well as frightened.

I went to stand between them, gripping both their hands in mine—to give and receive support, perhaps.

Plicton's grin turned to a sour frown.

They want to use us, if we have what they call mindspeak, Laren replied. *They intend to kill our families and some of the others, if we don't cooperate.*

They're outlaws, Kyal informed us.

Chapter 6

My breath stopped—we'd never heard Kyal do this before.

Help us, I sent out to anyone listening. Mindspeak. If they were looking for it, then others had it, too.

Would someone hear us?

Come.

The voice from my dream the night before, accompanied by the same instructions.

My grip tightened around Laren and Kyal's hands, and praying that the voice wasn't my imagination, I did as it instructed.

* * *

Merrin

"What the fuck just happened," I shouted at Plicton, when all three disappeared in front of us.

Plicton looked stunned—he hadn't guessed that this could happen. I had no idea which of the three could *step*, but one of them could and had taken the other two as well.

"It had to be the oldest boy," I fumed. Black rose girls didn't have a clue that they'd ever be able to *step*.

"What do we do now?" Plicton demanded.

"Go to the other outpost, you moron, and grab those young warriors before they get away, too. For all we know, the three we had could be on their way to Thorn right now. The boys know enough to get us all killed."

"Your fault for talking in front of them," Plicton's voice rose in anger.

"Shut the hell up, or I'll fry you where you stand."

Plicton didn't reply; he whirled and strode angrily from my office, cursing under his breath.

Chapter 7

*S*herra

"Run," Pottles shouted and bolted out the back door. We raced toward the catalpa trees—my steps quickened the moment I realized someone had received Kyri's message and *stepped* here—not at night, but during the middle of the day.

Kyri was already at the tiled rose, greeting a black rose girl—*and two warrior boys.* I understood they'd escaped Merrin's clutches the moment I saw their eyes and the terror they held.

Less than half an hour later, they sat at Kyri's kitchen table, eating honey cakes with weak tea while Pottles asked questions and Kyri and I listened.

"The head man has pale hair," the youngest—Kyal—answered Pottles' question. "They never said his name."

"His name is Merrin, and he has escaped the King's justice for committing treason and other crimes," Pottles explained carefully. None of us wanted to explain that he'd committed murder, or broken the law and taken advantage of a black rose trainee—with the help of the former Crown Prince.

"He talked about killing some of us," Laren explained. "Why would he do that?"

I could see that Pottles was working out in her mind what to tell the boy. How do you explain to someone who hadn't been given proper news in months, if not years, that Merrin wanted to take the King's throne for himself?

"He wants to kill the King and the Crown Prince," Pottles said. "For sentencing him, you understand. He is willing to use anyone or anything to achieve that goal, including the lives of the villagers. The King will not be willing to sacrifice any of you, so Merrin could use you as a bargaining chip."

"That's horrible," the girl, Anari, spoke.

"Hmmph. That's Merrin. Now you understand how terrible his crimes are? He's already tried to kill the King once, which resulted in Crown Prince Drenn's death. Now he's determined to try again—against the King and the new Crown Prince—Thorn."

"He killed the Crown Prince?" Kyal squeaked.

"He placed a weapon in the Crown Prince's hand, which ended up killing the Crown Prince," Pottles snorted. "He hoped to kill the King and Prince Thorn at the same time, but they were able to protect themselves."

"Because he wants the throne—isn't that right?" Anari had already sorted this out in her mind.

Chapter 7

"Yes. Merrin is related to the royal family—a cousin. In his mind, he deserves to take the throne from King Wulf. Nothing is further from the truth, but as you probably noticed, Merrin managed to gather a few allies from the army, where he was a former Captain."

"I saw six black rose escorts," Anari confirmed. "They acted so—obedient."

"Say subservient, and you'll be closer to the mark," Pottles said. "They're afraid of their own shadow, if my guess is correct."

"They do act afraid," Kyal agreed. "If one of the warriors orders them to do something, they run."

"Their power has been hampered by their training, which was insufficient," Kyri spoke for the first time. "If they'd been trained properly, they wouldn't behave like that."

"What do you mean?" Anari was more than curious—because that's what awaited her.

"Don't worry about poor training," I reassured her. "Between Doret and me, I think we can further your education."

"What about us?" Laren asked.

"Sherra knows more about warriors than most warriors know," Pottles huffed. "I think we can handle it."

"Things are moving strangely," A man walked through the back door into the kitchen. "Kyri, I must speak with you—alone."

* * *

"Don't worry, that's just Adahi," Pottles soothed our young guests. "He comes now and then to talk to Kyri."

As I hadn't seen Adahi before, I cataloged his image in my mind. Pottles' previous description of him was correct; he wore a hooded cloak, and the hood covered most of his face,

113

preventing us from seeing anything except his mouth and chin.

Things are moving strangely, he'd said. What did that mean?

Besides the obvious, of course—that Merrin was stooping to threatening children and killing more villagers.

"Want more tea?" Pottles asked, interrupting my thoughts. Three heads across the table nodded in unison.

* * *

Kyri

"Will you carry this news to Thorn?" I asked. "That we have two warrior boys and another black rose girl?" We'd moved to my suite, to have a private conversation.

"I'll take it, but that's not why I'm here," Adahi replied.

"Tell me." I crossed arms over my chest, as if that act would ward off bad news. Adahi wouldn't have walked through the door like he had if the news weren't important.

"I feel strange rumblings, and an echo from Ny-nes," Adahi growled. He hadn't bothered to lower his hood during this visit—a sure sign that he was upset by what he'd learned.

"Strange rumblings?"

"From—shall we say the slightly lesser of two evils?"

I went still.

Ruarke. Adahi had felt Ruarke, and that meant Ruarke had departed—well, that was the worst news I'd heard in a while, and I'd heard plenty of bad news in the past year or so.

There's no way I could inform Doret of this—she'd be more than upset.

She'll want to go after him herself, a small voice informed me. All the more reason to hold the information back—at least for now.

"You're sure of this?"

Chapter 7

"As sure as the blood that runs through Az-ca's royal family."

"What do you suppose is his reason for leaving?"

"A plot, surely."

"Will he have others with him?"

"Assuredly, and likely more troops on the way in a more ah, conventional manner."

"Then Ny-nes had another army held back and trained," I dropped my arms and rubbed my forehead as I turned away from Adahi. He and I knew the one behind this. I still couldn't say the name—it disturbed me so badly.

"How do you suppose they'll get around the power difficulty?"

"I am still considering that. It is evident that some way has been discovered."

"What will you tell Thorn?"

"That three young ones escaped Merrin. If I were he, I'd ask to see them—question them—to learn what he can and develop a strategy. There can be no attack—if he wishes those villagers to remain alive."

"I don't want to just turn the children over to Thorn—they're safe here," I countered.

"Then take them for a visit," Adahi shrugged beneath his cloak.

"If I go, he'll demand to see Sherra."

"As is his right."

"What do you suggest? I know when you disagree with me, even when you don't say it."

"Take Sherra back now—and leave those children with her in the King's City."

"I dislike that idea. You understand why."

"I think you fail to understand this time."

Rose and Thorn

"Just as I failed to understand last time? Is that what you're saying?"

"Examine your motives, Kyri, before it is too late. I tell you again; Ruarke is on the way. What he does when he arrives, and with whom he allies, will tell us much. Hold Sherra back at your own peril."

"And what do you see if I do hold her back?" I demanded.

"That way is splintered, depending upon when you decide—or she decides for you. Do not make enemies of allies. Consider carefully how you'd react in her place."

"What will happen if I release her now?"

"Then you will have a powerful ally in the days to come, and Thorn will live to mourn his father."

"You see his death?"

"I see his death if Sherra doesn't stand with him."

"You make my life more than difficult, Adahi."

"My existence is difficult enough already, as is yours. Stop complicating everything with your past and your fears."

"I need to think on this," I said. "I need some time."

"Taking time may kill Az-ca," Adahi growled and stalked out of my study. I should have pleaded with him to come back.

I didn't.

Lives are destroyed by hesitations. I suppose I still hadn't learned that lesson well enough.

* * *

Merrin

"I can't work with that," I hissed after sending an eight and nine-year-old boy out of the office. There'd been no black rose girl at the other outpost, only two young warrior boys.

Chapter 7

Plicton had barely spoken when I'd returned with both warrior boys in tow. Neither of the boys had the slightest inkling of mindspeak—what it was or how to go about it. I'd even threatened them, in case they were holding back. Both had burns on their wrists, now, but no mindspeaking ability had come to the surface.

"You know Thorn has heard everything from those other three," Plicton chose to speak now. "He and the army could be here at any moment, and blast this outpost to the ground. As for our plans to infiltrate the villages and spread our message, that effort may be badly crippled by these events."

"We can escape this outpost," I pointed out. "I have my perimeter up to warn me if they come."

"And they will keep coming, until we run out of places to hide."

I considered blasting Plicton, just to have enough silence to think properly. "Perhaps it's time we sent Thorn a message," I opened a desk drawer to search for paper and pen.

"You think a letter will keep him away?" Plicton tossed up a hand.

"It may—if the letter is delivered with burned villagers' bodies. If he sends the army, we'll leave the villagers here to be killed while we go straight to Secondary Camp. We'll take it if we can."

"And if we can't?"

"We burn it down. Go find three dissenters—the worst of the lot, Plicton. I have a message to send to Prince Thorn."

* * *

Secondary Camp
Armon

Rose and Thorn

Kage, Garkus and General Weren sat at our regular table for the midday meal. Kage and Weren were now adept at shield building—Garkus' shields were still weaker than any of us liked.

"Merrin has taken two outposts," I said, repeating information I'd gotten from Thorn and Hunter. "We're concerned he'll kill his hostages if we don't leave him alone. Prince Thorn wants his assassins back at the palace, because of this."

Weren didn't have mindspeak; that meant he depended upon me for that talent.

"I can be ready to go in five minutes," Garkus said.

"As can I," Kage agreed.

"Go after you've finished your meal, then," Weren instructed. "Report to Hunter; Armon will inform him of your pending arrival."

"Caral, how are the washouts faring?" Weren turned to other items.

"Ana is far ahead of the others," she said. "I think because of her dream."

"Dream?" Weren asked.

"She had a dream about Sherra, who told her she could make fire and do other things—like mindspeak. That's why she attempted to make fire the morning after, and succeeded, then contacted me with her news."

"Fascinating," Weren appeared thoughtful. "Have any of the others had a dream of Sherra?"

"None reported, sir," I replied.

"You'll let me know if that changes?"

"Of course."

* * *

"Do you think Ana is farther ahead because of her dream, or was it because diviners reawakened the power in the other washouts?" Misten asked on our walk back to the training fields.

"You think Ana wakened her power by herself?" Levi asked.

"I don't know what to think," Misten confessed. "If Sherra were alive, I'd say she did it. Since that's not true, I don't know how to explain it, other than Ana being really strong with talent. It makes me wonder why she washed out."

"Hmmph," Caral snorted. "Depending on who her instructor was, it might not be that difficult to determine."

"Armon, what do you think?" Levi asked.

"I don't know," I admitted. "I was more than shocked to get mindspeak from Ana, that's all I can say. If she hadn't told me to tell Thorn to clear out the training camps and outposts, well, you know where we'd be right now."

"I'm surprised Thorn was so ready to accept that information," Levi countered.

"I'm grateful," Caral said. "If Ana and the others had stayed at North Camp, they'd be dead, now."

"Do you think it was a dream-vision? Like some of the old diviners could do?" Levi asked.

"No idea," I shrugged.

"It sounds like something Sherra would do—if she were alive." Misten's voice held an unmistakable longing.

"It is something she'd do," I agreed. "Here we are. Let's get to work."

Caral squared her shoulders as she took in the crowd of former washouts. If not for Sherra, none of them would have any hope of being anything other than a drudge or, if they showed a talent for it, an instructor.

In a short amount of time, Sherra had changed so many things for the better.

* * *

King's Palace
Kerok

"I've already sent scouts to observe the outposts from a distance," I said. "We need to discuss what actions to take when Weren and Armon are here," I told Garkus. He and Kage sat in my office after they'd left Secondary Camp behind. Garkus wanted to present options on how to deal with Merrin's hostage situation at two outposts, and I wanted all my advisors with me before making important decisions.

Those advisors included Barth and Hunter. Both would be clear-headed as we considered our options.

"Whether we send in a small or large force, people will die," Kage refuted Garkus' suggestion of going in to take Merrin down, regardless of the loss of civilian lives. Kage was firmly in the negotiations camp, offering to go himself, if necessary.

"When will that be?" Garkus demanded.

"Tomorrow. Go home, put all your options on a list and bring them tomorrow at mid-morning. We'll discuss all ideas then. I'll send mindspeak to Armon in the meantime, to tell him and Weren the same. Something has to be done before they run out of food."

Garkus wasn't happy, but he rose when Kage did and was ushered out of my study by the guards posted at the door.

Chapter 7

"That one has always acted rashly," Adahi appeared and took Garkus' seat before my desk. "It's one of the reasons Linel offered him a position as an instructor, after his last escort died more than forty years ago."

"I've read Linel's records," I leaned back in my chair to study my visitor. This time, he'd left his hood up, instead of lowering it. I wondered why, but that thought was cut short when Hunter almost ran back inside my study, Garkus and Kage right behind him.

"There are burned bodies in the courtyard," Hunter's breaths were labored. "With a note addressed to you, Thorn."

* * *

"Who brought them here?" I demanded when we reached the ring of guards in the courtyard, who now surrounded three blackened bodies dropped haphazardly onto the flagstones. All were burned beyond recognition, and currently in that small period of time between the body remaining intact and dissolving into dark ashes.

"Only a brief sighting," my Prince, the guard captain bowed to me. "I only know it wasn't Merrin—this one had darker hair."

"Querl?" Barth arrived to survey the tragic pile of bodies.

"Most likely," I growled. "Captain, are the bodies cool enough to approach?"

"Yes, or the note would have burned, my Prince."

"I will retrieve it, then," I strode forward.

"No, my Prince," the captain held up a hand. "I merely waited for your approval before removing it myself." He turned toward the bodies and pulled out the dagger holding the paper to one of the bodies.

Rose and Thorn

The note was brought to me; I recognized Merrin's crabbed writing immediately. Adahi, still standing behind me, read over my shoulder when I opened the note.

Well, Thorn, you know what this message means, Merrin had written. *We have roughly two hundred more who can meet the same fate. Come after us and you'll regret it, I assure you.*

Merrin.

"No demands?" Barth read the note quickly after I handed it to him.

"Only that we leave him be," I hissed. Angry couldn't begin to describe how I felt.

"Perhaps we should offer a trade, anyway," Hunter's eyes met mine after reading the note.

"We need to negotiate for lives," Kage agreed.

"He'll kill them anyway—they're already dead," Garkus advised.

"Prince Thorn, I suggest taking this conversation back to your study," Adahi spoke quietly. "Call in your other advisors and make a decision."

"Hunter, send for Armon and Weren. Get them here as quickly as you can," I snapped.

"It will be done, my Prince."

"Captain," I turned back to the guard.

"Yes, my Prince?"

"See that these bodies receive a proper burial."

"It will be done, my Prince."

* * *

High Cleric Ruarke

"Things are moving quickly, my brothers," I announced to the soldier-clerics gathered about me. "I understand, too,

122

Chapter 7

that these are not the best of conditions, but I feel that will be remedied very soon."

Currently, our tents were spread across the northern edge of an enormous blast crater, left behind when Ny-nes' army was destroyed—before the weapon could be delivered by plane.

The actual events surrounding that destruction were hidden from me, but it was clear that all involved were dead, and rumors from within Az-ca verified it. We'd failed at a direct attack.

We would not fail this time—with an indirect assault that came from inside. Events were lining up spectacularly; the day I destroyed the King's City and handed the rest of Az-ca to Kaakos would be a glorious one.

"Will we have enough weapons to last until the vehicles arrive, Revered One?" A cleric asked.

"I believe so, brother. Everything else, the god will provide. The vehicles are on their way already. We must clear a path for them, you understand. This device will aid our work," I held up the gadget I'd brought with me—the one they all believed had transported them in moments to the edge of the enemy's lands.

"The god's will be done," the cleric dipped his head to me.

"As it has always been," I made the expected reply.

* * *

King's Palace
Kerok

"I dislike the idea of holding back and allowing Merrin free rein to do as he pleases," Weren sighed and handed the note to Armon. "I dislike even more that the lives of villagers hang in the balance."

"We have to make an attempt to negotiate," Kage said. "If Merrin refuses, then our choices are limited, but at least we'll know where we stand."

"What will you offer?" Barth asked. "Food? He has that already—for the moment. I have no desire to offer him freedom and absolution for his crimes."

"I say we allow him to take as much food and supplies as he wishes, if he leaves Az-ca," Hunter suggested. "If he returns, he will be hunted again."

"You'll be offering him time to gather more power about him," Adahi counseled. I suspected Adahi knew more than he was saying, but I refrained from asking.

"Do you think that's possible—that he can become more powerful?" Weren asked Adahi. Weren was still skeptical about allowing the phantom into our meeting, but I had no way of keeping him out of it—he *stepped* in whenever it suited him.

"What if he offers an exchange?" Armon said.

"An exchange? For food or gold?" Garkus asked.

"No. An exchange of prisoners. Thorn and Hunter—for two hundred villagers."

"Because Merrin wants the throne," Adahi nodded to Armon. "Very perceptive, Colonel."

"That offer will be refused," Garkus insisted. "I will never serve Merrin. He is a traitor to the Crown and a murderer."

"Calm down, assassin," Barth said. "Trading either of these will not be an option. If Merrin doesn't realize this yet, he should."

"It could get me inside the outpost," I said after considering it for a moment.

"No," Hunter and Barth objected simultaneously.

Chapter 7

"But I could," I started again.

"No," Garkus, Weren and Armon joined Barth and Hunter's protests.

"Never consider it, Prince Thorn," Adahi spoke. "Unless your rose is beside you."

"Do not speak of the dead to her grieving warrior," Weren snapped.

"You think her dead? You have much to learn," Adahi stood. "I will leave you now. I caution you to proceed carefully, Thorn, and do not offer yourself without her beside you."

Adahi strode toward the door, before *stepping* away.

* * *

Kyri

I was more than grateful that Adahi came when he did, while Sherra and Doret were busy finding beds, clothing and arranging baths for three unexpected guests.

"More betrayals will come, Kyri. Believe that, if nothing else," Adahi warned.

"I will be hunting Ruarke," I began.

"Tell Doret he is coming. She will not forgive if you withhold that information. Neither of you will find Ruarke, if he reaches Merrin's side."

"Does he know? That Merrin is unseeable?"

"I'm sure he has his spies. Doesn't everyone?"

"You make me weary," I sighed.

"I only give you truth, Kyri. This truth will weary anyone, including the powerful. Also, I am removing the shield around Sherra's bedroom. It has caused too much interference and I no longer agree with your reasons for placing it."

"You know she'll disappear the moment her dreamwalker discovers," I snapped.

"You cannot keep her forever, Kyri. You said this yourself—told Thorn this yourself."

"But I'm not done with her training," I argued.

"Hmmph. Better to let her go and remain allies, than attempt to hold her here and make an enemy."

"You make it sound so clear-cut," I complained. "When it is anything but."

"Nothing is decided, or can be from now on—I feel it. Only the actions of those involved will send events one way or another. Do not hold them back by your own fears and misgivings."

"Then tell me what you think I should do, Adahi. All of it."

"Take those three children to Thorn, so they can report what they've seen and heard directly to him. Tell Doret that Ruarke is coming. Let Sherra make up her own mind from now on."

"Doret will begin her search for Ruarke immediately."

"Not if you tell her that tomorrow, you are sending her and those three children to Thorn, where they belong. They need her training, as you both well know. All three have mindspeak, and that is a rare and desirable gift. Keep Doret away from Ruarke at all costs. I see this ending badly for her if she pursues him. You must convince her—tell her that she is needed by those children—and by Thorn. She has a sworn duty to the Crown, you know."

"Blackmail, Adahi?"

"If that's how you choose to see it."

"Fine. Leave the shield up for tonight, and I'll send Doret and the children to Thorn tomorrow."

Chapter 7

"Tell them while I am still here, and the shield will be removed, regardless."

"Distrustful?"

"Kyri, you may not be thinking clearly in the wake of this news concerning Ruarke."

"I suppose you want me to tell Doret about that, too, while you're here?"

"It will not go amiss, I promise. Doret shall make up her own mind in this, but your persuasion will count for much in her decision. This way, she will not count withheld information against you later."

"Have you become my conscience, then?"

"When yours does not act as it should."

"She'll leave. Sherra will leave," I quavered.

"Kyri, you will only be alone if you wish to be alone. Go with them, if you want to continue seeing them. Get back to living a normal life. Surely someone here can take charge in your frequent absences. They will understand there are things that need doing in these volatile and unpredictable times."

"You're asking me to ally with Thorn?"

"He is the best of many I have seen who are destined for the throne—if he survives."

"I have no stomach—or desire for that," I said. "What about you?" I pointed an accusing finger at Adahi.

"If it will make you feel better, I have offered to train Thorn, but have held back after I saw more than one path leading to his death. My training will not help him, should that occur. Sherra will be the best shield and protection for him, should it come to that."

"More blackmail." I turned away from Adahi again.

"I consider this the event we all knew would come. It requires that we stand or fall together."

"As it has always been," I quoted without thinking.

"As it has always been," Adahi agreed.

* * *

Doret

"Adahi and I must speak with you, Doret," Kyri walked into the spare bedroom, where we were putting fresh sheets onto two small cots for Laren and Kyal. Anari would share Sherra's room—she'd offered to sleep on the floor and give Anari her bed, if she wanted.

"Where?" I asked, my hands stilling on a folded blanket.

"In the kitchen. I need tea," Kyri sighed. I knew then the news wasn't good. All three children, washed and dressed for bed, looked up and blinked at Kyri. They'd sensed something amiss, too. Sherra wore a frown as she gazed at both. She certainly understood that something was wrong.

"Finish the beds," I handed the blanket to Sherra. "I'll be back." Taking a deep breath, I followed Kyri and Adahi down the hall, toward the kitchen.

* * *

"Doret, you must train those children," Kyri said.

"I agree," Adahi dipped his head in a single nod. "If you choose to search for Ruarke, I feel it will end badly for you."

Ruarke. I despised him with a hatred none could eclipse. Adahi said Ruarke could be coming to Az-ca himself, treading across the boundary of Ny-nes that he'd hidden behind for so long.

"There is also the difficulty concerning the Crown Prince," Kyri said. "Adahi says he needs good advice and a steady hand, or his death could come and serve to destroy Az-ca anyway."

Chapter 7

"I don't care if it ends badly for me." I discarded everything they'd told me in the last few moments.

"Doret, please listen to me," Adahi rumbled softly. "I do not wish for your death to feed that vile creature's unnatural pleasures and ego."

Those words shocked me into a momentary silence. "You mean he'll survive?" I breathed when I could speak again.

"I cannot see his death at your hands, Doret."

"You still owe the Crown of Az-ca your service," Kyri reminded me. "You swore an oath long ago to protect it. It will fall if we do nothing."

"Channel your anger into thwarting Ruarke's and Merrin's plans," Adahi suggested. "You have much to offer the army—and the Crown Prince."

"Do you think those two—Ruarke and Merrin?" I almost couldn't breathe at the thought of *that* alliance.

"It is certainly possible, and perhaps likely, given the circumstances."

"You can't help anyone if you're dead," Kyri gripped my hands with hers. "Promise me you'll stay alive."

Closing my eyes, I drew a deep breath. And then another. I had no idea how many breaths it would take to still my anger and hatred of Ruarke, but I would do it, in an attempt to bring about his downfall.

Chapter 8

Sherra

"Laren and I stay in contact, we just didn't know it was called mindspeak until we were herded into the outpost and met Merrin," Anari explained. "Neither of us knew that Kyal could do the same until there at the last, before we got away."

"I wish I'd had someone to speak to like that when I was younger," I laid a quilt and blanket on the floor. The bed was small and wouldn't fit both of us, so Anari had agreed to take it.

"What was training like?" Anari asked, settling under the blanket and turning on her pillow to look at me.

"Scary at first," I admitted. "I think things will be much better for you, especially if Pottles—Doret—trains you."

"Why do you call her Pottles?"

"A long story. Ask her to tell you, sometime."

"So it's a friendly name?"

"Yes. Exactly. She calls it a nickname, but I have no idea where that word came from."

"Did you have friends while you were training?"

"I had the best friends, and one or two of the worst enemies," I said.

"Who were your friends?"

"Caral. Misten. Jae. Wend. Others, too."

"That sounds nice."

"It helped me so much, to have good friends like that."

"Did you choose a warrior?"

"That's a story for another day," I said. "Time to sleep, now."

* * *

Doret

Ruarke was always a coward, unless he had the upper hand, a small voice reminded me as I readied myself for bed. I doubted I'd get much sleep, with Ruarke's threat looming as it was.

What would change that—to make Ruarke bold enough to come to Az-ca and leave his safety in Ny-nes behind?

What did Merrin have to offer that Ruarke couldn't obtain for himself? Ruarke was much more talented than Merrin ever would be.

There had to be something.

Thorn's Book.

Holy hell. What would Ruarke be able to accomplish with that thing in his possession?

Kyri?

Yes? Her answer was a sleepy one.

Adahi thinks Ruarke will get his hands on Thorn's Book. Doesn't he?

Chapter 8

That's one of his concerns, yes.

This isn't good. For all of King Thorn's talents, did he ever stop to think the book could fall into the worst hands of all?

I don't have an answer, Doret. Let's sleep on this and discuss it in the morning. We'll decide then when to send you and the children to the Crown Prince, too.

He probably should hear their story soon, I said.

I know. I'm not looking forward to being without you here.

You can travel, too, I pointed out.

Yes. I can, can't I?

It won't be as if I don't know my way around the palace, either.

Very true. Good-night, Doret.

* * *

King's Palace
Kerok

If I didn't go to bed soon, I'd not get any sleep. If I went to bed, the same could be true.

I wanted to curse Merrin until he couldn't move from the weight of my words. Damn him, blast him, strangle—the list was nearly endless.

"You'll be receiving guests soon." Adahi walked into my study and took a seat as if he were invited.

"Guests?" I cast a wary eye upon the phantom. Guests could be welcome or unwelcome, and I dared not pretend to know which these would be.

"Three young ones escaped Merrin's clutches; a black rose girl and two warrior boys. The girl *stepped* them away to a safe place. They will be returned to you soon, and you will hear their tale."

"You're sure they're safe?" I rose to my feet to stare at Adahi.

"As sure as I am of anything. Another will bring them. Sherra calls her Pottles, but her true name is Doret."

"What about Sherra? Why doesn't she return?" I demanded. I needed her with me now, to navigate what had become the most dangerous maze of treason and betrayal I'd ever dealt with.

"She will return in her own time, Prince Thorn. When she is ready."

"When will that be? You said earlier that I needed her at my side to deal with Merrin."

"Patience is a virtue, or so I've heard, dear Prince. No, that's not meant to goad you, or make you angrier than you are at this situation," Adahi held up a hand. "If I thought it appropriate and it wouldn't interfere with her own choices, I'd bring her to you now. Whether she returns tomorrow or takes longer than that, I cannot say."

"Why can't I get mindspeak to her?" I wanted to shake Adahi and force him to answer my questions, but for now, he was the only link, tentative as it was, to perpetuating my belief that Sherra still lived.

"Where she is, mindspeak is blocked from leaving the area. She must depart that haven to communicate with you in mindspeak."

"Then what do you suggest?" I'd come to the point of letting this overwhelm me, and I knew it.

"Sherra is a dreamwalker, and can contact you that way," Adahi said. "I suggest you get some sleep."

* * *

Central Outpost
Merrin

Chapter 8

"No news is good news," I told Querl. "Our message is working. If they decide to ignore the first one, we'll just send another."

He and I sat around the outpost commander's desk, sharing a bottle of whiskey he'd scrounged from somewhere.

"I say we offer to trade a few live ones for mindspeakers," Querl hiccupped. "Young ones. You know how that will make their hearts bleed—to see young ones fried."

"Something to consider—when we're less drunk," I pointed a finger at Querl and laughed.

"We need to be drunker," he lifted the bottle with an unsteady hand and poured more whiskey in his glass. The fireblast that hit the outer walls shook the outpost so badly, Querl dropped the bottle. The shattering of glass and the screams of villagers reached my ears simultaneously.

* * *

King's Palace
Kerok

Thorn!

Hunter's mental shout woke me from a dream, the clouds of which reminded me that I'd been calling Sherra's name.

"What?" I said aloud, before the door to my bedchamber was thrust open and Hunter, closely followed by Barth, stumbled in.

Kage, still fully dressed and wide-awake, stepped in behind them.

"Garkus is missing, my Prince," Kage said. He'd wakened Hunter and Barth first, that was clear.

"Where is he?" I slid off the bed and reached for the trousers I'd worn earlier.

"I think he went to Central Outpost," Kage held out a written note.

"Tell me," I snapped.

"Garkus wrote that he's going to do what nobody else has the courage to do," Hunter breathed. "I think that means he's gone to attack Merrin, no matter what the consequences may be."

"Fucking hell," I snarled and snatched my shirt off the chair. "Let me get my boots on, and we'll see what he's up to."

"My Prince?" The night Captain of the guard now stood at my doorway.

"Yes, Captain?" I wanted to shout, but that would do no good.

"Two scouts recently arrived. They say Central Outpost is on fire."

"Garkus," Hunter and Barth said in unison.

"Let's go," I said, shoving boots on my feet without bothering to find socks. "We'll have to pull the fool away—if he's still alive. What's the status of the fire—is the entire outpost engulfed?" I barked at the Captain.

"They said the initial fireblast was quite large, my Prince."

"Let's go. I'm *stepping* out of here. Who's coming with me?"

"I've sent mindspeak to Armon. He and some of the others will meet us there," Hunter said.

"Stay here, Hunt," I dropped a hand on his shoulder. "You know why."

"I'll stay here," he nodded. "By your command. Be safe, Prince Thorn."

* * *

Chapter 8

Merrin

Thorn thought to attack me at night, eh?

That left the palace guarded by those who held no power.

A perfect time to destroy it.

"Come," I pulled Querl up by the shirt collar. I didn't give a damn that villagers were running out the gate—they'd survived the initial blast and were now running like stampeding cattle.

"What are your orders?" Gram appeared in the office doorway, still dressed in sleep clothes.

"Leave one warrior and his escort here—to fire back for a few minutes," I barked at him. "The rest of us are taking a trip to the palace—wouldn't you rather have it than Secondary Camp?"

"Let's go," Plicton's mind was made up quickly.

Outside, another blast hit the outpost, shaking the ground beneath the building.

"I thought you'd see things my way," I grinned. "Tell the others to *step* you; Querl and I are going now."

* * *

Central Outpost

Kerok

"What the bloody, feces-covered hell do you think you're doing?" I shouted at Garkus, who'd just leveled another blast at what remained of the outpost's walls.

"What you don't have the balls to do," Garkus turned toward me, grimacing as he forced another blast into the air.

From where we stood, less than a quarter mile away, I could hear screaming. Garkus hadn't killed all of them, but not from a lack of trying.

"Stop now, or I'll fry you where you stand," I shouted.

Rose and Thorn

"Try," Garkus laughed.

My exchange had given Barth time to approach Garkus' unguarded side. When Barth gripped Garkus' shoulders from behind, the assassin's power died with his laugh.

* * *

King's Palace

Hunter

I sat in Thorn's study, waiting to hear an update.

Garkus' power has been stilled, Thorn sent mindspeak. *Armon and Weren are assessing the damage and calling for physicians to tend the wounded. More than half the hostages are either dead or dying, thanks to Garkus' attack.*

What about Merrin and his sycophants?

Not here—ran like the cowards they are. I've sent Levi and a few others to Northeast Outpost to warn the messengers—Merrin probably went there the moment Garkus began firing blasts at him here. If you receive word of their whereabouts, notify me immediately.

Suddenly, Thorn's study was filled with people.

The first to arrive I recognized easily enough.

They're here, I sent, as Merrin leveled a fireblast directly at me. The bloom of light and fire that came next informed me that I was about to die.

Chapter 9

K ing's Palace
Hunter

It was a dream—perhaps that's what happened as you died—that you dreamed of your salvation as your body was left behind on a burning floor somewhere.

"They're gone," she said. "Your shield was a good one, Hunter. I only had to help a little."

Sherra. Sherra's face floated over mine as I blinked up at her.

"I can see through you," I croaked. "Am I dead? Are we ghosts?"

"You're not a ghost." She smiled at me. "I'm not a ghost, even though you can see through me now."

"How are you here?"

"Come now, sit up—I can't lift you physically at the moment."

Rose and Thorn

"What did you do? Did you scare them away?" I grunted as I struggled to sit up on Thorn's decorative rug.

It hadn't burned. Nearby, his desk stood, unscathed.

"I sent power against them. If it made them afraid, then they deserved that and more," she said. "I must go—I'm dreaming this where I am."

"But Thorn—he needs you. Desperately," I sighed.

"I know. I will consider that. There are other things that need attention, Hunter. Terrible things. This is only the beginning. I have to go."

She'd faded from my sight already when Barth and Thorn arrived to pull me to my feet.

* * *

Merrin

"What in the name of the first warrior was that?" Plicton exploded. I'd taken us back to the shack near the border temporarily, to gather my thoughts and consider my next move.

Plicton must have felt what I had inside Thorn's study— the feeling that thousands of claws were digging into my body, so painfully that I'd wanted to scream.

The bloom of light that came at that same moment had swallowed my fireblast as if it were a candle flame to be snuffed out.

What had Thorn done to protect the palace against me? He'd discovered the pilfering of Drenn's room—and the treasury, no doubt. This bit of work—I'd never seen its like before.

I wanted this ability for myself. Perhaps *Thorn's Book* could explain—I cursed long and loudly, then.

Thorn's Book had been beneath my bed at Central Outpost, with the dagger and coronet. The book was likely ash, now, and the dagger and crown little more than twisted, melted metal.

"What's wrong?" Querl asked.

"Never mind," I snarled. "Let's go to Northeast Outpost. I want to know if it's still intact and in our possession."

* * *

Northeast Outpost
Ruarke

"Just leave them there," I waved a hand after pretending to shut off the small device. A warrior and his escort lay dead on the floor, with scorch marks all about them. I wanted Merrin to find them on his way to the commander's office. If he attempted to level a blast at me, I could easily thwart his efforts.

My clerics surrounded me as I strode toward the office in question—and the desk and chair that surely waited.

I wanted Merrin to know exactly where he stood in my presence. After all, he'd failed to protect one outpost already, from a single attacker.

That attacker didn't have half the talent I held, or ties to Ny-nes' Sovereign Leader and his entire army.

I also held something Merrin thought lost—and that, if nothing else, could prove to him that I was more than familiar with his tricks and could walk through them at will. While that wasn't particularly true now, I'm sure it would be in the future. All it had taken was the divination of a fire at Central Outpost and his expected, hasty exit.

"Set the box down on the corner of the desk," I nodded at my cleric, who'd carried the small chest as if it contained deadly snakes. "Our quarry approaches. We will pretend to be allies, just as I've instructed. He won't know we mean him harm until we have exactly what we want—the complete destruction of Az-ca."

* * *

Sherra

My head was still clouded with my dreams as I drank tea at the breakfast table. Something had interrupted one dream, which morphed quickly into another. Only now I recalled that I'd dreamed that Kerok was calling my name, which served to set up the second dream.

A dream more terrifying than the first, if that were possible. In the first dream, I'd stood inside an unfamiliar outpost and watched as an enemy I hadn't known marched through it, followed by men dressed in black robes that hung to their ankles.

My focus had been on a small chest that a black robe carried, when Kerok's mental anguish pulled me away—he'd been shouting my name for some reason, and he'd sounded desperately unhappy.

My dream had transferred from the outpost to the King's palace quickly; only to find Hunter under attack from Merrin and several others. I recalled repelling them in the dream and then speaking to Hunter afterward, before Anari shifted on the bed nearby and woke me with a start.

"We're taking the young ones to Prince Thorn tomorrow," Pottles announced as she walked into the kitchen. "I'm going with them, to make sure they're trained properly."

"But," I sputtered.

"It's what Kyri and Adahi want—they say it needs to happen," Pottles shrugged. There was something hidden beneath her words, but I didn't ask what that could be.

"Want tea?" I asked, rising from my seat. "I'll get it, and fix breakfast for you."

"Thank you," Pottles settled on a chair with a sigh. "I'm out of sorts this morning."

"May I have tea?" Anari shuffled into the kitchen.

"Of course. Take a seat, I'll get it," I waved toward an empty chair.

"Central Outpost burned to the ground last night, and half of Merrin's hostages died in the fire," Kyri strode into the kitchen. "Things aren't looking good, Doret."

"What happened?" Anari begged. "What about?" She didn't finish, although I was sure she wanted to know whether her parents survived.

"Your parents are alive, according to Adahi. Sadly, neither Laren's nor Kyal's still live."

"Oh, no," I moaned.

"Should we postpone the journey?" Pottles asked.

"No. Taking them to Thorn is still our best option."

"What?" Anari sounded confused.

"I am taking you to the Crown Prince," Pottles attempted to soothe Anari. "You belong there, and I will stay with you, to make sure you are trained as you should be. Mindspeak is a rare and valuable talent, young one. It's a talent which could aid the Prince in the coming days. To find three of you with the ability in the same village—that is extremely unusual."

"Is he mean? The Crown Prince?"

"Ask Sherra. She knows him better than anyone here."

"He isn't mean—or scary. He will be overjoyed to see you," I told Anari. "You must tell him what you saw and heard while at the outpost—he'll need that information."

Rose and Thorn

Laren and Kyal walked into the kitchen then. Pottles and Kyri got them seated at the table, while I poured tea and set about making breakfast. I wondered how Kyri intended to tell them about their parents, until I saw that Anari had informed both in mindspeak.

Kyal's gaze was downcast; Laren appeared to be stunned.

They need help, I think, I informed Pottles. It was fortunate, perhaps, that Anari sat between both boys—I could see she was gripping their hands beneath the table.

"Here, something warm," I set tea down for all three.

"Loss is never easy, young ones," Pottles sighed. "We will do what we can to help you through this."

* * *

King's Palace

Kerok

"Garkus is still shouting in the lockup," Hunter appeared harried as he walked into my study. "The messengers report that they've seen movement at Northeast Outpost, so Merrin is likely there, now."

"*Stepped* straight from here to there, most likely," I said. None of us had slept, which resulted in a weary early morning, during which decisions would have to be made. "Are you ready to tell me how you survived an attack from Merrin and Querl, now?"

"I'm not sure I believe it myself," Hunter said. He was unwilling to tell this story; anyone could see that.

"Tell me anyway. I need cheering up before discussing Garkus' fate."

"Ah, well, I saw Sherra, only it wasn't really her," Hunter's voice wobbled. "I could see right through her image."

Chapter 9

I blinked at Hunter in confusion for several moments, before my exhausted mind recalled that I should bring Barth in to hear this story.

Several more moments passed until Barth could reach us—he looked as tired as the rest of us did. "I asked for tea to be brought," Barth said before taking a seat. "What's this about seeing through Sherra? Did I hear that correctly?"

Barth turned bloodshot eyes on me.

"It's what Hunter said—that he saw her and saw through her."

"She said she was asleep where she was," Hunter's second admission confused me more than the first one had.

It took Barth a moment to digest the information. I could see after a few seconds of silence that he had a possible explanation. "Well?" I asked my Chief Diviner.

"It's such an old story, I thought it was a myth," Barth shrugged.

"I like stories." I recalled that the story about Kyri appeared to be true. Maybe this held truth—or the seeds of truth.

"Dreamwalking," Barth said. "My teacher told me about it when I was first beginning to learn, years ago. He said a dreamwalker may have abilities the real person hasn't developed yet. I found that difficult to believe, my Prince. Then and now."

"Did you get a better explanation than that?" Hunter grimaced at Barth. "I saw Sherra last night, but I saw right through her, even though she was talking and making sense. Merrin tried to blast me. I don't know why I didn't get burned to a crisp, and this room with me."

"I really don't want to send mindspeak, but I figure Adahi could explain this," I said, covering my face with both hands.

Why hadn't I *seen Sherra?* In my befuddled state of weariness, I felt slighted that she'd come to Hunter instead of me.

Hunter's life was the one in danger, I reminded myself. Still, that realization made me feel no better. As tired and angry as I felt about the night's events, the worst of it was that I felt abandoned.

Adahi was right about Garkus acting rashly—his words had been proven true in less than a day's passing.

"Do you think Merrin's plan to attack here was impulsive—after Garkus attacked the outpost?" I asked, dropping my hands and gazing blearily at Barth.

"I think it was precipitated by Garkus' actions, and doesn't surprise me that he imagined the entire army had been sent to attack him," Barth replied. "He expected you to be poorly-guarded as a result, and came here to capitalize on that supposition."

"I can't say whether I'm glad I wasn't here, or that I should have been here so Hunter wouldn't have to face Merrin's attack by himself—without discounting the ah, unexpected help," I amended, when Hunter looked ready to burst with a rebuttal.

"That still leaves us with the problem at Northeast Outpost," Barth intervened before Hunter and I began to argue.

"How do we explain to the villagers who survived last night why half their number died in what they currently believe was a botched rescue attempt?" I pointed my argument at Barth instead. "Garkus was the King's

Chapter 9

Assassin—until he chose to go rogue. That means we're responsible, whether we knew of his plans or only learned of them after the damage was done."

"Some Council members are pushing back and lodging protests," Hunter admitted reluctantly. "They believe we did this without thinking it through, and they're now concerned for dead villagers, whereas they weren't concerned about any of the live ones before."

"Then convene the fucking Council," I snapped at Hunter. "We'll give them the truth, and see how it goes."

"They'll still blame you, Thorn," Barth said. "They'll bring up Drenn, who will now attain abilities he never displayed while he lived. The dead will always make a better choice and do a better job, you know."

"I wish Father were stronger," I sighed. "I'd ask for advice. This—is on us, regardless of whether we initiated it."

"Then hold a public trial for Garkus, instead of shouldering all the blame yourself," Adahi walked into my suite.

When that idea filtered into my brain, which was undeniably slow at grasping anything at the moment, I realized he was right.

Let the Council question Garkus and his motives. Any diviner would know if he spoke the truth.

A public trial of military personnel hadn't happened in a very long time. In this case, where civilian deaths were concerned, it could be considered appropriate.

"Then we'll do that," I said. "Hunter, take the message to the Council. We'll convene tomorrow, to discuss a time and place. Today, we must discuss how to handle Merrin's presence at Northeast Outpost."

"Have the physicians testify as to the damage caused by Garkus' attack," Adahi went on. He'd lowered his hood today, so we could see his face. "If I were you, I'd also ask them to testify regarding the neglect of those villages by their ah, representative Council members."

"We can summon the villagers, too, to corroborate that testimony," Barth suggested.

"Excellent idea, Diviner," Adahi nodded to Barth.

"Tea, my Prince," one of the guards tapped on the door.

"Bring it in," I said. "Adahi, will you join us?"

"Certainly."

* * *

Northeast Outpost

Merrin

He'd killed another of my warriors—and his escort—while I watched. *How in the name of the first warrior had the enemy created a device that could do what a warrior did?*

"I did that to get your attention, Merrin," he'd said.

Ruarke. He called himself Ruarke. Described himself as the Chief Cleric to the Sovereign Leader of Ny-nes.

Then, he'd offered me protection, the throne of Az-ca, and control of thousands of Ny-nes' troops to keep the peace among the rabble—if I cooperated and helped him destroy the King, the Crown Prince, and every warrior and escort in existence.

Granted, the idea had merit.

A great deal of merit.

Gram was somewhat skeptical—but if I promised him a role as my First Advisor, why should he quibble if Az-ca's army was destroyed and Ny-nes annexed our lands? If I were

Chapter 9

left in charge as Ruarke said, I'd see that the remaining population followed my desired path anyway.

It greatly intrigued me to be one of only a handful remaining in Az-ca with a warrior's talents.

Ruarke didn't seem to mind that I'd remain powerful. He had a device, after all. Who knew—everyone in Ny-nes could now own one of those things. Power in the hands of the rabble? Nobody could have guessed that.

As for Ruarke's black-robed clerics, they were silent more often than not. Their faces were like masks—neither approving or disapproving. They merely obeyed Ruarke's every whim in every matter, and I admired that level of submission.

Gram, Querl and the others had a penchant for arguing against everything I put forward. If Ny-nes were in charge, I'd expect to see that subservience in everyone about me.

"You can have that and more," Ruarke spoke aloud after reading my expression. I followed his gaze to the small chest lying on a corner of the outpost commander's desk. "You may read the book anytime you wish, after I've read through it. Never forget, too, that you will be left in charge, here. Neither I nor my people want that position."

A slow smile spread across my face at his words. "I've considered your offer, Chief Cleric," I said. "I'll stand with Ny-nes; as will my followers."

* * *

Sherra

"Will we get more clothes when we get to the King's City?" Anari stepped through my open door sounding lost.

"Of course," I said, motioning for her to come in. "Sit there on the bed. I think you can have a few of my things before you go—if you want them. They may be a little long, but they'll fit."

"I like this," she pointed to a blue top I'd just folded.

"Then it's yours," I handed it to her. "There are dark blue trousers to go with it," I rummaged through a stack until I found them.

"Those are nice," she agreed and pulled both items to her chest, as if she were afraid I'd take them back.

"You should see the uniforms for the escort trainees," I smiled at her. "And those they give to escort officers, if you get a promotion."

"Did you get a promotion?"

"I was a captain," I said. "In the King's Army."

"Az-ca still exists because of Sherra," Pottles walked in. "I see you already have an outfit for tomorrow," Pottles smiled at Anari, who clutched the clothing to her chest. "Come with me; I'll find other things for you."

"What about Kyal and Laren?" I asked as Anari slid off my bed to follow Pottles.

"I've asked for help in the matter. Cole is sending something for them."

"Good."

"There will be baths tonight and clean clothes tomorrow," Pottles patted Anari's shoulder. "We can't go to the Crown Prince dirty."

I didn't miss the sudden hero-worship in Anari's eyes; Pottles had made a definite friend.

I laid out two other outfits so Anari could choose something else, but all the while, I couldn't shake a feeling that something had gone horribly wrong in Az-ca.

It has to do with your dreams, I told myself. A part of me wanted to tell Kyri. Another part wanted to hold the

Chapter 9

information back. Both halves warred with the other, which ended up rendering me helpless and undecided in the matter.

"I'll take the yellow outfit, too," Anari decided.

"Yes—it'll look good on you," I agreed.

"Have you been to the palace?"

"I have."

"I wish you were coming, too," Anari sighed. "Doret is nice and I look forward to learning from her, but having someone else to talk to would be good, too."

She meant someone closer to her own age—I read the wistfulness in her voice.

What if I did go back with her?

Would that be a bad thing?

Kerok had been calling my name—that's what sent me in his direction in my dream the night before. It's just that other things drew my attention away, and I hadn't seen him after all.

I'd seen Hunter—and the one called Ruarke.

Who was Ruarke? I needed information on that one. Would Kerok know who he was? I knew one thing that others perhaps didn't, though. If my dream were true, he now held a very dangerous book.

There's one way to find out if Kerok really wants to see you, a small voice said.

Ever since I'd breached Kyri's perimeter divination, I'd held the key to breaking through the shield she held around her city.

I could get past it, now, either by *stepping* or in mindspeak.

I hadn't forgotten the vision of the boy I'd seen in her necklace, either. I wanted so badly to ask who he was, but held back. She didn't know that I could see that memory in her belongings. Neither did Pottles realize I'd seen her memory.

Perhaps it was time to consider other memories, of other people. Merrin I also wanted to see again, but handling the rosewood box and dagger sheath could be telling if Kyri or Pottles found me with either.

Perhaps there was a way to deal with everything at once.

If I returned the sheath and box to the King's palace, where they belonged.

If Kyri didn't want me to go, what then? Would it be ungrateful of me to go against her wishes? Where was my loyalty in all this? If Kerok needed me, if Az-ca were in as much danger as I imagined it to be, that decision could be an easy one to make.

You owe it to the black rose girls who are afraid to come here, the small voice insisted. *They are in terrible danger, as are the warrior boys.*

"I need to find Kyri," I told Anari. "Try on those clothes—we may be able to hem them before you leave."

* * *

Kyri

"I dislike this."

"You cannot—and should not—hold her here against her will. She is needed by the Crown Prince and all of Az-ca. The visions are fracturing all around us and you know this. I cannot see Ruarke's hand in anything—not since he breached the barrier between us and Ny-nes. I know not where he is. He is close to Az-ca, I feel it, but that is the best I can do."

"You think to pit her against that viper? You know what he is," I hissed.

Chapter 9

"We fight with what we have," Adahi quoted the old adage. "If she is successful against Ruarke," he began.

"*If* she is successful," I snapped. "She needs more time and training."

"Because you want her able to take on the one who is worse than Ruarke. Admit it—you wanted her to breach the barrier around Ny-nes, and get you past it, too. That's why you've focused her recently on the perimeter divinations. How long has it been since you were locked out of Ny-nes?"

Adahi knew just where to dig to find the sorest part of *that* festering wound. "Admit that you may not be strong enough, Kyri, to stand against him again," he added.

"He deserves to die," I hissed.

"As do many. We all meet our match—or the one who is stronger, eventually. Then it no longer matters who is right—only who is powerful enough to survive."

"Selling me platitudes from the End-War, Adahi?"

"It bears saying again. We know who won, by killing nearly everything in their path."

"Too bad those fanatics from Ny-nes can no longer read the book they believe so desperately in," I snorted. "Judgment and purgatory for those who are evil? What a load of tripe. Every day, they're led around and subjugated by evil, and they don't have a clue."

"Kyri?" Sherra's voice floated into my study—she was looking for me.

"Bring her in," Adahi said. "I think she may have something to tell you."

"In here," I called out, even as I frowned at Adahi.

"Kyri? Oh, sorry," Sherra stepped back after discovering Adahi standing nearby.

"Do not fear," Adahi held up a hand. "Ask your question—I see it in your eyes, young one."

"Uh," she looked from Adahi to me and then back again. "Do you ah, know anyone by the name of Ruarke?"

* * *

Sherra

"You're sure he has the book?" Kyri asked the question for perhaps the fourth time. Every time, my answer was the same.

"He has the book, the dagger and the coronet. And Merrin, too, I think. I didn't see Merrin, but it's logical to me," I said. "I don't know the name of the outpost, either, but it was an outpost, I'm sure of it."

"Our worst fears," Adahi turned his back to me as we sat inside Kyri's study. That's when I understood that Kyri and Adahi were holding a silent conversation in mindspeak.

"Did you see anyone else?" Adahi turned back to ask.

"I ah, saw Hunter, when he was attacked by Merrin and someone else in Kerok's study," I said. These two were taking my dreams and treating them as if they were more real than reality, if that were possible.

"Hunter still lives," Adahi confirmed before I could say it. "I saw him earlier. He remains confused about his rescue, but this—Kyri, you can no longer doubt."

"How long will it take Ruarke to get through the book?" Kyri whispered, her eyes begging Adahi to give her hope.

"Perhaps a few days," Adahi rumbled. "After that, who can guess what he'll do?"

"Why will Ruarke read the book? What can he do with it?" I asked.

"We must approach the Crown Prince, before it is too late," Adahi said. "We are wasting time as it is."

Chapter 9

"I'll go with Doret in the morning," Kyri said. She sounded defeated. "Sherra, go pack your things—you must come with me."

"Kyri," I began as I stood to go.

"What is it?"

"I think we should gather the older black rose girls still in Az-ca—and the warrior boys, too. I am afraid for them." My voice became a whisper at the end, as if speaking those words aloud made them truer than they'd ever been.

"It's prudent," Adahi agreed.

"Then you tell Thorn to get on that," Kyri snapped at Adahi. "Tell him he'll have visitors tomorrow morning. Early."

She was angry about all of this, and spitting her anger at Adahi and me, when we'd had nothing to do with it.

"Kyri, it isn't their fault," Pottles appeared in the doorway. "Put the blame where it belongs—on Ruarke's and Merrin's shoulders."

"Doret, make sure the children are ready early tomorrow. We'll go. I may not stay, but I'll go for a meeting with Thorn," Kyri sighed. "Meanwhile, don't tell the children of this—they have enough to deal with as it is."

"I'll see to it. Sherra, you need tea and something to eat. Come with me—the young ones are eating in the kitchen."

* * *

King's Palace
Kerok

"He didn't say who's coming?" Hunter asked a second time. Adahi had come and gone, after delivering a rather cryptic message.

"He didn't. He only specified the number and type of suites."

"One with two beds means two are sharing. Two others with one bed means either two couples, or two that aren't sharing. It could mean at least four, or as many as six."

"True."

A part of me held hope that one of our visitors would be Sherra, but why would Adahi ask for a separate suite if that were the case? If Sherra came, there was only one place I was willing to allow her to stay, and that was with me. I hadn't set aside our vows. Only death or the actions of the King or Crown Prince could do that.

I certainly wasn't willing to take that action. Even if Sherra were dead, I'd be unwilling. I'd had enough of pain, and had grown tired of losing what I loved.

"Get the rooms ready, and select those close together if possible. I don't want to set up extra guards if it's not warranted."

"I've already given it some thought," Hunter said. "I have staff working to prepare four rooms on third floor east."

He'd named suites farthest from Father's and mine. That satisfied me well enough. Whether Adahi thought these guests trustworthy, I would make my own determinations—with help from Barth and Hunter.

"The kitchen will serve drinks and small treats for the breakfast meeting tomorrow morning," Hunter added. "I've included Weren, Armon, Levi and several others in the number expected."

"Good. Thank you, Hunter. I hadn't considered that."

"You should also consider what you'll wear, Crown Prince Thorn," Hunter pointed out. "You're still wearing your uniforms, you know."

"Hmmph. Do you think I'll start dressing like Drenn?"

Chapter 9

"Nobody should dress like Drenn," Hunter sniffed. "Not even Drenn should have dressed like Drenn."

"Then order clothing—in black. Make a new design, marking me as the Crown Prince and ultimate Commander of the Army."

"Making a change?"

"It will be made," I growled. "I know what I'm doing on the battlefield—who better to do it?"

"None that I know," Hunter agreed. "We have Council members who want to do what Garkus did and attack Northeast Outpost. I told them that was out of the question, with so many civilian lives at stake. On another note, how is the training of washouts coming? We need extra troops to guard villages. We can't risk Merrin taking more than he has already."

"Armon says they have to work around convincing some of them—men and women—that they actually have the talent in them, it only needs to be brought out better."

"I'm assuming the men had better training to begin with?"

"They did. I wish Sherra were here—maybe they were never meant to be warriors, but messengers or something else, instead."

"You think she could touch them and tell you what they were suited for?"

"I do. I wish I'd considered it before. Especially in light of recent events. We needed more messengers; messengers working directly for the Crown instead of worthless Council members, who took the money provided by the Crown and kept it, instead of paying the messengers."

"I have a suggestion, then," Hunter said.

"What's that?"

"To allow the villages to send their own representatives to comprise the Council, rather than appointing overfed politicians from the King's City to consider their interests—because they don't. They're self-serving, and it's the real reason you don't want anything to do with them—admit it."

"That's something to consider," I agreed. "But first, we have to deal with other problems."

"Merrin—and Garkus' trial date."

"Merrin and Garkus," I repeated Hunter's answer. "Merrin, who holds villagers and an outpost hostage, even as we speak. I'm surprised he hasn't sent another note, yet."

"Give him time—he was always slow at writing anything."

I barked an unwilling laugh; not only was it an excellent insult, but all the better because it was true.

* * *

Secondary Camp
Armon

"I want you and Misten to come to the meeting with us tomorrow," I told Caral. "We can't be too careful, you know."

"What about the trainees?" she asked.

"Wend and Marc can oversee training for half a day," I said. "I know you're worried about more than half our trainees, but they can wait a few hours for you to stand over them and glare if they're not trying."

Caral turned away so I wouldn't see the grin.

"Thorn says there'll be a few extra guests, but he didn't say who they were. It almost sounded as if he didn't know himself, but unless I miss my guess, there'll be tea and a nice breakfast, with honey cakes, perhaps."

"Food is always good at the palace," Caral turned back to me. She was still smiling.

Chapter 9

"Yes, it is. Wear your new uniform, Captain."
"I will."

* * *

Sherra

"It's fried squash, fresh from the garden, and sliced tomatoes," Pottles told Kyal, who couldn't get enough of the vegetables on his plate during evening meal.

"It's wonderful," Anari confirmed. "I don't think I've ever had squash before."

"Good," Laren confirmed around a mouthful of food. At least they were eating, instead of staring morosely at their plate.

"Wait until you swallow your food to speak," Pottles reminded Laren. He nodded and kept eating.

I recognized their hunger—I'd had it myself at their age. It wasn't until I arrived at North Camp that I'd ever been full after a meal.

"You'll have enough food from now on—especially if you're in training," I told them.

"Baths and bed after we finish cleaning the kitchen," Pottles warned. "Tomorrow, we wake early."

"Yes'm," Kyal nodded.

Chapter 10

*K*erok

"I don't fidget," I told my image in the mirror. "I am the Crown Prince of Az-ca, and former Prince Commander of Az-ca's Army. I do not fidget."

I'd risen long before breakfast, because I couldn't sleep. I'd tended to unwelcome paperwork, while my mind wandered often to the guests scheduled to arrive for breakfast.

Silently, I begged for one of them to be Sherra, but why wouldn't Adahi say she was coming, if she were? After all, I was dependent upon his words being truth about her continued existence.

Why would he not report on the guests?

It made no sense and I struggled to contain my hope, lest it lead to substantial disappointment.

Kage has arrived, Hunter informed me.

Rose and Thorn

I will be there shortly.

We'd chosen a meeting room near Drenn's suite—it was a small library that held a long table and chairs. Drenn should have used it to meet with Council members of this sector or that, but he'd left it to collect dust and went to the Council chambers instead, to conduct his business.

All of which was self-serving, as it turned out.

Hunter had the room cleaned and made ready; I'm sure the kitchen was prepared to deliver tea and food the moment he called.

I forced myself to walk at a steady, normal pace as I left my suite in the west wing. There were hallways and stairs to navigate before arriving at the meeting room. As yet, our guests had not arrived or Hunter would have alerted me, I'm sure.

When I walked into the small library, I found Kage sitting on the left, near my seat at the head of the table.

"General Weren, Colonel Armon, Captains Levi and Caral, and escort Misten, my Prince," Hunter ushered those five into the room.

"Please, sit," I motioned toward the table. "Breakfast is on the way."

"My Prince," Barth dipped his head as he entered on Misten's heels.

"Barth, good morning," I told him.

"Prince Thorn," Adahi, his hood already down, strode through the door. Following him were several others; Kyri followed Adahi. Three young ones—two boys and one girl— followed Kyri, then came Doret, whom Sherra called Pottles.

My knees threatened to give way beneath my weight.

Sherra.

Chapter 10

I'll never know whether I *stepped*, jumped or ran; all I remember is the scent of her as I crushed her in my arms, and the tears as her arms wrapped around my neck in return.

* * *

Sherra

If the meeting hadn't been so important, I'd have gone anywhere Kerok wanted to take me after his greeting. He'd kissed me, over and over, in front of all the others.

I don't think either of us cared.

I now sat to his right as the breakfast meeting commenced.

"These three young ones escaped Merrin's clutches," Kyri indicated the two boys and the girl. "Anari *stepped* them away. The boys' parents died later—in the attack."

"I am most sorry about your parents," Kerok closed his eyes for a moment while regret washed through him. When he blinked again, he focused on Laren and Kyal. "Will you tell us what you saw and heard at the outpost?" he asked. "We seek justice in the loss of innocent lives, and hope to prevent other deaths, too."

"Kyal and I heard the one you call Merrin say many things," Laren admitted. "He wanted to kill those he kidnapped. He wants to kill you, too," Laren hesitated over those words. "Kyal and I have talked—we're grateful that some escaped. We don't think Merrin wanted any of us to live."

"Don't be afraid—I already know Merrin wants me dead," Kerok held up a hand. "Tell me what else you heard."

"The uh, Council man said he'd separated the villagers into two groups," Kyal spoke, now. "He divided those who believed him from those who didn't. Merrin called the Council man Plicton. I've never heard that name before."

"I know who that is, and he is no longer a Council member," Kerok said, keeping his voice calm so as not to upset the boy. "Go on."

"Merrin said the ones who didn't believe Plicton should be killed when the army arrived. I think he intended to burn them and uh, cut them apart," Laren took up the tale while Kyal nodded.

"Then Plicton wanted to know what would happen if the army attacked both outposts at once. Merrin said he had a—perimeter around the outposts." Kyal stumbled on the word perimeter, as if it were a term he'd never used before.

Barth, Hunter and Armon were nodding at the boy's words—they'd already known about the perimeters Merrin could set, to alert him to encroachers.

"They said they wanted to take someplace—second camp?" Kyal went on. "Merrin said that while the army was attacking the outposts, he and Plicton would get away to take second camp."

"Secondary Camp," Weren's frown was deep. "I'm not surprised he covets it."

I watched as the fist Weren rested on the table curled and uncurled, as if he wanted Merrin's neck in his grip. Garkus' unplanned attack had accomplished one thing, at least—Merrin's initial plans had been diverted. It made me wonder what Levi and Armon were doing to protect Secondary Camp.

"Merrin told Plicton to get Anari, then," Laren said. "When she came in, I knew she wasn't safe with Merrin or Plicton."

"I heard Kyri's message—to go to her," Anari took up the story. "I grabbed Kyal's and Laren's hands and *stepped* us away."

Chapter 10

"Very brave—all three of you," Kerok said. "I have rooms for you, and, if I understand correctly, training will be provided?" He turned toward Pottles, who nodded.

"I want to place a shield around Secondary Camp, if there aren't enough people left behind to protect it," I stated.

"May I suggest another tack?" Adahi held up a hand.

"What's that?" Hunter asked.

"Sherra may be able to get past Merrin's perimeter divination," Kyri said.

"But," Adahi objected.

"What if—*he* plants a perimeter divination before she gets there?" Pottles hissed. "Sherra may not be able to get past what *he* can do."

I turned to Kerok—he had no idea what Pottles meant. Kyri glowered, as if the one Pottles mentioned were an affront—even if his name had been left out completely. They were talking about Ruarke—I understood that quickly.

"Who?" Kerok turned back to Pottles.

"A boil on the ass of all living things," Pottles mumbled.

"She speaks of one called Ruarke. He is ah, Chief Cleric for the Sovereign Leader of Ny-nes," Adahi explained. "He is, according to reliable reports, now allied with Merrin at Northeast Outpost."

* * *

Hunter had taken Kyal, Anari and Laren to the kitchen for a honey cake while Kerok waited to learn about a person he hadn't known existed.

"Ruarke. Kyri and I have known about him—for a long time. Occasionally, we see refugees from Ny-nes," Pottles sighed. "They tell us the same tale about Ruarke, a heartless, cruel creature who has set himself up as the head of the religion practiced in Ny-nes, because that puts him in charge of the torture and killing of any who are found in Ny-nes with power. Including small children."

"There are those in Ny-nes born with power?" Kerok disliked that idea greatly.

"Yes," Kyri said simply. "There are no boundaries on power, Prince Thorn. The trouble comes when those in charge of Ny-nes see it as a terrible crime against their religion. They torture and kill anyone rumored to have power, before they have a chance to develop their talents—or live their lives."

"That's sickening," Misten whispered.

"Hmmph. You don't know Ruarke like we do," Pottles snorted. "Take the worst evils you can imagine and multiply them by thousands. You may get close to what Ruarke is and does. Merrin's tricks can't come close to Ruarke's disturbed behavior."

"Why are you so concerned about him—Ruarke?" Barth asked. "Even if he is allied with Merrin, he is only a cleric—by your own description."

"What you don't understand, and what is most dangerous of all, perhaps, is that Ruarke was born with power—and survived," Pottles interjected.

"But how? You say all in Ny-nes are tortured and killed who have power," Weren argued.

"He's quite cunning," Pottles muttered. "He can fool even the best among us. Merrin will only be a stepping stone when Ruarke decides to act, and mark my words, he is coming for the King's City. Adahi has felt it."

"So. Ruarke is still alive and fooling everyone in Ny-nes, and we have to deal with this now, because?" Kerok asked.

"Ruarke wants to destroy Az-ca, in any way he can," Kyri explained. "Somehow, he'd gotten wind of Merrin's acts of treason, and the fact that he's still running loose. Now that they've found one another, I can't imagine a more terrifying alliance."

"With Ruarke's hands on Thorn's Book, it will be worse than that," Adahi said quietly.

"Thorn's Book?" Weren asked.

"King Thorn," Adahi corrected himself. "The one Prince Thorn is named after. The book he wrote enables Merrin to set those perimeter divinations mentioned earlier. To our benefit, Merrin has limited talent to use the book. Ruarke has no such limitations."

"How do we go about finding Ruarke, then?" Kerok asked.

"If we approach Northeast Outpost, they'll know and desert it—after killing the villagers, no doubt. Afterward, it's anyone's guess where they'll go. Even the best diviner won't see it," Pottles said.

"You don't find Ruarke—for the same reason you don't find Merrin by employing divination. They're unseeables," Kyri explained.

"That's frightening," Barth rumbled.

"More so than you think, Diviner," Kyri said.

"You say Ruarke has a great deal of power—how does he get around the laws preventing it in Ny-nes?" Armon asked.

"He doesn't employ power until it's time to torture," Adahi grimaced. "Then, he claims it is the power of their god working through him which creates the despicable acts. It ah, serves to convince the population of Ny-nes."

"How the hell do we fight that?" Kerok tossed out a hand in frustration. "He seems to have an answer for everything. I thought we were fighting an enemy who only had bombs and mechanical weapons. If Merrin, the lying treasonous bastard, has truly allied himself with this abomination, we could be doomed faster than anyone expected."

* * *

Kerok

"Adahi and I won't be staying," Kyri informed me. Misten and Caral had spirited Sherra away for a reunion of sorts; Weren, Armon and Levi had joined Kage and Hunter for a midday meal, Doret had gone to find the three young ones, and I'd been left with Kyri and Adahi.

I'd been in more comfortable situations in the midst of heavy battle.

"We will return often—I have things to teach," Adahi rumbled.

"I hope you keep me abreast of happenings with Cleric Ruarke," I said. "As much as you can." For whatever reason, I felt as if they'd told the truth about the cleric, but only a partial truth. They knew more about Ruarke than they'd said; I was certain of it.

"Don't wander far down that path, Prince Thorn," Adahi warned. "You won't like what you find there."

"I dislike what I've discovered so far," I snapped. "Tell me how to destroy them before they find a way to kill us all."

"We don't have an answer, just as you don't," Kyri sounded angry. "Not unless you want a swath of innocent bodies strewn across Az-ca, and most of the villages on fire."

"Consider this," Adahi said. "You can take your army and distribute it among the villages, and that leaves the King's City vulnerable. Concentrate the troops in the King's City and the villages will surely die. Tread carefully, Prince Thorn. The ultimate desire of Merrin is to take the King's

Chapter 10

City. Ruarke's ultimate desire is to see it fall. Use all weapons at your disposal, including your black rose."

"When Ny-nes' army returns, as it surely will, you will be forced to defeat them, too," Kyri said. "I may be able to bring others who are willing to fight beside you, but if that happens, then you must accept them as your own countrymen afterward."

"Allies will be welcome, no matter what," I said.

"I'll remember you said that, Prince Thorn."

* * *

Sherra

"There you are." Kerok found us in the palace gardens. I was teaching Misten and Caral how to make a mirror shield. For the moment, Misten was completely invisible. Kerok walked right through her bubble shield as he approached.

"It really works," Caral breathed as Kerok joined us. Misten released her shield with a laugh.

"You just walked through Misten's mirror shield," I told him. He was completely disinterested in that. Taking my left hand, he raised it to his lips and kissed the black rose on my wrist.

"Sherra, will you come to Secondary Camp?" Misten asked.

"Kerok?" I placed a hand on his shoulder. "May I have dinner there with them tonight?"

"Tomorrow, after breakfast," Kerok mumbled distractedly against my wrist before kissing it again.

"Put up your strongest shields," I told them as Armon and Levi appeared to take them away. "In layers. Don't let anyone you don't know *step* inside."

"Come with me," Kerok breathed against my ear the moment they *stepped* away.

"I have to put up shields, first," I told him. His breath against my ear was doing strange things to my body.

"Hurry," he kissed my cheek and then my throat.

I hurried.

* * *

Kerok

"My rose, wake." I nuzzled Sherra's bare shoulder before kissing it. "Breakfast, then work," I mumbled while my body made other demands. Those desires had to be forced back; I'd already taken much of her time, and, as she wasn't used to my loving, I didn't want to make her sore.

Sherra curled into a ball—a clear signal that she wanted to sleep more. I chuckled, kissed her shoulder again and rolled off the bed.

Watching her straighten her body, stretch, yawn and then sit up was worth everything I owned.

"If you hurry with your shower, we can have breakfast with Hunter and Barth," I teased as she turned toward me.

"I'll hurry." Sliding off the bed, she trotted around it, past me and into my private bath before I could stop her.

* * *

Sherra

"Just hand her the entire dish of butter and don't ask questions," Kerok grinned at Hunter.

"It's not that bad, really," I said while accepting the dish of butter from Hunter. Barth, sitting next to Hunter at a small breakfast table in Kerok's sitting room, ducked his head and snickered.

"I'll have new uniforms made for you," Kerok turned to me with a smile. "With the Crown Prince's insignia on them."

"But," I protested.

Chapter 10

"You can keep the others and have the bars replaced if you want," he said. "If you can pry them away from your friends—they kept all your things to remember you."

"Oh, no, I forgot to tell Caral and Armon I was coming this morning," I sighed.

"They know—I sent mindspeak."

"I love you," I blinked at him.

Hunter snickered this time.

* * *

Secondary Camp
Armon

Wend shouted with joy and ran to Sherra the moment she appeared in the mess hall. Several others followed, while most of those present stood and cheered.

Sherra had made a name for herself, that was clear, and if there were any who hadn't seen the massive hole left behind after she destroyed the enemy army, they'd been told about it by those who had.

Weren wanted a meeting with her and the rest of the officers the moment we could pull her away, and then we'd take her to assess former washouts to determine what, if anything, they could do for the army.

Merrin and an alliance with the enemy troubled all of us, and while Levi and I hadn't discussed it at length, it felt like a bomb waiting to explode in our midst.

Ruarke—the faceless, powerful enemy, wanted all of Az-ca destroyed, according to Kyri and Adahi. As no diviner from here had ever assessed his power and ability, we may as well be fighting a mythical monster in his stead.

Merrin's strengths and weaknesses were known to us, but that was before he'd gotten his hands on a forbidden book.

Rose and Thorn

Adahi called it Thorn's Book, after the ancient King whose name Thorn was given. Merrin should never have had it, according to the Thorn I knew. Was never meant to have it, either.

Would it be used to kill us? I silently cursed the words on its pages and the King who'd written them.

* * *

Sherra

"I wish Crown Prince Thorn could be here, too, but whatever is discussed will be sent to him by messenger," Weren announced after the officers were seated in the mess hall. Wend and Marc sat at a table nearby; I sat with Levi, Armon and Caral, near Weren's table.

Next to Weren sat Linel's former messenger, Dayl. A messenger's satchel lay on the table beside him, and several sheets of paper lay under his hand.

Dayl? I sent mindspeak.

His head came up immediately and he blinked at me. *Sherra?* he responded.

Have you been trained to protect yourself? I asked him.

There has been little time, he began.

I'll see that you're trained, I said. *To protect yourself only.* I knew that Dayl wanted no part of battle. Being a messenger suited him. If I had my way, all messengers would be able to protect themselves in a matter of days.

Thank you. Dayl lowered his head and began to write as Weren spoke.

* * *

While the meeting served to inform the officers of what we were now facing after Merrin's alliance with the enemy, we were no closer to a real solution. Several officers had spoken in favor of Garkus' method, of a surprise attack.

Chapter 10

Weren had pointed out the major flaws in that plan—those of innocent lives sacrificed and the fact that Merrin, Ruarke and their small horde of followers could *step* away when the army arrived, because of Merrin's new talent of perimeter divination. There would be no surprise in our surprise attack—not after Garkus' unplanned efforts in that area. No mention was made of Thorn's Book—by design.

I couldn't decide whether that was a good or bad thing.

Caral, Misten and I decided to walk to the training field afterward, while Armon and Levi *stepped* there to see how everything was going.

"Where is Kyri's City?" Misten asked.

"Far to the north," I said. "I didn't see a map while I was there, so I couldn't point it out to you. It gets rain regularly, is much cooler and there are plants and ferns growing among the trees that we don't see in Az-ca. I saw the sea, too—it's close by."

"That sounds nice," Misten sighed.

"Maybe Kyri will let you visit sometime," I said.

"We missed you," Caral said softly.

"I know. I really missed you, too. If Kyri hadn't kept me so busy with training after I recovered, I probably would have moped the whole time."

"Ana's doing very well," Misten said as the training field came into view. "The others are somewhat slower."

"I'll take a look," I said. "Tell me who to go to first."

"Best or worst?" Caral asked.

"Let's go with worst. If we can get him or her going, maybe the others will be more enthusiastic."

"Barney," Misten said quickly.

"What's wrong with him?" I asked.

"Not him. Her. Real name is Barna, but prefers Barney," Caral explained.

"I see. She's ah, not of the Bulldog variety, is she?"

"I don't think so—she just isn't catching on. At all."

"What can she do?"

"Well, we got her to make fire, but that's about it," Caral frowned.

"So she's a washout from the beginning?"

"From about twenty years ago, yes."

"And she still wanted to try this again?"

"She wants to, but it's just not happening for her."

"We were hoping you could put your hands on her—like you did in the past," Misten pleaded. "She's not really popular with the others, because she can't do anything."

"I know how that feels—to be excluded," I blew out a breath. "Take me to her. We'll see what she has."

We found Barney sitting beneath a tree on the edge of the training field while others were practicing their shielding. Ana was helping another instructor; I could see it from a distance.

There was plenty of work to be done here, that was obvious.

"Barney, this is Sherra," Caral introduced me.

"Sorry," Barney jumped to her feet and brushed off her trousers before offering me a hand, which was now covered in dust.

"Sorry," she pulled the hand back immediately and wiped it on her shirt.

"Barney, Caral tells me you really want to learn," I said, ignoring her nervousness and discomfort.

"I do. But I just—can't."

"Will you let me touch your hands—so I can see what level your power is?"

"What if I don't have any?" Tears were forming in her eyes as she hid her hands behind her back.

"You can make fire. You have power," I assured her. "If I touch you, your power will be revealed," I added. "Don't worry, I won't hurt you."

"You saved Az-ca. Everybody says so." She hung her head.

"Barney, take my hands," I held them out to her.

Reluctantly, she brought her hands around, then hesitated for several moments before gripping my fingers with hers.

A simmering pool of power, previously untapped, lay within her. I was surprised she'd been able to make fire, because of the disconnect between the power and her mind.

A pathway was there, but it took a few turns instead of being straight, as another's would be.

"Let me show you the path to your power," I blinked into deep green eyes. "Close your eyes, I'm about to connect with you to show you what you have and how to reach it."

"I have power?" she breathed.

"You have power," I smiled. "Now, close your eyes. We'll travel this path together."

Chapter 11

*S*herra

"You mean that the way she reads or writes—misspelling words and such, is a reflection of how she connects with her power?" Caral asked as we walked into the mess hall for midday meal.

"Yes. Now that she knows how to get to it, I think she'll learn quickly."

"She sure surprised everybody, when she made a shield strong enough to knock those wooden balls away," Misten said. "And that was right after you showed her how to do it."

"I think some of the others will be lining up for Sherra this afternoon," Armon said as he and Levi followed us in. "Nice job, taking the worst of the lot and working a miracle."

"She wasn't the worst, I'd bet on it," I said. "She just didn't understand. Now she does."

Rose and Thorn

"We only have to deal with weak shields and self-doubt in the others," Levi grinned.

"Have I hugged you lately?" I turned to ask him.

"No," Levi's grin grew wider.

"You only get a few minutes before we have to report excessive contact to the Crown Prince," Armon teased as Levi lifted me off my feet in a bone-cracking hug.

Pottles' mindspeak came after Levi set me down.

Sherra, I'd like to bring the young ones to Secondary Camp for a short visit—they're curious, she said.

That's fine. Tonight, though, when I get back, I want to see the lists of all the talented young ones in Az-ca. Feel like going through it with me?

If you'll let us watch the training.

Done. Bring them in an hour—we're about to eat right now.

I will.

"Pottles is bringing the young ones—they want to see the camp," I said.

"Really?" Misten asked.

"Yes. Let's eat; they'll be here in an hour."

* * *

Merrin

"Those clerics can cook," Plicton patted his stomach after our midday meal. "I like being served," he added.

During our meal, which Ruarke's clerics had prepared, they'd silently served us, anticipating our requests and keeping cups filled with the beer we'd found in the outpost's cellar.

Ruarke hadn't joined us—two clerics served him in the commander's office. He'd be engrossed in Thorn's Book, I imagined, and wondered if he'd tell me the important things he'd read, rather than making me read them for myself.

I hated reading, actually. Thorn was always the one who studied; I never cared for it, myself. I'd done the minimum of what was required during my training, just to get to the more physical aspects of using my power.

I'd gotten enjoyment from blasting things to atoms, early on. Thorn was one of the few who could surpass me during our field training, and it made me angry most of the time.

I'd carried that anger to Drenn, who not only agreed with me, but helped to plot small ways to dig at Thorn. We always laughed about it afterward, too.

Thorn would regret Drenn's death—I'd make sure of it. Drenn and I should have been brothers, and Thorn should have been a lesser cousin to the royal family. It angered me still that I hadn't been able to kill Uncle Hunter—just to eliminate his path to the throne and destroy Thorn's only legitimate heir.

Except for me.

I was a legitimate heir, once Uncle Hunter died. I hoped Ruarke would find the passages in the book—the ones about the talent employed to prevent me from killing Hunter in Thorn's study. I wanted to learn that for myself.

Most urgently.

With the ability to destroy blasts that way, I could take on Thorn's army and defeat them single-handed.

Since Ruarke's power was contained in a small device, I had no worries that he'd learn anything useful from the book. He was from Ny-nes, and everybody knew they had no power; they only had devices and machinery. His device would only make blasts, *step* him and his clerics elsewhere and form shields. Anything else was beyond its capability—by his own admission and by the marks on the device's dials.

Ruarke must depend on me to employ the book's subtler secrets. The thought brought a smile to my lips.

* * *

Secondary Camp
Sherra

By nightfall, shielding lessons were going better and faster. Armon was more than happy with the progress made, and told me that the warrior washouts needed my attention the following day.

Pottles and the young ones had sat at the edge of the training grounds, while Anari, Laren and Kyal watched wide-eyed as the trainees worked on their shielding.

Occasionally, I'd glance their way, wishing all of the black rose girls and warrior boys were sitting on the sidelines watching, instead of the boys scattered among the villages, and the older black rose girls too terrified to go to Kyri.

I wondered how I'd have felt if her invitation had come to me when I was younger. I suppose Pottles' presence had negated the need for it, but had she not been there, I'd have been very tempted to make that journey.

And Az-ca could be destroyed by now, I reminded myself. The enemy could have killed or overrun Kerok's army, and Az-ca would be taken by that malevolent horde.

Had Kyri known I'd be needed where I was and hadn't interfered? Perhaps that was a question for Pottles later.

I couldn't shake the feeling that I still didn't have all the information concerning Ruarke—and other things. I hoped someone would tell me if it were needed.

My rose?
Kerok?

Chapter 11

Will you have dinner with me tonight?

I'll be there shortly, I said. *I'm returning with Pottles and the young ones.*

Good. I need you to myself for a while.

May I have the lists of the older black rose girls and all the warrior boys? I asked.

Yes, but not until we've had dinner.

All right. Thank you.

* * *

Northeast Outpost

Ruarke

It only takes a small amount of the powder to make even the strongest mind compliant, and serving it in beer was more than easy, as the brew masked the powder's taste. Merrin was already immersed in his own self-importance; it only took a bit of the powder to add to his delusions, followed by a small nudge from me to convince him that I only had his best intentions at heart.

I'm sure Az-ca may have wondered for years why Ny-nes' army was so focused on killing them—and why those troops would willingly die in that effort.

Too bad they'd never learn the truth—that ingrained dogma, combined with the drug, would produce the desired results.

How very easy it had been to usurp a religion, interpret and misinterpret it too many times to count, and then combine it with a drug its followers willingly accepted. All Kaakos and I had to do was point to a book the population could no longer read, and it was accepted as fact.

Moving my cup of tea aside, I turned a page in Thorn's Book to keep reading. How I wished I'd had this earlier in my life—so many things could have gone differently, and Az-ca would have fallen long ago.

* * *

King's Palace
Kerok

I wanted Sherra in my arms; she wanted to talk laws and business during our meal. "Kerok, the trainees need the book. Isn't there some way to rescind the law and make copies?"

We were discussing *The Rose Mark*.

I was an unwilling participant.

"There's something else," she said. "I'd like to see the law changed about roses being with other roses. It's only fair—the warriors can choose to be with other warriors."

"My love, can we do this after dinner?" I complained as gently as I could.

"All right." Her eyes dropped to her plate.

"Did they feed you well at Secondary Camp?" I pointed our discussion in a different direction.

"Of course. The food is good, there. Did you know Caral's sister works in the kitchens?"

"I do—I gave permission," I said.

"Caral is really happy about that," she said. "I think all the troops—warriors and escorts alike, should be allowed to visit family now and then."

We were back to laws and business.

Again.

"Tell me why." I cut into the lamb we'd been served.

"Well, it may have gone a long way toward getting needed information to the villagers—that your Council didn't think important enough to carry to them in the past few years," she pointed out bluntly.

Chapter 11

My fork poised halfway to my mouth. "Granted," I said after a moment, before placing the food in my mouth and chewing. Clearly, she'd learned many things from Armon and Levi while at Secondary Camp.

"You're saying you'll do it, or just agreeing with me?"

The agreeing part, I sent mindspeak, as I was still chewing. I watched her frown while I considered what Kyri and Pottles had done to make her as forward as she was, now.

"Hmmph," she sniffed aloud.

"I'm not King yet," I growled once I'd swallowed my food. "Father is failing, but he still holds that title."

"And you're unwilling to set things right."

"You're saying things aren't right?"

"Some things, yes. I'm not hungry." She rose from the table, dropped her napkin on the chair and stalked out of my suite.

* * *

"I have no idea where she is. What did you do to upset her?"

Pottles—*Doret*—glared at me as if I were not only wrong, but so deeply mired in it I might never get out. That glare certainly belonged to a former Queen of Az-ca; there was no doubt in my mind.

I'd gone looking for Sherra *after* finishing my food because I was frustrated, angry and not in the mood to chase anyone, including my black rose.

"My Prince," Hunter joined me in the hallway outside Doret's open door. She chose to glare at him, too, until something in his expression softened her anger.

"What happened?" she asked immediately.

Rose and Thorn

"The scouts keeping a watch outside Northeast Outpost are dead, except for one and he's badly wounded."

* * *

Doret must have sent mindspeak to Sherra; she walked into the meeting room and sat beside Doret without speaking to me or anyone else.

Hunter and Barth exchanged a glance but refused to say anything. Kage had joined us quickly once Hunter sent for him.

Five scouts were dead; the sixth had barely escaped with his life, but was severely burned by one of Merrin's rogue warriors. He was in the infirmary, now, being cared for.

"Merrin knew every landing spot around the outpost, didn't he?" Doret's voice was accusing.

I wanted to sink into my chair at her words. She was right, of course. Those scouts had been easy to pick off, and once Merrin and his allies learned of the times the scouts arrived to change shifts, they'd struck, killing five of the six.

Likely, they didn't care that one had survived to tell the tale. Who knew what they planned if we sent more spies?

"They probably want us to attack them, now," Hunter grumbled. "So they can show us how good they are at picking us off."

"I'll take suggestions," I said with a troubled sigh.

"Send those who can make mirror shields," Sherra snapped. "None of those scouts were able to make a shield—admit it. If it requires a warrior and his escort, so be it. An escort can place a bubble shield before a warrior *steps*; that way, it won't matter where he sets his feet—he'll be safe enough. If the shield is a mirror shield, as long as it's set down outside the perimeter divination, they'll be able to watch for hours while remaining hidden."

184

Chapter 11

"You're saying it's possible to set a shield around someone who *steps*—before they *step*?" Barth asked.

"Yes. It's easy," Sherra said. "I've shielded myself when I *step*. I don't need a designated place to set down, as long as it's in an open area."

"How will we know where Merrin set the perimeter?" Barth asked.

"I'm assuming his power may be limited, and doesn't extend very far outside the walls," Sherra said. "That's how Garkus surprised him before—by setting down far enough away and firing blasts from around a quarter mile outside Central Outpost."

"How do you know about that?" I snapped at her.

"I went to talk to Garkus, that's how."

"He was willing to answer questions?" Hunter sounded surprised.

"I think he knows how desperately he fucked up by now," Doret snorted.

"I told him that Merrin is allied with the enemy, now, and it's partly due to his foolish interference," Sherra said. "He should have stayed put. People would still be alive and we'd be discussing how to alleviate a hostage situation rather than engaging in an all-out war with an enemy who's taken up with some of our own."

"How can you say that for sure?" I demanded.

"Because if Garkus hadn't intervened, I could have gotten past Merrin's perimeter," Sherra snapped. "As it is, we now have to contend with an enemy power wielder who has possession of Thorn's Book. I have no way to get past his perimeter, if he sets one. I'd need something of his to make an attempt, and I have nothing."

Her voice had gotten louder the longer she spoke, until it was a half-shout.

"Fucking hell," I stood and shoved my chair across the floor in a teeth-jarring scrape.

"Is that true?" Hunter whispered in the ensuing silence.

"Yes," Doret sounded defeated. "I wish now we'd sent Sherra back days ago. Hindsight is always clearest, is it not?"

* * *

Ketchi

Kyri

"Some want assurances," Cole said. He and I stood amid trees west of the village, where we could see the ocean in the distance.

"I understand—I just can't guarantee anything at the moment," I told him.

"If we're willing to fight—and give our lives to their cause, why shouldn't we be welcome?"

"Old prejudices, my friend."

"We've dealt with that from our childhood," he muttered. "I was hoping for better."

"This is no fault of yours—it is the fault in others," I explained. "Changing hearts or minds is often the most difficult task of all."

"So. If we go to help, all they'll see is the enemy."

"I think there will be some who won't see it that way. Sherra is there, now."

"One ally out of many?" Cole was skeptical, just as I would be in his place.

"What will convince you?"

"I will serve with Sherra, as will the others. We stand together—under her command. You say she is an officer in the army? We will follow her."

Chapter 11

"I—may be able to offer that," I agreed. "Give me two days, perhaps."

"We will be waiting."

* * *

"Have you convinced Cole to take his troops?" Adahi sat at my kitchen table, waiting for my return.

Removing my jacket and draping it on the back of a chair, I frowned at my uninvited guest. "He says they'll serve under Sherra's command."

"Cole is adept at reading others. I believe it is because he was so terrified as a child, that it developed in him unawares."

"However it happened, he can sense insecurity and prevarication from miles away." I shuffled to the stove to boil water for tea. "Sherra made an impression on him—a very good one, it appears."

"Are they trained well enough?"

"I believe so, but Sherra is adept at bringing troops to their full potential."

"An unusual talent in one so young."

"I don't know that she's ever been young, Adahi. Much like Cole was never young. I think he was born aware of the dangers around him."

"I should never have placed the shield around Sherra's room."

He'd just spoken aloud what I'd castigated myself for the past few hours. Had I allowed Sherra's dreamwalker to roam, Merrin may have been contained, or a warning given of the threat Ruarke presented.

I hesitated over Thorn's Book, and what damage it could cause in Ruarke's hands. So far, questions hadn't been asked about those two together.

Important questions.

Questions neither I, Adahi nor Doret wanted to answer.

"You want to tell her, don't you? That she's a dreamwalker." I pulled two cups from the cupboard and set them on the counter.

"She needs to know, Kyri. A dreamwalker can find themselves in danger, if proper warning isn't given."

"Too many things to worry about, and all too close together," I said. "We'll tell her tomorrow. Want tea?"

"Please."

* * *

King's Palace
Sherra

I was still angry with Kerok. He was still angry with me. I suppose it was a fair and even distribution of anger between us. We also had five needless deaths to consider, plus a wounded man in the training camp infirmary.

Kerok found me pacing inside Pottles' suite after the meeting.

"Sherra, please come with me to the infirmary," his voice was even and held no anger. My head jerked up and my eyes met his across the room.

He's actually behaving like an adult, Pottles sent mindspeak.

Then I have to be an adult, too, I replied.

"Is the scout conscious?" I asked Kerok.

"Hunter says yes. Let's ask questions." He held out a hand.

Unsure whether I wanted his touch, I hesitated before placing my hand in his when I reached the doorway where he stood. Without a pause, he raised my hand to his lips and kissed the black rose tattoo.

188

Chapter 11

Choosing not to speak, he walked me along the hallway, my hand still in his as he sought the stairs to take us to the ground floor of the palace. Once outside in the courtyard, I imagined he'd *step* us to the infirmary.

Halfway down the first flight of steps, Kerok stopped and turned to me.

"My rose, I love you too much to argue—especially tonight. Consider that I am only a man, no matter what title others give me. As a man, I will make mistakes. I beg you to overlook as many as you can, and accept my apologies for those you cannot."

In the dim light illuminating the steps, I reached out with my free hand to touch the scar on his face. "I'm sorry, too," I said. "It's just—other things are so important right now."

"I know, and I'll try to do better next time."

"Kerok?"

"What, my love?"

"This." I stood on tiptoes to kiss him.

* * *

Kerok

"I knew him—the one who tried to kill me," Harel, the surviving scout, confessed. He was sitting up in bed, his arms and torso wrapped in bandages from the burns he'd received. "I think he almost pulled the blast back because of that, so I only got burned instead of killed."

"I take it you *stepped* away quickly before he could change his mind?" I asked.

"Yes, my Prince. My arms, chest and the front of my legs are burned. The physician says he is hopeful for a recovery, although there will be scars."

"Can you give me the name of the one who harmed you? For the record?"

"Yes. Narvin is his name. I assume his escort is there with him."

"Her name?" Sherra asked.

"Willa."

"Did you see any of the others?" I asked.

"No. The landings are too far apart, as you know. I only saw two other fireblasts before I was attacked and *stepped away*."

"You did well," I nodded. "Thank you for answering questions. Is there anything we can do for you?"

"Hope for a swift healing," Harel sighed. "Burns can be tricky things. As a former warrior, I know this as well as anyone."

What is he saying? Sherra silently asked.

He probably won't live through the night; the burns are likely too deep. For now, he's in shock. His body won't be able to handle the damage, my rose.

She stood there, straight and tall, gazing at Harel. "May the winds bless you," she said. "May the sun watch over you. May the earth carry you, now and always."

It was an old blessing—for births, deaths and other occasions. Like Sherra, I felt it was warranted. Harel closed his eyes and nodded his gratitude.

* * *

Sherra

"I think he knew—even when he said that the physicians hoped he'd recover," I breathed when we left the infirmary behind. We found ourselves walking for a distance instead of *stepping* back to the palace courtyard.

Chapter 11

My left hand was enveloped by Kerok's again as we walked, although he remained silent. He nodded to acknowledge my words, but appeared lost in thought.

He'd likely seen so many deaths through the years, and not just those of black rose escorts. As for Merrin, I could only imagine what Kerok thought of his treasonous acts. It made me think of the old riddle that Pottles told me—the one about evil murderers and whether you'd be willing to kill someone like that early in their life, when you knew they'd commit heinous acts in the future.

"I wish we could storm Northeast Outpost and just—you know," I waved my free hand in a helpless gesture.

"Shhh," Kerok pulled me closer and *stepped* us to the courtyard. At least he waited until we were up the stairs and the door of his suite was shut to pull my clothing away and kiss whatever he uncovered.

* * *

Northeast Outpost
Merrin
"Did you get the book back?" Plicton set his mug of beer down on the mess hall table where I sat, my feet propped on the table's surface.

"No. But I didn't ask for it, yet."

"That belongs to the royal house of Az-ca, you know."

"What do you suggest I do about it?"

"Ask for it. Why does Ruarke need it, anyway? It isn't as if he can do what you can do with the instructions in it."

"My thoughts exactly," I lifted my own mug and saluted him with it before drinking. "Do you think there are any girls or women among the villagers we could have fun with tonight?"

Rose and Thorn

"There are a few I've had my eye on," Plicton agreed. "I'm not sure about getting them into our quarters, though—those damn clerics are everywhere."

"I can blast them if they try to stop us."

"I'm not sure that's a good idea—to anger our allies so soon."

"When do you think Ruarke's army will get here?" I asked. "I really want to see the look on Thorn's face when that happens."

"I hope Thorn's dead by that time," Plicton huffed and drank more beer. "That means you'll already have the King's City. We don't care what happens to the peasants, now do we?"

"Not even a little," I laughed. That's when a cold wind swept through the mess hall, making me shiver.

"What the hell was that?" Plicton scooted his chair back. It was summer in Az-ca, and as hot as it usually was this time of year. A cold wind wasn't possible. This had felt—*frigid*.

On a table farther away, a napkin left behind lifted for a moment as the wind passed it, too.

"What the hell?" Plicton growled before striding in the wind's direction.

Rising from my chair, I cautiously followed Plicton. Perhaps he wasn't concerned by something so unusual but I, even half-drunk, was alarmed. If this were something formed by an enemy from the outside, it should have triggered my perimeter divination.

No alarms had sounded in my mind.

A memory rose unbidden, then.

The phantom. I hadn't bothered to hide myself lately, depending solely on the perimeter divination to protect me well enough.

Chapter 11

"Plicton," I shouted after him, but he was already on his way into the kitchen. That's when I ran after him, forming a fireball in my hands as I went.

* * *

King's Palace
Kerok

Sherra leaned back in my arms with a satisfied sigh. I'd sent mindspeak to Hunter, asking him to have wine delivered and left outside my door. I'd just gone to retrieve it and the glasses, before pouring wine for both of us and settling on the bed again.

"It's the connecting," I brushed Sherra's cheek with my lips. "That's why it's so," I hesitated, looking for the proper word.

"Consuming?" Sherra leaned back and smiled at me.

"That's sufficient," I agreed. "It doesn't happen for everyone—just those who were meant to be, I think."

"Do I have to keep cutting my hair?" she asked as I lifted a strand of dark curls over her ear.

"No." I pulled her against me again. "Sometimes, being with me has its advantages." I didn't tell her that Grae had asked for—and received—the same benefit. That was so long ago, and too many things had happened since then.

"Drink your wine, love, then we need sleep," I yawned. "We've stayed up far too late as it is."

"Whose fault is that?" I didn't fail to hear the humor in her words.

"I take full responsibility, and it was worth every second of lost sleep. Why do you ask?" I teased her gently.

"I just wanted to hear you say it," she said.

* * *

Northeast Outpost

Rose and Thorn

Merrin

The kitchen was filled with a freezing, opaque mist, and I hesitated at the doorway. So far, it was contained within the kitchen, and I wasn't willing to enter.

Plicton was nowhere to be seen, and there was no noise from his moving about. "Plicton?" I called his name aloud. There was no answer.

What should I do? I still held the small fireball in my hands, and could make it larger whenever I wished.

Fire destroys frost, my addled brain informed me. Without another thought, I built my fireball until it was more than large enough to destroy what lay before me.

I let it loose with a shout for my enemy, the phantom, to die in my fire.

Thorn always said, *never employ power when you're drunk*. For once, I should have listened to him.

Chapter 12

K*ing's Palace*
Kerok
Sherra and I leapt off the bed from a dead sleep when someone pounded on my outer door.

Pulling a robe from a nearby chair, I ran for the door while Sherra searched for clothing behind me.

Hunter, looking disheveled, stood outside. "Northeast Outpost is on fire," he said.

It couldn't be Garkus this time; he'd been relieved of his power and was still in the lockup.

"What the bloody hell happened?" I turned to search for clothing, only to find that Sherra had gathered pants, shirt and boots for me and held them out. How she'd dressed so quickly I couldn't guess, but she had.

"One of the warriors we posted came to report it," Hunter said, following me while I dressed in haste. "He and his escort are downstairs, in case you want to speak with them."

"I want to go to Northeast Outpost," I growled.

"I'll shield us," Sherra said.

"My rose?"

"I can hide us, Kerok. It'll be easy. We should probably tell the others there to pull back, just in case."

"I'll send mindspeak on your command," Hunter offered.

"Then it's given," I said. "Send for Armon and Weren. What's the word on the hostages?"

"None were seen escaping," Hunter grimaced.

"First warrior knows what's happening to them," I hissed. "Sherra, are you ready?"

"Yes."

"Let's go, then." I *stepped* us away.

* * *

Sherra

We landed on a high outcropping, far away from the burning outpost. My shield protected us well enough from the uneven surface—I'd shaped the outer bubble shield to conform with the surface, while holding Kerok and myself inside a safer, inner shield. Both shields were mirrored, in case someone was near enough to see.

By this time, the entire outpost was ablaze; it didn't take much to burn dry wood in the summer—the evidence lay on the valley floor below us, with flames shooting high into the sky.

"What the fuck happened?" Kerok growled. He was furious at this turn of events.

"I don't think somebody decided to do as Garkus did, this time," I told him.

Chapter 12

"Why? How do you know?" he demanded.

"Because the walls are only half burned all around, while the inner buildings are nearly gone," I pointed out. "I'd say the fire started near the center. Garkus blasted the walls first, remember?"

"True," Kerok considered my words. "Do you think there are survivors?"

"I don't know if the villagers escaped, if that's what you're asking," I said. "As for Merrin and Ruarke, those two can get away easily."

"And where they'll end up is anybody's guess."

"Yes." My shoulders sagged at the truth of his statement. At least we'd known where they were—until now.

"I don't think there's anything left to save," he said. "I'll keep the warrior and escort spies here until daylight, and we'll search the remains of the outpost for bodies. At this point, I think that's all we can accomplish."

"I think I can place a shield over it, and cut off the air feeding the fire," I suggested.

Kerok turned toward me; I could only see the outline of his face in the light of a half-moon overhead and the blazing fire in the distance.

"Do it," he said.

He watched as I sent power toward the outpost, covering the entire compound in a domed shield and then reducing it quickly.

We observed as the fire dissipated and died in a matter of minutes.

* * *

Ruarke

"It was time to move anyway," I waved away Merrin's concern over his fireblasts setting the outpost ablaze. I didn't express condolences for his accidental blasting of Plicton—the man was beginning to annoy me anyway.

My freezing mist spell had performed perfectly, too—Merrin, in his drugged stated, believed it to be the work of some vigilante called the phantom, and I allowed him his fantasies.

Besides, camping on the other side of the border would ensure that Ny-nes' army could find us easily when they arrived. A raid on the nearest supply outpost would also ensure that we had enough food to last until the army joined us.

As for the villagers, I sent half of them to Kaakos for public executions. The other half remained with us, in case we needed to send messages to the King's City.

I only kept two young ones; the warrior boys. The rest of the children went to Kaakos. He'd be more than willing to do what needed to be done with that lot.

"We can find another outpost—I know where they all are," Merrin suggested.

"No, we stay here, remember?" Perhaps I should reduce the amount of the drug he was getting—it addled his brain too easily. The other warriors and former Council members willingly followed his lead, and the escorts were too frightened to do anything other than to serve the men.

All of which worked perfectly for me. For now, I left the warriors' power intact—in case I wanted to use it in some way. They were under the drug's influence and were easily manipulated.

Things were going quite well, actually, and Kaakos, in mindspeak, had expressed his appreciation for my efforts.

As for Thorn's Book—I couldn't wait to explore more of the talents and spells I'd found inside it. The freezing mist

Chapter 12

was a work of genius, after all, and it had been carefully explained in the book.

Merrin had no idea what treasure had fallen into his hands—the perimeter divination had been the simplest of its secrets to create.

* * *

King's City
Kerok

"The only body we found was Gram Plicton's," Barth slid onto a chair in my study with a weary sigh. He'd had to touch the crusted ash of it—I knew without asking—just to determine who it was.

"So. They're elsewhere, now, and nobody has an idea where that could be."

"I got nothing from Gram's body, other than Merrin fireblasted him to death. I did get confusing divination from a few metal objects in the kitchen around the body, however."

"What's that?"

"A feeling of intense cold—before Merrin fired his foolish blasts. I also got something else from Plicton—a confusion, as if he'd been drunk when he died."

"Perhaps he and Merrin had a disagreement about their new overlord," I snorted.

"No idea—I only found confusion in Plicton's reading."

"He must have been very drunk, then, for you not to see past it."

"Just what I was thinking."

"Did you find anything belonging to the enemy to divine—that we might use against him?"

"Nothing yet, although we still have troops sifting through the ashes."

"Do you think this was planned in any way?"

"I didn't get that feel from anything I touched," Barth shrugged. "Everything so far points to it being a drunken brawl that went wrong."

"I always told Merrin not to employ power after drinking."

"When did Merrin ever heed good advice?"

"True enough. At least Plicton is no longer a worry."

"True enough."

* * *

Secondary Camp
Sherra

Training was the last thing on my mind when I arrived at Secondary Camp for breakfast. Neither Kerok nor I had slept again after watching the fire die at Northeast Outpost.

The latest word from Barth was that Merrin had foolishly blasted Plicton and set the entire post ablaze. Kerok sent mindspeak shortly before I left, while I was dressing and he was meeting with Barth, Hunter and Kage over breakfast. He had also planned a visit with his father afterward.

I wondered what they'd discuss instead of current events.

"You're miles away this morning," Armon said, pushing my tea mug closer to my elbow. "Drink that. It'll help after a long night spent awake."

"Your eggs are getting cold," Levi added. Caral, sitting next to Armon at the table, nodded her agreement.

"I know. At least no villagers died in the fire last night. I can't help but feel—strange about the whole thing anyway."

"Strange how?" Misten asked. She lifted her roll and set it on Levi's plate—she'd never been as fond of bread as he was.

Chapter 12

"I feel a remnant, I suppose, of the hatred I felt when the enemy army was here before they were destroyed," I said. "I can't really explain it better than that, and I didn't get that feel yesterday. I suppose it could be because I'm tired and my shield may be weaker."

"General Weren is sending teams to the other outposts, looking for signs of occupation. So far, they've found nothing," Levi said. "Who knows where Merrin's clutch of enemies are?"

"What if they're no longer in Az-ca?" Caral asked. "What if they're outside for a while, just to confuse us?"

"It would be difficult to hide that many hostages," Armon's brow furrowed as he considered Caral's questions.

"They wouldn't have to kill them at the outpost," Levi pointed out. "What if they died elsewhere, and the whole fire thing was a ruse?"

"Barth says Merrin may have fired blasts after a drunken argument with Plicton," I said.

"Then Merrin probably started the fire," Levi acknowledged. "Still doesn't mean we know everything there is to know."

"I think that's a given," I agreed. "We don't know enough about Ruarke to gauge his part in this."

Levi's words had given me pause, however. There were people who *did* know more about Ruarke—by their own admission. Perhaps it was time to corner at least one of them, and ask serious questions. Pottles would be easier to approach than Kyri. If I weren't completely exhausted at the end of the day, I'd find her and have a discussion.

"Are you thinking too much again, instead of eating?" Armon lifted an accusing eyebrow.

"It's tired thinking. Does that count?" I asked.

"Usually. Finish your food—we have troops to train."

* * *

"That's outstanding—to make a game out of it," Levi chuckled as we watched trainees lob wooden balls back and forth using only their shields.

At any point in time, there were at least fifteen balls in the air or bouncing off someone's shield. If the trainee allowed a ball to get past their shield, or they dropped it to the ground, they were out of the game.

Nobody wanted to be taken out of the game, and it served to make them better, faster and capable of making stronger, more pliable shields.

"I wish we could have trained this way at North Camp," Falia grinned after walking off the field toward us. We stood next to the water buckets, so we were able to speak with each trainee as they were declared out by either Caral or Misten.

"Handling three balls at once is never easy," I said. "You did very well."

"I can't wait to train the next batch," she said after filling a cup with water and drinking. "It's going to be so different from now on."

"You'll be able to show them everything," I agreed. "Nobody will go without a meal from now on because they can't make fire."

"I always disliked that practice," Levi said.

"I had a problem with it, but it was the way we were trained, so," Falia shook her head.

The Bulldog's image and the sound of her voice shouting at trainees filled my memory, but I didn't say anything. She'd taken pleasure in refusing food to those of us who hadn't performed.

Chapter 12

Pottles called the Bulldog's death karma, although I still didn't have a full grasp of the word's meaning.

Perhaps karma was another name for Adahi. I'd have to ask him sometime, if I could gather enough courage to speak with him about it.

"I think we should begin teaching the warrior trainees how to shield," I told Levi. "I know their training is more structured; they're taught by those who have been in battle and can actually perform the things they're teaching. The trainees may need shields before they finish warrior training, though, just to be safe."

"My shields are certainly a comfort, as well as a practicality," Levi's grin lit his face. "I'll suggest it to Armon, and he can carry the idea to Weren."

"How did Weren's lessons in shielding go?"

"He and Kage did very well. Garkus was the obstinate one."

I didn't point out where Garkus was at the moment; Levi was more than aware of just where Garkus' opinions and stubbornness had placed him.

Kyri and Adahi will be visiting the palace tonight, Pottles informed me. *They wish to speak with us.*

All right. Did you offer them a meal?

Yes. They accepted.

Does Kerok know?

I was hoping you'd tell him.

I will. Thank you for letting me know.

I sent mindspeak to Kerok while watching the last few trainees struggle to capture flying balls in their shields before the objects hit the ground.

* * *

King's Palace

Rose and Thorn

Kerok

"I don't have much appetite nowadays," Father sighed. We'd moved his chair to the garden because he asked to have the midday meal with me there. I forced myself not to dwell on his withered hands or shrunken countenance—the disease was taking a terrible toll before it claimed his life.

I considered asking Sherra to come back to the palace to sit and talk with us, but I didn't.

Kerok, Pottles says Kyri and Adahi are joining us for the evening meal, Sherra sent mindspeak just as I was thinking of her.

My love, can you get away for a little while? I'm having a meal with Father, and would like you to join us.

I'll be there soon, let me tell Levi.

All right.

Sherra walked toward us minutes later, still dressed in her uniform. At least it bore the Crown Prince's insignia, in addition to her captain's bars.

"Ah, I was hoping to see you," Father's face lit in the first smile I'd seen all day as Sherra dipped her head to him and took the chair I offered at the table.

"King Wulf," Sherra reached out to take his offered hand.

"Daughter, I am more than happy that you survived," Father told her. "Please, eat—this food will go to waste if you don't."

"This looks so good," Sherra smiled at him before reaching for a roll and the butter plate.

"I hear you're training those who failed the first time. Are they doing better?" Father asked as Sherra dipped food onto her plate.

Chapter 12

"They're doing very well, Sir. Some of them just needed a nudge here and there to build their confidence. Some of the warrior washouts will be better suited for things other than fighting—many of them will likely be able to provide shields and messenger or scouting services for everyone else."

"They have decent shielding talent?" Father hadn't shown this much interest in anything for days.

"From what I've seen so far."

"This will help on the battlefield, won't it?" Father turned to me.

"It will. It may bring changes, so that the ones providing shields can trade off with someone else, to give those fighting long hours a much-needed break."

"Using the new method, of course," Father suggested.

"Of course. We're only teaching to the new method now," Sherra bit into her buttered bread.

"We'll teach the trainees the old way after they've learned everything else, just in case," I told Father. "Everybody from the instructors on down recognize what a time and energy saver the new method is."

"Have you considered giving your rose the honor medal?" Father asked.

"I," I leaned back in my chair as it hit me—she was certainly deserving, and many who'd done far less had received the award for meritorious service on the battlefield.

"I think you should do it soon," Father waved a hand. "I would do it, but I can't stand for more than a few seconds at a time."

I don't need a medal, Sherra protested in mindspeak.

The King has spoken, I argued.

Fine.

Fine. See, my sarcasm works just as well as yours, I retorted. *Besides, it will make Father happy.*

Fine.

I looked away to hide my grin.

* * *

Secondary Camp

Armon

"How was your meal with Thorn and his father?" Levi asked as Sherra met us on the training field.

"Fine."

"Weren has reports from all the warriors sent to the remaining outposts. They're all empty," I told her.

"What about the training posts?"

"Same—empty," I said. "Messengers are going out to the larger villages now, and they'll look at the smaller ones after that, but so far, no sign of the enemy has turned up."

"Do you think they crossed the border?" Sherra asked.

"It's possible, just to throw us off," Levi agreed. "That means they could be anywhere along the safe zone, between the sea and the poisoned lands."

"There are plenty of mountains and valleys in the safe zone, from the border northward. They could effectively hide from even our best spotters," I said.

"They'll need food and shelter for the extra mouths," Sherra pointed out.

"Unless they're already dead," Levi grumbled.

"I hope that's not true," Sherra wrapped arms about herself.

"I sent Weren's report to Hunter; Thorn likely has it in his hands by now," I said. "If we could only challenge them to a fair fight, and leave the villagers out of this," I shook my head.

"There's nothing fair about any of this," Sherra whispered. "Nothing. They'll kill whatever stands in their way, to satisfy their sick desires and destroy Az-ca."

"Are you feeling their anger again?" Levi thought to ask.

"It's worse, now," she admitted.

"Levi, gather our best. If I'm right, they're probably hitting Vale right now."

"I'm going," Sherra announced as Levi *stepped* toward the east corner of the camp where new warriors were being trained. He'd select our best, most seasoned troops to take with us.

"Good. I need your shields," I told Sherra. "Caral," I shouted at her. "Bring Misten. We're going to Vale."

I sent hasty mindspeak to Hunter, too, letting him know where we were headed. *Tread carefully, Colonel*, he warned in return.

As always, I replied. Less than five minutes later, I and forty others, warriors and escorts, *stepped* to the outskirts of Vale.

* * *

Vale

Ruarke

We'd never have known they were there except for the perimeter divination I'd set after our arrival at the supply outpost.

From a window in the outermost cabin, I felt them.

I failed to see them, though.

Somehow, they'd learned how to mask their presence from sight. They couldn't fool a perimeter divination, however, and certainly not one I'd set myself.

Half the small town's residents were dead—we'd seen to that the moment we'd *stepped* to the center of it. The rest cowered before Merrin and his rogues, who threatened to burn all of them to ashes if they didn't do as we said.

The entire episode was laughable, as my clerics forced the hostages we'd brought with us to gather food and supplies—as much as they could carry. I could transport men; large piles of goods were more difficult to *step*.

"Do you see something, esteemed one?" Cleric Ward stood at my elbow.

"See? No," I snorted a laugh. "They're out there, though; the god assures me of this. You see what demons they are?"

"They are truly demons, as you say," Ward whispered in terror. "May the god continue to protect us from invisible enemies."

"He will, I assure you," I said. "Bring one of the children—a girl. Bring one of Merrin's warriors and his escort, too. We shall deliver a message to these demons."

"As you say." Ward dipped his head and hurried away.

* * *

Sherra

"They know we're here," Levi's voice was soft as we stared at the five walking along the dirt-and-gravel road through the supply village.

Straight toward us.

One of those five was a young girl—perhaps eight years old.

"Do you see what I see?" Armon nodded at Levi.

"Yes. That's Narvin and Willa," he named the two dressed in army uniforms. "You can bet Willa has a shield up around all of them."

"What about the other two?" I hissed. One of those two held the girl's arm in one of his hands and was practically

Chapter 12

dragging her along the road. I saw she was crying. In his other hand, he carried a long knife.

Fuck.

"The two dressed in black robes," Armon breathed, "those are clerics from Ny-nes. The one walking alone is probably their chief."

"How strong are Willa's shields?" I asked, narrowing my eyes at the scene unfolding before us. I also wondered how close they'd come before delivering the message they surely intended us to see.

"Strong enough, I suppose," Armon replied. "She's been with Narvin for maybe two years. Why? What do you have in mind?"

"Armon, if you could kill one person and save another at the same time, which would you choose? Answer quickly," I breathed.

"I'd save the girl—she has nothing to do with this," Armon's anger sounded in his voice.

"My choice as well," I nodded. "Caral?"

"Sherra?" Caral stepped up beside me.

Keep your shields up and tight, all right? I told her in mindspeak. *You have my signature, so my blast will go through. On the count of three.*

Two.

One.

* * *

Ruarke

I'd already told the others to go back to our camp across the border while Ward, Narvin and I dealt with the troops sent against us.

Rose and Thorn

I'd told Narvin to *step* his escort away the moment the girl was beheaded, as the troops would surely attack. I'd *step* Ward away; we'd be safe and the town would be doomed.

It gave me pleasure to think the troops would attempt to blast an enemy who'd already left, leaving its remaining inhabitants behind to die in the ensuing barrage of fireballs.

Az-ca's army was so predictable that way—all they knew to do was to level fireblasts at what attacked them. If the rest were at Merrin's level of intelligence, I wondered how they'd lasted as long as they had.

"Stop here," I held up a hand. "Narvin, ensure that your escort's shield is up," I added.

"It is."

"Good. Ward, you know what to do."

Ward pulled the crying girl against him, preparing to cut her throat. I imagined her head could be severed; she was so thin and the blade that sharp.

"This is what will happen to all of you," I shouted into the emptiness ahead of us. They were there, I could almost hear them breathing.

"Now," I turned to Ward, with a flip of my hand to signal the girl's death.

Instead, a barely audible whine sounded, and slowly, so slowly, Ward's hand fell, releasing the now-screaming child.

There was so little blood, and only the minutest amount of fire to tell me how this had been accomplished.

"Retreat," I shouted, almost before Ward's body fell back and hit the dirt, raising dust about him in a cloud. Did I consider going after the girl, who ran as fast as she could to get away from us?

Not even for a moment.

Chapter 12

Someone had designed a way to pierce an escort's shield with the thinnest, sharpest fireblast I'd ever seen. It had penetrated Ward's forehead and gone through his skull as if his head were made of cotton fluff instead of bone and brain matter.

The surprised look on Ward's face as he died spoke volumes.

By the time I landed awkwardly inside my tent at the camp, tripping and falling over my cot in the process, I was breathing with difficulty while my heart refused to slow down for a very long while.

***

King's Palace
Kerok

"Half the people, mostly the men and older boys, were already dead when we arrived," Armon reported. "We've spoken with those still alive, after transporting them and any remaining supplies to Secondary Camp."

"What about the body—of the one Sherra killed?" I asked.

"It's here. Barth and two physicians are looking at it. Barth asked for Sherra to be with him while he attempted divination—that's why she's not here reporting with me."

"I'll speak with her when she's done," I waved a hand. "I figure Merrin gave information to that cretin he's allied himself with, and that's why they attacked Vale. I should have seen this coming."

"Thorn, nobody can know what they'll do next. We searched outposts and training camps, because those were logical. After that, they could have hit any village anywhere, to supply themselves. It's my opinion that they're camped somewhere across the border and won't be easy to find."

"How much did they get away with? Do you know?"

"They had to carry what they could, and the townspeople said Merrin and the rest of those who came had already gone by the time the girl was dragged into the street. It's my guess that we crossed their perimeter divination, letting them know of our arrival. I hoped we'd set down far enough away so they wouldn't know, but that wasn't to be."

"You say that some of those who came were kidnapped villagers that they'd kept with them after Northeast Outpost was destroyed?"

"Yes. At least twenty or thirty of those—there are conflicting reports on those numbers."

My Prince? Hunter sent mindspeak.

Hunter?

Barth asks that you come to the physician's examination room right away.

Armon and I will be there shortly.

"Armon, Barth is asking for us to come."

"Of course." Armon rose from his seat and we strode out of my study.

* * *

Sherra

Kerok and Armon arrived quickly. I sat on a stool against the wall, trying to even out my breathing. Barth leaned against the wall nearby, silently attempting to accept and digest what we'd both seen.

Barth had requested my help when he performed his divination on the cleric I'd killed in Vale. Too many things had flown through my mind after Barth placed his hands on the body, and I'd placed my hands on Barth's shoulders.

"Tell me," Kerok said.

Chapter 12

"His name was Ward," I croaked. I felt as though I'd not had water in a week, my throat was so parched.

"And?"

"They call the white dust they consume *the prophet's bones*," I whispered.

Chapter 13

*K*erok

"I believe the white granules make them more—amenable to their commanders," Barth held a cup of tea in his hands. He and Sherra were now inside the chief physician's private study in the infirmary, and both had cups of tea to drink.

I probably should have asked for wine to be served— both had been deeply affected by what they'd seen in the cleric's divination.

At least cleric Ward was easier to read than the troops we'd captured in the past. Sherra hadn't helped with those divinations, I reminded myself. Would we know more now, if that had been the case?

"What else did you see?" I asked.

"Torturing. Ceremonies with other clerics. Ruarke's image, of course," Barth mumbled. "An all-consuming desire to please their god, to keep Ruarke happy, and to murder all of us. They imagine us to be spawn from hell, who must be destroyed at all costs."

"Sherra, explain the hole in his head," I turned to her.

"I formed a long, small tube with my shield," she sighed. "I sent a forceful blast through it, straight at Ward's forehead. He never knew what hit him."

"That's terrifying," the chief physician said. I considered that I should have sent him out of the room earlier.

"It was necessary," I frowned at the physician. "He was about to behead a nine-year-old. What would you do in Sherra's place?"

"The same, if I could," he shrugged.

I made a mental note to ask her how she'd come up with the idea. It had been a sound one, and something I hoped I could duplicate if necessary. She'd pierced another escort's shield with her own, and then brought down an enemy about to commit murder.

"Is there anything else you found in your divination?" I asked Barth.

"Yes. Perhaps the worst of all," Barth mumbled. "Ny-nes is sending another army against us, and they are scheduled to arrive at the border soon."

* * *

Border Camp
Ruarke

"Bring Merrin to me," I commanded my newly-appointed first assistant, Niles. Ward's death angered me, and the way he died angered me more. I wanted to know exactly how this method of killing had been developed, and by whom.

Chapter 13

The one responsible would become a target of my recently-acquired divination techniques, and I would have my revenge. As yet, I hadn't contacted Kaakos; that could wait until I had further information from Merrin to pass along.

"Merrin is here, esteemed one," Niles escorted Merrin into my tent.

"Ah, friend Merrin," I greeted him.

"Is there something amiss?" he asked.

"No, I merely wish to ask questions about our mutual enemy," I held out a hand, inviting him to sit on a nearby camp stool. "Niles, bring something for our friend to drink."

That drink would be laced with the drug, to make Merrin even more cooperative. Niles left, but was back shortly with a mug of tea for Merrin.

"Ah, good," I nodded as Merrin drank. "Now," I began, "You know they killed my beloved first assistant, Ward."

"Yes, I heard that news. I'm sorry."

His condolences were false; I expected nothing else from this one. "Well, I wish to discuss how they were able to breach Willa's shield to deliver a small, well-aimed blast to Ward's forehead. I watched him die. As you may imagine, I am greatly incensed by this heinous act."

"Hmmph. If Sherra hadn't died when you sent the huge bomb against Az-ca, I'd say it was her work. She did train several before her death, however, so this talent could be attributed to any of her closest followers."

"Sherra? I haven't heard that name before." He was about to tell me how the bomb had failed to eliminate Az-ca's army. Kaakos would be more than interested in hearing this, as Merrin appeared convinced that it was accomplished by a single person.

And a woman, no less.

Had things changed? Were women allowed to become warriors again? That couldn't be. Surely the old laws were still in place concerning the training of warriors and escorts.

"She's dead—everybody said so, and the last I heard, it was more than six months after the bombing and there was still no sign of her. She died. This—maybe Caral, Wend or one of the others who trained with her managed this."

"Caral? Wend?"

"They are quite talented with their shields. I can only imagine that they did this with stronger shields than Willa can make."

"You're saying that an escort's shield pierced another escort's shield?"

"How else would it happen?" Merrin gulped more of his tea.

"Something to consider," I said. "Niles, take Merrin back to his tent. I must think on this."

* * *

King's Palace
Sherra

"Because I asked Pottles how that weapon that your father kept in his desk worked," I explained to Kerok. He and I sat in his study with Barth, Armon, Hunter and General Weren.

We'd left the physician's study after Barth told the biggest secret we'd found in Ward's divination—that the enemy army was on the way.

Kerok said Weren needed to be in the meeting, sent Armon after him and moved the rest of us to the palace. I was glad to leave the physician behind, actually. I felt bad enough about killing the way I had, and he'd pointed out how horrible he thought it was, too.

I'd done it to save a life—one who was much more innocent than Ward had been for most of his existence.

"You wanted to know more about Drenn's death, didn't you?" Kerok asked me. He didn't sound upset.

"I did. Pottles explained about ricochet, too—how the bullets can bounce off one surface and hit another. We had a discussion about redirecting fireblasts with shields at the same time, to accomplish the same result. I'd just never connected those two in my mind, until she pointed it out."

"You formed a narrow tube with your shield, you say?" Weren asked.

"Yes, General. Like the barrel of a pistol—that the enemy carries. I sent the small blast forcefully through the tube I formed. It exited not far from Ward's forehead and killed him before he could kill the girl."

"Was it difficult to breach Willa's shield?" Armon asked.

"Not really; she was prepared for much larger blasts. A small, forced piercing of her shield didn't concern her. I doubt she even felt it."

Kerok, Armon and Weren exchanged glances, while Barth and Hunter focused on me with growing interest. I felt compelled to explain.

"It's the way they were taught," I said. "To concentrate on protecting against bombs and larger blasts. They weren't as concerned about bullets and small projectiles, because they weren't trained to be."

"And they never expected to get this close to the enemy, either," Kerok nodded thoughtfully. "That's why some shields held around the few enemies who managed to invade our camps, while others didn't. The escort really didn't know what to expect and hadn't prepared for such an event."

"Yes. We talked about that at Secondary Camp," I acknowledged. "You said that everybody ran after a shield was placed around an armed enemy, because nobody knew if the shield would hold their small bombs or bullets back. I've had time to think about it since then."

"I can see that," Weren agreed. "That is exceptional observation, young woman."

"Do you think the escorts with Merrin will be able to prevent something like that from happening again? I want your honest opinion, Sherra," Kerok said.

"Willa won't ever be able to hold me back," I sighed. "Her shielding talent isn't strong enough. Caral can probably get through, too. Wend, yes, probably some of the others. As for the other escorts with Merrin's bunch, I can't say, because I didn't go against them."

"Which escorts are with Merrin?" Kerok turned toward Weren and Armon.

"Willa, Calli and Reva," Weren replied.

"Are the other two stronger than Willa? Weaker?" Kerok asked Armon.

"About the same—if I were grading them, I'd have said Willa was the strongest of the three, though."

"Probably why Ruarke chose her to place a shield around them," Adahi and Kyri walked into my study. "We've been listening to rumors," he held up a hand to silence Kerok's annoyed growl. "We're hoping to learn the truth of the matter, if you don't mind."

"I suggest we adjourn to the meeting room, then," Hunter said. "We can have a meal there and discuss the day's events."

* * *

"Did Ward know the numbers being sent by Ny-nes?" Weren asked after we'd been seated around the meeting table and plates of food were set before us.

"He didn't," Barth answered. "I believe only Ruarke may have that information, and he hasn't shared it with his clerics."

"What he did know is that they held back some of their troops last time," I said. "Somehow, they knew to do that, in case something went wrong. They were training replacement troops, too, for the same reason."

"You saw that?" Barth turned to me.

"Sherra has an unusual talent to see others past the divination subject," Kyri said.

"I don't see everybody," I said, hoping to fend off additional questions. That talent wasn't a reliable one, and I'd hoped to keep it to myself until I knew more about it.

"Who?" Kerok asked.

"It's unreliable," I admitted what I didn't want to reveal. "Some things just come during the divination, and I can't predict who it'll be or command it in any way."

"Could still be useful," Barth said. "No matter who or what."

"I didn't see Ruarke," I pointed out. "I wish I had, so we'd know more about him. It's as if he were closed off to me. What I saw was someone else who'd said those things within Ward's hearing—back in Ny-nes. Perhaps it was a conversation that Ruarke had with another, but Ward was listening, too."

I didn't add that Ward wasn't supposed to be listening. He'd been spying, actually. I wondered if Ruarke knew about that.

"We've never seen past the prophet's bones—or whatever that drug is, on any other divination of the enemy," Barth observed. "Sherra and I together can do it. That will change things going forward."

"The prophet's bones is a mind-altering drug," Kyri sniffed. "Those fools."

"Which ones—the ones giving it or the ones taking it?" Kerok asked.

"Both. Granted it does what their Sovereign Leader wants it to do in the short term, which is to develop an obsessed hatred for their enemies. At times, one of the recipients goes berserk and kills anything in his path—including his closest friends and colleagues. This is why the officers and leaders never take it, once they've left the common ranks behind," Kyri said.

"They learn what it is and how dangerous it can be, and still they give it freely to their troops," Adahi didn't hide his scorn.

"Because it achieves the desired results," Kyri added. "Those in power desire to stay in power, and rise in the ranks. Better benefits and living conditions are offered, you understand."

"The same goes for the clerical order," Adahi agreed. "While they form an army of sorts, their method of destruction is generally relegated to information gathered on Ny-nes' subjects, and the torture of those who hold power or withhold desired information."

"Until now," Kerok said. "Why do you suppose Ruarke and his clerics decided to come this time?"

"Merrin," Kyri answered quickly. "Ruarke saw an opening with one of our own who has gone rogue. You can be assured that Ruarke has offered Merrin your place, Prince

Thorn. Merrin has likely been given the drug unknowingly, to make him more cooperative. As for Ruarke, he has no intention of giving Merrin anything other than a tortured death after the rest of us are destroyed."

"How close were you to this Ruarke person earlier?" Kerok turned back to Armon and me.

"Perhaps thirty yards," Armon said. I nodded my agreement. We could see him, but not well enough to sort out identifying marks on his face. Mostly he'd been wrapped in long, black robes, which brushed his booted feet.

"I was much more focused on the girl and the knife Ward held," I confessed.

"Sherra, I know how you feel about situations like these," Kerok sighed as he studied me. "If you find yourself in the same situation again, I order you to kill Ruarke first and forget the others. Do you understand?"

* * *

I recognized the wisdom in Kerok's command; I merely didn't want to accept it. That's why I walked outside the palace later, after paying a short visit to Pottles and her young trainees.

Anari and the boys were thriving and getting enough to eat for the first time in their lives, I imagined. I didn't stay long, choosing to go downstairs instead of up, and walking out of a side door in the palace and into the gardens there.

The guards thought nothing of it, merely nodding as I passed them on my way out. I knew where the outside table and chairs were, if I wanted to sit.

I didn't.

I wanted to walk and think—about everything I'd seen in Ward's divination, what I'd seen that Barth hadn't, and finally, Kerok's command to kill Ruarke first, no matter what the situation.

In my short span of life experiences, there was always an exception to nearly every rule. Something more important, perhaps, that took precedence. Too many possibilities crowded my mind, of whose life I'd consider more important than Ruarke's death.

Where are you? Kerok sounded gruff.

Walking in the gardens, I replied stiffly. I wanted to ask for a separate suite—one I could retire to on nights like this, when something troubled me and served to hold me away from him.

Sherra?

Kyri's voice.

I'm in the gardens, I replied absently.

Good. Adahi and I need to speak with you alone. Seconds later, they appeared nearby.

"What is it?" I asked as they approached.

"We have something to tell you. Something that you are that is—unexpected," Kyri said. "Come, sit with us. We'll explain as well as we can."

We found the garden table and chairs not far away. I shivered in the night air as I took a seat; the way Kyri spoke didn't sound as if she had pleasant news to deliver.

"Do you recall the dreams you had—and the rescue of Hunter when he was attacked by Merrin?" Kyri asked once she was settled on a chair opposite mine.

"I do. I still don't know what that was, or how it happened."

"We do," Kyri said. "Sherra, you are a dreamwalker. That means you can carry your power away from your body while it sleeps. Your body stays behind, but your spirit and your power can travel elsewhere, sometimes faster than *stepping*. You really did save Hunter's life that night."

"A dreamwalker?"

"There are dangers to being a dreamwalker," Adahi rumbled. "Never let the enemy know what you are. With Thorn's Book in his hands, there may be a way to trap a dreamwalker, keeping his or her spirit in a prison of sorts, until the body dies."

"That's horrible," I whispered.

"Much of the time, the dreamwalker knows more and can be more powerful than the conscious person realizes. We tell you this now, so that if you find you are dreamwalking, you'll know what you're doing, and also know to protect yourself at all costs. Do you understand?"

"I can see why it would be so important," I agreed. Leaving my body behind to die while my spirit was held captive frightened me a great deal. "How do you know this about me? Other than the saving Hunter's life?"

"You remember the nightmares you had—of being trapped?" Adahi asked.

"Yes. Those were horrible. I felt as if I were suffocating."

"In a way, you were," he said. "I placed a shield around your bedroom, keeping your dreamwalker inside while your body rested. I apologize for doing that, now. I removed it before you returned to Az-ca, because it was wrong to place it in the beginning."

In the dim light of the King's gardens, I watched Kyri's head turn swiftly toward Adahi, before turning back toward me.

She asked him to do it, I realized. Somehow, that made me sadder than it should have.

* * *

Rose and Thorn

Kerok

Perhaps they didn't know I'd *stepped* into the garden with a bottle of wine, breaking Father's rule while I searched for my rose. Therefore, I heard what Kyri and Adahi said to Sherra.

It was meant for her ears only; I heard it, too. A part of me was angry that they'd left me out of this meeting.

Another part understood how dangerous this information could be. The thought of Sherra's spirit trapped by the enemy while her body died terrified and angered me. I had no idea what to do about it, either. She was already upset that I'd ordered her to kill Ruarke no matter what, if she saw him again.

"I need to go. I have to think about this," Sherra scooted her chair back on the flagstones. Like a coward, I *stepped* back to my suite, as if I'd never stumbled upon a conversation I wasn't meant to hear.

* * *

Sherra

"Did you need something?" Hunter found me walking down the hall toward Kerok's suite. After the events of the day, even though I still felt a little out of sorts with him, I wanted Kerok's arms around me.

"No, just—bed, I suppose," I said.

"Good. Kerok will be pleased to have your company—he may have thought you weren't coming. I just delivered a book to his suite."

"He's reading?"

"I think it was a distraction," Hunter shrugged. He was smiling, however. Perhaps he and I should have a talk about the night I'd saved him. Both of us could learn things, maybe.

"I'll see if he has a bottle of wine," I said. I needed something to help me sleep.

"I believe he does. And an extra glass. Good-night." Hunter continued along the hall, away from Kerok's suite.

"Kerok?" I tapped on his door.

Come in, he sent.

Just as Hunter said, I found him reading in bed, several pillows propping him up. Covers were pulled up to his waist, but his chest was bare as he turned a page. A scar on his body disappeared beneath the blanket. It made me sigh.

"Please say that's an open wine bottle," I moved toward the bed, waving a hand at the bottle and glasses on his bedside table.

"It is," he stuck a thumb in the book to hold his place. "Come have a glass with me."

"Thank you."

"Hold on, I have a bookmark somewhere," he moved about, searching for the bookmark in question. "Ah." He held up a scrap of paper. Stuffing that in the book, he set the volume on the table before reaching for the wine bottle.

"Come, fill your glass and then lean against me—you've had a terrible day, my rose."

"No worse than yours," I sighed and did as he asked. His skin felt good—warm—as I leaned against him and sipped my wine.

"Weren will be expediting the training in the next few days," Kerok whispered against my hair. "We have no idea when the enemy army will arrive to attack us."

"So many things happening at once, and we're not prepared for even half of it," I turned my head into the hollow of his shoulder and closed my eyes. His presence was

Rose and Thorn

a comfort that I couldn't describe at that moment. It merely was.

* * *

Doret

While the young ones slept, I *stepped* away to Kyri's City—at her request. Waiting there with Kyri were three black rose girls—they'd finally answered Kyri's call.

"This is Doret," Kyri introduced me to the girls. "She will take you to the King's palace, where you'll be made comfortable. You'll train with the others who've come away."

Kyri had given them a meal before she called for me, and they'd had a bath and wore fresh clothing. It made me grateful to the residents of Kyri's City for providing in an emergency.

I'll send mindspeak to Hunter to prepare another bedroom, I informed Kyri. One of these can stay with Anari, the other two can share.

I'll let Sherra know tomorrow that she'll be in charge of Cole's troops—they'll arrive at Secondary Camp on her command.

Will they survive? I asked the direct question.

I don't know. Things are too fractured to see much. Adahi says the same.

Whenever Kyri said that, it meant the future was balanced upon the breadth of a hair, and could fall either way.

Would any of us survive? I doubted anyone had an answer.

* * *

Border Camp
Ruarke

228

Chapter 13

I had two names, Thorn's Book, and a desire to exact revenge for Ward's death. Except for the guards at the perimeter, everyone else was asleep. Thorn's Book held so many delightful possibilities; compelling someone to come to me was among them.

Merrin had given me the names; I'd gotten descriptions from one of the escorts. Caral and Wend were as good as in my hands as I set about sending messages into their dreams. I considered the pleasure I'd have, torturing both until they screamed and begged for death.

Placing the King's heavy dagger across the book to hold it open, I began my preparations.

* * *

Sherra

I felt the uneasiness in my dreams; they'd turned quickly from harmless randomness to focused fear—for Caral and Wend. I'm not sure how I'd connected their dreams to mine, but both were being pulled away—coerced to go elsewhere.

Suddenly, I stood beside the bed where Marc lay with Wend in his arms. Constructing the most powerful shield I could, I cut off the coercion to her dream and pulled it toward myself instead.

He was on the other end, I felt sure of it.

Next, I went to Caral, who was shielded better but still in danger.

I didn't bother with the fact that Misten slept in Caral's arms. That information would never come from me or go to another if I could help it. As for breaking the law—the law was unjust, cruel, and deserved to be broken.

Cutting off the coercion in Caral's dreams, I transferred it to myself, too.

Rose and Thorn

He had no idea I was only using it to locate him—I saw his hiding place easily. He waited inside a tent across the border, casting a spell from Thorn's Book to ensnare two unsuspecting black roses.

Did he realize the coercion would allow the visions to work both ways? *For someone powerful enough to force it to do so?*

With no second thoughts, I shifted my location to his tent. I smiled, because he expected corporeal bodies to appear before him, instead of a half-visible wraith.

There he sat, Thorn's Book laid open on a small table before him, the King's dagger set across it to hold the pages open while he chanted the words of the spell.

His death would be mine.

Something stirred at my back.

Wait.

Kerok was attempting to wake my physical body.

No!

Grasping the dagger swiftly, I stabbed downward, the point piercing Ruarke's hand and pinning it to half of Thorn's Book, while I ripped the other half of the book away with power and disappeared with my body's waking.

Ruarke's howl of pain followed me the entire way.

Chapter 14

K*ing's Palace*
Kerok

A loud thump sounded next to the bed and Sherra, whom I'd attempted to wake in an amorous fashion, leapt from the bed with a shriek.

"What the bloody hell?" I half-shouted as she raced toward the location of the noise.

Flipping on the solar light on the bedside table, I saw Sherra standing nearby, naked and holding half of a large book in her hands.

What terrified me most was the blood dripping from the book's pages.

"Prince Thorn?" A guard, banging on my outer door, drew my attention away. Sliding off the bed, I grabbed a dressing robe and strode toward the door. "Coming," I shouted. I'd have to sort this out quickly or the entire palace would be awake in seconds, thinking we were under attack.

Throwing the door open, I saw the concerned look on two guard's faces. "We're all right," I waved away their concern. "Will you ask Barth and Hunter to come? Have wine and tea brought, too. Please."

"Of course, my Prince," the guard who'd knocked dipped his head to me. I closed the door and walked quickly back to the bedroom, where Sherra still stood, holding the book—half of it, anyway—as if it were a live snake.

"Tell me," I said, attempting to calm my voice.

"I ah," she swallowed. "I was away," she whispered. "He was trying to take Wend and Caral. I, uh, got there first. I stabbed his hand onto the other half of the book and took this." She held the book higher.

"That explains the blood, then," I said, my words dry.

"I know where they are, or were. He isn't stupid. I figure he'll move the camp quickly, so we won't find him."

"He?" I had a good guess, but wanted to verify my thoughts.

"Ruarke. He was using a spell from the book to bring Caral and Wend to him, so he could hurt them. I stopped him and stole half the book—and half the spell with it."

"My love, you need clothing. Hunter and Barth are on the way," I said, moving carefully toward her. Her eyes looked wild to me—almost desperate. She'd been afraid for her friends, I saw that much.

Kyri was correct—Sherra had gone dreamwalking and I'd wakened her. "Were you going to kill him?" I asked.

"I intended to. I was ah, pulled away."

Meaning I'd wakened her before she could accomplish her goal. Silently, I cursed myself.

Chapter 14

"Clothing, love," I gestured for her to put the bloody, half-book on my bedside table so she could clean her hands and get dressed.

"Oh. All right." She set the book down carefully before searching for a robe and disappearing into the bathroom.

Barth and Hunter knocked on the outer door before Sherra's return, so I went to let them in.

* * *

Ruarke

Niles wrapped my hand after we'd moved camp; I wasn't willing to stay in the original location any longer—they could find us if we didn't move.

Merrin was especially unhappy about being wakened, but he gathered his things eventually and came along.

At least most of the bleeding in my hand had stopped; I'd waved the bloody thing enough to spray red on anything and everything that failed to cooperate immediately.

I hadn't even gotten a good look at my attacker, and that concerned me a great deal. While I had a desire to discuss the event with Kaakos, I worried that he'd command us to return to Ny-nes. My imagination had run wild, too, and my thoughts on the matter were so improbable he'd call me delusional.

Worst of all, half of Thorn's Book had been taken by my attacker. That alone infuriated me—far simpler spells were in the pages I retained, and many of those were now covered in my own blood.

We'd settled in a valley farther away from the border, and made it as difficult as possible to find us by nesting the tents among thick stands of trees.

Kaakos would call the wound in my hand just, for attempting the spell without testing it first.

I no longer had the entire spell to try it again. I cursed softly, causing Niles to stop his wrapping for a moment.

"Not you," I gestured angrily for him to continue his work. He was bursting with questions—I saw them in his eyes. He knew better than to ask, because I was unwilling to answer, even on the best of days.

This was certainly not the best of days. Perhaps one of the women I'd called was more powerful than I imagined, or there was someone else—someone to be very concerned about—among my enemies.

* * *

King's Palace
Sherra
"You stabbed his hand?" Hunter asked.

"Onto the other half of the book," I said, holding a warm mug of tea against my chest as if it would warm my entire body, which felt chilled to the bone.

"At least we know Ruarke bleeds red, just like the rest of us," Kerok shook his head.

"How did you know where to find him?" Barth asked the important question.

"He was calling Wend and Caral to him," I said. "He was showing them where to come. I intercepted his message and followed his instructions. He never saw me," I said. "I doubt he'll understand what or who attacked him—at least for a while."

"What about Caral and Wend?" Kerok asked.

"Safe. I placed extra shields around them, so his message wouldn't get through."

"That's extraordinary," Hunter admitted. "I wouldn't think it possible."

Chapter 14

"I don't know how I knew to do it," I confessed. "My dreamwalker knew." *Just as Kyri said.*

"So, Ruarke has the King's dagger, instead of Merrin," Barth said. "I'm not surprised. Likely he has the coronet, too."

"It makes sense—he had the book, obviously," Kerok pointed out. "Now he's leading Merrin around by the nose, and Merrin's too stupid to realize it."

"Don't forget that Merrin is probably under the influence of the drug, too," Barth said.

"You think he's any less to blame because of that?" Kerok was angry. Part of that anger was directed at himself, for some reason.

"No, my Prince. Merrin holds the blame in this, start to finish," Hunter soothed. "Had he not done as he did, he wouldn't have attracted Ruarke's attention. I firmly believe this."

"Then place part of that blame on my brother, who helped him," Kerok snarled, before rising to pace.

"Kerok, we have to find a way forward, not retread the paths behind us," I said, rising to go to him. "I think we've had enough discussion for tonight."

"We'll continue this at breakfast," Kerok waved a hand, dismissing Barth and Hunter.

* * *

Kerok

I asked Armon and Weren to meet with us over breakfast, after sleeping fitfully for what remained of the night.

Sherra had to deal with my tossing and turning, but never said a word. "Thorn," Hunter said as he walked into my study, "There are bodies outside the northern dome."

Rose and Thorn

* * *

"I locked the shields against Merrin and the others," Sherra admitted later. Six villager's bodies, hostages of Merrin's, lay outside the northern dome. They'd been found by guards when day broke. I didn't ask her about that feat then—perhaps I should have.

"The bodies were just dumped here, when they found they couldn't get inside?" I fumed. Sherra, Barth and I stood outside the dome, where the bodies had been dumped in a haphazard fashion.

"I believe it was retaliation for last night's events," Barth ventured.

Of course it was. The bodies showed burn marks, so it could be Merrin's work, even if it weren't Merrin's decision to kill them. Frankly, it could be either Ruarke or Merrin, in my mind.

Ruarke would have tortured Wend and Caral before they died—of that I had no doubt. Sherra's dreamwalker had put a stop to that, and now six villagers were dead in their place.

Outside the dome where the bodies lay, there was nothing but dry desert and the morning heat reflecting off the dome's surface. Only stubborn plants and small reptiles survived for any length of time.

"Have the guards gather the bodies and deliver them to the infirmary. Barth will do a divination there," I said. Sherra stood silently at my side while I issued orders. *You had nothing to do with this—those poor villagers are marked for death, no matter what we do,* I reminded her. *Come now, Armon and Weren are on the way; we'll discuss this latest atrocity at breakfast.*

* * *

Chapter 14

Sherra

We sat at the meeting table, food in front of us as Kerok explained what he knew of the night's events. I hoped the others asked no questions of me; this way I could consider six deaths I'd caused, instead of the two Ruarke intended.

If I could only find Merrin, now, things would not go well for him.

Or Ruarke.

Or any of the others who followed either. I wanted to curse that I'd been pulled away from Ruarke too soon; my dreamwalker desired his death, just as Kerok did. Would I ever find him again so easily?

I doubted it greatly. Ruarke knew to guard himself after last night. He had a hole in his left hand to remind him, should he forget. He'd carry that scar the full length of his life, however long that might be.

"You're positive that he wanted Caral and Wend?" General Weren asked.

"I am, sir," I replied. "I—my dreamwalker—intercepted his spell that called out to them. That's how I found him."

"What is this spell, exactly?" Armon asked.

"We only have half the book, so I can't say for certain," Kerok began. "Sherra probably knows more."

"Sherra?" Weren turned to me.

"I think it's similar to the one Kyri uses—to issue invitations to those who are welcome to come to her city," I said. "And the one time that she pulled all the youngest roses to her, when they were threatened by Merrin."

"You know this how?" Kerok frowned at me, then.

"Because I provided extra power for her, while she did it," I said. We'd been connected. It was very similar to what

Ruarke had performed the night before, to pull Caral and Wend away from Secondary Camp.

I'd hoped they'd ask no questions. It appeared to be all they wanted to do. I was compelled to answer, as I'd been in the middle of it all.

At least my dreamwalker had, and I was left with the memories of it.

"How did you keep them from getting past the domes?" Barth asked. "I thought you had to touch them to recognize their power before doing something like this."

"I did it last night, after Kerok fell asleep again," I admitted, hanging my head. "I only need something they've touched, you see. I found all that in the half-book my dreamwalker stole from Ruarke. Almost all of Merrin's and Ruarke's people have touched it."

The meeting room erupted, as everyone attempted to speak at once.

* * *

The headache I'd developed hadn't eased any, an hour after I'd gotten the pain-killing powder delivered in a cup of tea. At least the others had gone about their business, leaving me alone with Kerok.

"If we locate Ruarke's camp, you may be able to get past the perimeter divination, no matter who set it?" Kerok asked for the third time.

"I think so," I replied for the third time. "Ruarke may be more—unpredictable than Merrin, but I believe I can work around that. The trouble comes from finding them, first," I pointed out.

"You know they can strike elsewhere—any village is vulnerable," Kerok growled.

Chapter 14

"I know that. I think you should stop haranguing me and let me go place shields," I snapped. He jerked around as I spoke; I hadn't expected my words to sound so waspish, but I was weary, my head hurt and I was more than ready for the inquisition to cease.

"We should sleep in separate bedrooms from now on."

I'd wounded him; he'd struck back.

"If that's what you want. May I be dismissed?"

He waved a hand before turning his back on me. I walked out of his study, my anger seething, my head pounding. With or without his permission, I could lay shields around ten villages before the midday meal.

* * *

Valley Camp

Ruarke

When Merrin's warrior returned, telling me that he'd been prevented from passing through the domes, I didn't believe him. I sent Merrin in his place—to deliver the bodies to the palace himself.

In only a few moments, he'd returned with the same tale. I cursed, then, called them fools, collected Niles to move bodies for me and went myself.

I found the bodies outside the northern dome; I couldn't get past that perimeter any better than the others. Something strange was happening—how was this even possible? Kaakos was able to set an alarm at his perimeter around Ny-nes, which alerted him to certain persons crossing into Ny-nes, but he had no way to keep them out.

He would know where they crossed, however, which made them easy to find and kill. That particular talent ensured we hadn't been attacked in two centuries or more.

Rose and Thorn

This—I had no idea how it was accomplished, but wanted more than anything to learn how it was done. So many things would come to me if I could perform this miracle.

Had the same one who'd stabbed me done this?

That question ran a regular track in my mind. Perhaps it was time to question Merrin again—and those leeches who used to be Council members. Somebody had to know something about this.

Meanwhile, I considered how to take further revenge against the Crown of Az-ca. The army was scheduled to arrive soon and Kaakos' generals would begin issuing orders. I needed to show Kaakos some progress, or he could ask me to return to Ny-nes. I had things yet to do and vengeance to be had before I left.

* * *

Sherra

Pottles volunteered to go with me, and I was grateful for her presence. Kerok had managed to wound my heart, and that pain, coupled with the headache, served to make me less than pleasant to be around.

Therefore, in the villages we visited, she handled the leaders' questions, explaining that we were protecting them as best we could from Merrin. Pottles never told them about Ruarke or the enemy army—she didn't want to panic the villagers.

"Of course you'll be able to go in and out if you want," Pottles soothed yet another village head. "There's nothing to stop you—only something to stop him from entering and harming you and the others."

"I heard about the burning of that village," the man frowned at her.

"We're trying to prevent that very thing," Pottles said. "Sherra, are you finished here?" She was tired of making explanations.

"Yes." My answer was short, like my temper.

"Good day to you, sir," Pottles told him. "We have other villages to visit before the day is over."

I let Pottles *step* us to our next destination; it took a few moments to realize we stood inside Kyri's kitchen.

"It's about time," Kyri said, setting plates on the small table. "Do you still have a headache, Sherra?"

"Yes," I sighed as I took a chair.

"I have something for that," Kyri said and handed me a small square of folded paper with powder inside it. "Drop that in your tea; it'll help. It's stronger than what they give at the palace."

"Wonderful. That stuff they gave me did no good at all," I grumbled and unwrapped the paper carefully before dumping the contents in my cup of tea. "Thank you."

"Thank me when the headache goes away," Kyri said. "Now, eat. It'll put the powder to work faster."

That day, I learned about the marching draught and what it could accomplish when combined with the pain powder. Before nightfall, Pottles and I visited sixty other villages. At times, I was able to place the shield without anyone noticing, we were so quick about our business.

"Those are the most populous; we can tackle smaller ones tomorrow," Pottles said when she *stepped* us back to the palace courtyard. I should have expected Kerok to be waiting for me; his face was dark with anger, making his scar stand out.

"Before you get on your high horse," Pottles warned, "there are seventy villages with protection now, whereas none of them were protected before. If you wanted to know her whereabouts, next time use your brain and send mindspeak."

"What she said," I breathed as I walked past him toward the side door of the palace. "I'm going to pick out my separate bedroom, now."

* * *

"I think he meant choose a bedroom near his, not on another floor," Hunter attempted to stop me as I carried my things into a third-floor suite, not far from Pottles'.

"Then why didn't he say that?" I snapped at Hunter. "Look, I'm sorry," I held out a hand. "I don't—I'm not angry with you."

"Just him, is that right?"

"He's the one who said we'd sleep in separate bedrooms from now on."

"Why don't you ask him why?"

"Are you serious? You weren't there when he said it. He was certainly serious." I flung my clothing onto the bed and glared at Hunter.

"Look, you were both tired from last night, and he learned things he didn't know were possible. I know I certainly did. It takes time to digest this, Princess. Give one another some room to understand, all right?"

"Princess? Hunter, you're delusional."

"No. It hasn't been formally declared as yet, but you and he spoke the vows. The title is yours, whether you want it or not."

"I don't. Please, leave." I covered my face with both hands.

"Denying it doesn't make it untrue." Hunter swept out of my new suite, closing the door softly behind him.

Chapter 14

* * *

Kerok

Sherra and I needed to talk. I should apologize, but my anger still seethed, so now wasn't the time.

As for guilt—I had that and more. Why in the first warrior's name did I tell her we needed separate bedrooms? Yes, I felt the guilt of waking her before her dreamwalker accomplished a vital mission. That was the reason behind the separate bedroom demand, but I realized later that it was more than foolish. All I had to do was rein in my night-time desires, once she fell asleep.

She'd left the palace to go place shields around villages, and it upset me more than I wanted to admit that she hadn't kept me advised. She hadn't returned for the midday meal, either, and that made it worse.

Hunter, I sent mindspeak, *will you ask for the names of the shielded villages so we can keep records?*

I'll ask Doret. Sherra isn't in the mood to answer more questions, he replied. *She ah, chose a suite on the third floor of the east wing*, he added.

Fuck.

As you say, my Prince.

"I take it things aren't going well between you and your rose?" Adahi appeared inside my study and seated himself before my desk.

"I'm an idiot. You don't have to point it out," I said.

"The best advice in the world means nothing if it isn't heeded."

"Have you become a philosopher, in addition to being the phantom?"

"I've been a philosopher far longer than I've been the phantom, although I dislike that term."

"Then what do you want to be called?"

"Adahi."

"This day will be recorded in the historical record as the ultimate peak of obviousness," I rose from my chair to stare out the window. "I decree it." I waved an arm.

Adahi surprised me by laughing.

"Come now," he said after a few moments. "I will teach you how to set a perimeter divination."

* * *

"Can you show me how to do what Sherra did? Hunter says she dissipated Merrin's fireblasts in my study."

"I can't say it will be exact," Adahi said. He and I sat at the garden table, after I'd spent a great deal of frustrated energy by building several perimeter divinations.

"But you can show me something, can't you?"

"Yes. It involves wrapping a shield about the fireblast itself and starving it of oxygen—very, very quickly."

"You're saying I need to work on my shields, then."

"You do. You need to practice shaping them. When you can wrap a shield around a falling vase and prevent it from breaking, I will teach you how to smother fireblasts."

"I need Sherra's help," I admitted.

"Her help will get you to your goal swiftly, Prince Thorn. You could fumble for days and still not get it right without her assistance."

"How do you suggest I approach her, then?"

"With the truth. Tell her you feel guilty about waking her. Tell her this was your attempt at not letting that happen again, you just went about it in the worst way. Your shields could work wonders by holding you back while she sleeps, unless you consciously choose to remove them."

"Well, I wish I'd thought of *that* sooner," I grumbled.

Chapter 14

"You didn't think of it; I'm giving you advice because you asked. And, there's always wine and honey cakes—with flowers, of course. The apology and the way it is delivered, however, will be your strongest advocate."

"I think I know what to do," I said, almost interrupting Adahi's speech. "I have to write and sign something. Thank you for the advice."

Adahi gave me a skeptical look as I walked toward the side door, leaving him standing in the garden.

* * *

Valley Camp
Ruarke

They are bringing three planes, with three bombs, Kaakos informed me. I'd asked because it was becoming increasingly clear that we needed them—Az-ca had become more insufferable than I'd ever imagined.

Unless we eliminated the source of the special shields, we'd never destroy the King's City, and that was a particularly important goal for Kaakos—and for me. The last time, they'd destroyed one plane and one bomb. Merrin said the one who'd done that was now dead.

We'd see how they dealt with three at the same time; all dropped at night, while they slept.

Perhaps we'd have our army attack in the traditional way, keeping the warriors busy while the bombs destroyed the rest of the country. It would be quite pleasing to see the enemy's army scatter after that turn of events.

We have three more bombs in the making, Kaakos added. *Should they be needed.*

You are the wisest, as always, I replied. It never hurt to stroke Kaakos' ego.

Never.

Rose and Thorn

Besides, I wanted to retrieve the other half of a certain book. Perhaps a trade of human lives would suffice? *Wise Kaakos*, I sent, *Are the enemy children I sent you still alive? I have a use for them if this is so.*

* * *

King's Palace
Sherra

"Your breakfast, Princess." Hunter led three servants into my suite the following morning. One held a tray of food, the second a huge bouquet of flowers and the third held a paper packet in his hands.

"What's this?" I frowned at Hunter.

"See for yourself," he gestured as the tray of food was set on a small table by my window.

I watched as the food was set out, the flowers arranged in their vase to be appealing, and the packet set beside the flowers.

"I suggest reading while you eat," Hunter dipped his head before ushering the servants out of my quarters.

Tea first, I thought as I approached the table; I hadn't slept well the night before, and needed something to wake me up.

After pouring and sipping tea, I opened the packet to read. I had no idea what it contained.

Inside the outer wrapping lay copies of a decree that Kerok had apparently written the night before.

Let it be known, it began, *that* The Rose Mark, *a book previously banned in all forms, is no longer unlawful.*

Let it be known that The Rose Mark, *henceforth, will be recognized as a legitimate training manual for all escorts.*

Let it be known that the Crown will provide copies of The Rose Mark *to all trainees from this day forward.*

Chapter 14

Decreed by Thorn Wulfson Kerok Rex, Crown Prince of Az-ca and Supreme Commander of Az-ca's Army.

The date and his signature followed.

The second page was a letter addressed to me.

My love, Kerok wrote. *I am sorry for ill words spoken in haste. I merely worried that I would interrupt your dreamwalker during important acts in the future, and made a poor decision without discussing it with you, first.*

The error of my words has been succinctly pointed out to me; therefore, I wish to discuss this subject with you now, as possible solutions have been brought to light.

Please accept my humble apologies, and consider coming back to me.

Your humbled Prince,

Kerok.

Kerok? I sent mindspeak to him.

My rose?

Will you join me for breakfast? I believe Hunter had enough food delivered to feed two.

I would be overjoyed.

The door to my suite flew open, and without knowing how it happened, we were in one another's arms. Breakfast was forgotten the moment Kerok appeared, and I believe the guards outside had to close the door, lest they see things not meant for their eyes.

Chapter 15

Secondary Camp
Armon

"I received this from Prince Thorn before breakfast this morning," General Weren handed a packet of papers to me. "I'd like you to give the information to the troops tonight at dinner."

"What is it?" I asked, staring at the papers in my hand.

"Something that needed doing, I believe," Weren smiled. "I also received a private message from the Prince, and you and I will discuss that one at the midday meal—just between us."

"I'll be there—where did you want to meet?"

"I'll have a meal delivered to my cabin—we can talk there. How's the training coming?"

"As expected, some are learning faster than others. I'm considering combining some of them together—to form shields or blasts together," I said.

"Work on that," Weren agreed. "If three or four together can accomplish the same thing, that's more troops we can place on the battlefield."

"My thinking exactly, General."

* * *

King's Palace
Sherra

"Kyri sent this," Pottles handed a message to me when I met her mid-morning for tea.

I had to find someone else to travel with me today—Pottles had taken a day away from training her charges to help me shield villages the day before. I couldn't ask her to spend a second day with me; Anari and the others needed her.

"What is it?" I asked, unfolding the second message I'd received in a matter of hours.

"Read it for yourself," she made a face at me. "Take action soon; if Kyri feels their approach, then we should pay heed."

The enemy army is approaching, the first line of Kyri's message jumped out at me. *Cole and his followers are prepared to stand with Az-ca, but they will only follow your command. Prepare to receive them at a place of your choosing; they await your orders.*

"I have to take this to Kerok," I breathed, before walking quickly out of Pottles' suite.

* * *

Kerok

Chapter 15

"How many?" I demanded. This new development threatened to place another rift in my relationship with Sherra. I recalled Kyri's offer of allies, but she hadn't told me they were from Ny-nes, originally.

"I don't know. Perhaps a hundred or so?" Sherra replied. I could see that my questioning of the loyalty of former residents of Ny-nes troubled her. She trusted them; I did not. Her face was pale, except for two bright spots of color high in her cheeks. I was upsetting her again, but this—I felt as if I had very good reason.

"They are committed to standing beside your warriors and escorts," Adahi joined us at the garden table. "They are willing to give their lives in your defense, Prince Thorn," he added, a tinge of sarcasm in his voice.

"Fine. You don't want them at Secondary Camp? I can send them elsewhere, but I *will* be going with them," Sherra snapped.

"Where will that be?" I was just as adamant as she.

"I believe we can operate from his village," Sherra replied. "All I ask is for mindspeak when the enemy attacks. We will join the army, then."

"I dislike that idea," Hunter said before I could form words expressing the same thoughts.

"Then what do you suggest?" Sherra turned to him.

"I suggest you welcome them to the King's City," Adahi said before Hunter could reply. "Sherra will be responsible for them. House them at the trainee camp—it stands empty at the moment. New trainees are not scheduled to arrive for two months."

"I can place shields around the trainee camp," Sherra said immediately. "You will be offering hospitality to friends, not housing enemies."

"Your shields will keep them on the grounds of the training camp?" I frowned at Sherra.

"When have I ever failed you in that?" she retorted.

I dislike fighting with you, I sent.

Then stop doing it, she replied.

"I will be staying at the training camp with them," she said aloud. "The entire time they are here."

"Adahi, do you have an idea of when the enemy army will arrive?"

"Soon," he rumbled. "I worry that Ruarke will have more wicked mischief to deliver before their arrival, too."

"Why do you think that?" Barth spoke for the first time.

"Because we now have in our possession half of something that has become quite important to him—Thorn's Book."

"He can't get past the shields on the city," I sputtered.

"Ah, but he has other bargaining chips, does he not?"

"How do you know this?" Hunter demanded.

"I am very old, dear Prince-Heir. I can explain the potential thoughts and decisions of nearly anyone you care to name. People follow patterns after a while, and I have seen more than my share of them."

"When will you bring them here?" I turned back to Sherra with a sigh of resignation.

"I'll send mindspeak to Cole and ask him when they wish to come. I'll join them when they arrive at the camp. We wouldn't want anyone to run away in terror, now would we?"

"When he arrives, ask Cole to dine with us," Hunter said. "Will he submit to Barth's divination?"

"I'll ask. I warn you, Barth, you may not like what you see," Sherra said. "Not that he's bad," she held up a hand in denial. "He ah, experienced torture in Ny-nes, for having the power that is outlawed there. He was seven when he came to Kyri. Tell me he has anything but contempt for those who'd torture a child."

"Is that true?" Hunter asked.

"It is true," Adahi answered. "There are graves in Kyri's City, where she has had to bury children who came from their torture too late for her to save them. They spent the last bit of energy they had, getting away from those monsters in Ny-nes."

"May the first warrior save us," Barth mumbled.

"The first warrior?" Adahi snorted. "Ask those who stand with you now to save you. You'll be far better off."

"Does that include those Sherra is supporting?" I demanded.

"It does. I have the advantage, here, because I know Cole. You do not. Cole is more than adept at knowing how those around him perceive him and recognizes those who stand with him. Rethink your perception of what makes an enemy, Thorn. One whom you once considered a friend has allied with a proven enemy. Some who began their lives in the same country as the enemy, now wish to fight beside you because your enemy is the same as theirs. Cole's parents handed him to the authorities to torture, because he made fire at a young age. Tell me that is evil, Prince Thorn. The enemy believes it is. Cole sees you and your warriors and escorts as validation; that his talents are not evil, but natural. That you have morals and the ability to love, just as he does."

"Acceptance may be difficult," Barth sighed. "I will try."

"Ask Cole to dine with us—at his convenience," I said. "I will meet with him."

"With your permission, Sherra," Adahi turned to her, "I will carry your invitation to Cole. He will contact you afterward with his decision."

"Thank you," Sherra said.

* * *

Sherra

Because he felt guilty, Kerok asked that Hunter accompany me on my journey to shield more villages after the meeting. Hunter had a list of the smaller places with him, with those villages marked on a map.

"You've met Cole?" Hunter asked after we arrived at our first village. I set the shields without alerting anyone to our presence—I'd hidden inside a mirrored bubble shield to accomplish my goals.

"Yes. If someone didn't tell you in advance that he was from Ny-nes originally, you might not guess it. His accent is somewhat different, but he speaks the same language, as they all do. He is also quite literate, although I understand that isn't the case with the normal population growing to adulthood in that country."

"They're not educated?"

"Hunter, I think that's by design," I sighed. "I'm done, here. Which village is next?"

We moved on the next one, and the next after that; the shields were smaller because the villages were smaller, and therefore took less time to protect.

By the time we were done for the day, after a brief stop at Secondary Camp for a midday meal, we arrived at the palace feeling sweaty, covered in dust and quite hungry.

"I've informed the Prince that we've returned," Hunter told me as we walked past the guards at the side door. "He says to meet him in his suite for dinner."

"All right. Thank you for going with me, today," I told him. "Your map and information made the journey much faster."

"I'm astounded by your stamina," Hunter said. "I'm exhausted."

"I think you should get out more," I smiled at him. "To build up your own stamina. I think I could teach you how to make mirror shields and tube shields—to fire aimed blasts."

"I would very much enjoy learning those things. Teach Thorn at the same time. Please."

"Tomorrow, unless something else comes along."

"Like Cole?"

"Yes."

"Perhaps he'd like to learn those things, too."

I blinked at Hunter for a moment as the possibilities hit me. "Excellent idea, dear Prince-Heir," I said. "I'll see you tomorrow morning."

* * *

"You want to teach Cole, too?" Kerok tried to keep the skepticism from his voice as we ate dinner in his sitting room.

"You've never met him," I said. "I have, and Kyri and Adahi trust him. He's an unexpected ally in this, and be honest, can we really afford to turn away allies?"

"Can you speak for all his troops?"

"I haven't met them," I admitted. "I can't imagine that Cole hasn't gauged their loyalties, though."

"On your head be it, since they want to serve under your command—specifically."

"Are we going to argue about that, too?" I didn't keep the plaintiveness from my voice. I was tired to death of arguing with Kerok. Tired, too, after a long day of shielding villages from attacks by Merrin and Ruarke.

"No." He pinched the bridge of his nose for a moment, as if staving off a headache.

"Are you all right?" I asked, suddenly concerned.

"I just feel—out of my element," he dropped his hand and blinked dark eyes at me. Even with the scar down his cheek, he was more than handsome to me—and too dear for words.

"You're not alone, Kerok, no matter how much you think you may be. People are willing to die for you. I am one of them."

"My rose, please don't place that burden upon me," he whispered before taking my hand across the small table. "I cannot bear it."

"I will make sure that none of our new allies threaten you or Az-ca in any way. All I ask in return is that you get to know them and accept them in friendship, as that is what is offered, in addition to their agreement to go to war beside us."

Kerok didn't reply, he merely nodded and dropped his eyes to his plate. Slowly, I watched as his shoulders settled a notch lower—he'd been so tense before.

"Come to bed with me," I breathed. "I think we both need that respite."

* * *

Kerok

She was right—we needed the lovemaking, as hurried and feverish as it was the first time, and as gentle and leisurely the second. She'd traced my scars the second time— the ones from my ribs downward—with careful fingers, as they were the deepest.

Chapter 15

I considered that none of my previous escorts may have had the courage to do that. Sherra appeared to find something to love in them, as horrible as they were.

Grae may have held my heart in the past, but Sherra was a piece of my soul, as well as the peace in my soul. I couldn't deny that, even if I wanted to do so. She'd become my conscience, too, and I'd admit that to anyone who asked.

"My love," I whispered against Sherra's forehead as she slept with her head on my shoulder.

"Kerok?" Sherra breathed against my shoulder.

"What is it, my rose?"

"I'm hungry."

I laughed.

* * *

Ketchi

Cole

"I believe you'll find that you're welcome to learn a new technique from Sherra, if you're willing to stand beside the Prince and the Prince-Heir while she teaches," Adahi's dark eyes held a light in their depths.

All along, I knew Adahi held more secrets than anyone; I merely didn't remark on what I knew. I couldn't gauge how old he was, either, and while that might trouble me with anyone else, I had no qualms in his case.

"You're quite pleased with this turn of events, aren't you?" I ventured.

"I am," a smile touched his lips. "A dreamwalker—again after so many centuries. It can be both blessing and curse, you understand. The ability will separate her from others because of its very nature."

"I understand about separation," I agreed and sipped my tea. I'd offered tea to Adahi, but he'd refused, preferring to sit at my table and talk, rather than drinking tea while he did so.

"Yes—your talent also sets you apart," Adahi agreed. "You are more valuable than you believe, friend Cole."

"Hmmph," I snorted around a mouthful of tea before swallowing. "Most people find it annoying."

"Perhaps one day, you can offer your services to Sherra, as her personal advisor," Adahi suggested. "I think that pairing would be a wise one."

"One can only try," I said. "First, we must be accepted by her mate."

"And by his army," Adahi gave voice to my unspoken words. "I know this. Caution your people to be steadfast in this. Sherra will protect you as much as she can; ask them to cooperate with her, and take their concerns to you and to her, to sort them out."

"I hope all goes well," I breathed a sigh. "For the obvious reasons."

* * *

Sherra

Not only did Kerok set a shield between us before falling asleep; I set one, too, so I wouldn't be awakened.

Something troubled me, and I had no idea what I'd learn—or that my dreamwalker would learn—once I fell asleep.

I wasn't disappointed. I found myself—or my dreamwalking self, anyway, staring at the couple on the bed as if they were strangers for a moment, before heeding the call of one who was terrified beyond belief.

The terror emanated from one who hadn't realized he could mindspeak—until now.

Chapter 15

Ruarke was planning to torture a young warrior to death, and then send his body to Kerok as a warning—and a bargaining chip—for the half of Thorn's Book we held.

Relocating to the sound of the mindspoken call for help, I found myself standing on the outside of Ruarke's camp. Hidden well inside a tree-covered valley in enemy territory, the tents were spaced carefully so that any attacker would be hard-pressed to defend themselves if they approached even one of those tents. The other tents' inhabitants would come running from many directions, making a rescue more than difficult.

With that in mind, I considered how best to make my entrance. Cool winds blew past my dreamwalker, making the evergreens creak overhead. Somewhere nearby, an owl made his nightly noises as the wind gusted faster for a moment.

Rain was coming—the scent of it reached me and I marveled that my sense of smell worked while in this state. My dreamwalker recognized the scent easily, although my physical nose was very far away.

That's when Adahi appeared at my side. I had no idea how he knew to come, except that perhaps he'd heard the mindspeak and felt the terror of the young warrior, just as I had. What surprised me was this; I could see through Adahi as well as I could see through my own hand.

Hmmph, he sent mindspeak, as if acknowledging what I'd discovered.

But, I responded in kind.

We will discuss this another time. This one I will deal with, he added. *It is time.*

Time? I didn't understand.

Rose and Thorn

Time that Ruarke and the one who holds his leash understand at last that one more old enemy has survived in some way. They believe me dead, you see.

We will have to talk, I agreed. *But he's about to*, I didn't finish as he held up a hand to stop me.

When I take a step forward, his perimeter divination will alert him to my presence. After that, I will have limited time to act. I can either gather the children and the villagers to me, or kill him. Killing Ruarke will leave the villagers vulnerable to Merrin and the others. I prefer to err on the side of caution and perform a rescue rather than a killing. Go back to your bed, dear Princess. I have this.

I wasn't sure how Adahi managed it, but I was flung back to bed, just as he'd suggested, and found myself sitting up next to Kerok while all the hells broke loose in Ruarke's camp.

* * *

Ny-nes
Kaakos

Are you sure? I snapped at Ruarke in mindspeak. *This is impossible.* I tore through my suite, searching for a robe to fling across my shoulders before stalking through my palace.

I saw him. He laughed at me as he took the boy away.

That's preposterous, I fumed. Guards scrambled to follow me as I strode angrily down a hallway toward the stairs and the sanctuary one floor below. Their booted footsteps echoed on the steps behind me as I raced downward barefoot, determined to get to the sanctuary.

If I *stepped* while in their presence, well, it was better if I did not. I didn't have my device in my hand, and that would give secrets away. Flinging open the sanctuary doors, I hastened toward the glass box on the dais at the end.

Chapter 15

Upon reaching it, I carefully examined its contents. It looked like any other rotting corpse to me, and the locks and seals had certainly not been tampered with—my power still radiated about them.

It is untouched, I informed Ruarke. *Tell me how he appeared in front of you. You must be suffering delusions.*

I tell you it was him, Ruarke argued. *I know not how it is, but he has returned.*

He is dead and lying in front of me. It was a master stroke to exchange his body for that of the Prophet, so we could watch him daily. He is still here. You saw an imposter. Have you moved the camp?

Of course. Immediately. We await the arrival of the army, as you commanded.

Too bad about the undelivered message—I wanted to know their reaction to a tortured warrior boy. Do not fear—we will still make them pay.

Dearly.

"My Lord, is all well?" My chief guard ventured to ask.

"All is well," I said. "It was merely a bad dream—that someone had harmed the prophet's body. As you see—he is untouched."

"Glory to the prophet—and to you," the guard dipped his head in reverence to the body inside the case.

I stifled a laugh at the immense gullibility of those about me.

* * *

Kerok

I found Sherra standing at my window when I woke the next morning, gazing down at the garden below.

"How long have you been awake?" I yawned.

"Several hours, I think," she kept her back turned toward me. "I heard from Adahi last night. The enemy camp has been moved in haste again—after he rescued the villagers Ruarke and Merrin held captive. I believe Ruarke is incensed over it."

"Adahi rescued them? Where are they?"

"With Cole and his people. They will arrive at the King's City training camp after breakfast. I'll meet them there, and Cole will return to the palace with me, to train with you and Hunter."

"Are the villagers safe?"

"They are safe, and Cole's people are tending to them. They've been starved, as you may imagine. The people were fed and clothed after their rescue, according to Adahi's mindspeak. Cole has healers among his people, and they have cared for them in that way, too."

"How did Adahi accomplish this?"

"One of the warrior boys has mindspeak. He called out in terror. Adahi and I heard him. Adahi told me he would take care of the situation."

"You've been having frequent mindspoken conversations with Adahi," I slid off the bed to approach her.

"Kerok, that's all it is," she hunched her shoulders. "It's only mindspeak, and all of it about issues that need addressing in Az-ca."

"I'm not accusing you of anything." I sounded defensive and winced at my own words.

"Kerok, you have nothing to be concerned about. Adahi—I'm not sure he could or would have a relationship with anyone."

Chapter 15

Her words were weighted with an unspoken explanation. I held my questions back. She would tell me or not; I'd let her choose.

* * *

Sherra

Breakfast was quiet for the most part. Kerok wanted to ask questions; he held them back. I understood his frustrations with me—I'd be frustrated with me, too, if I were he. *How had I changed so much?* I wasn't the woman he'd met at North Camp that first time, although I had called him a jackass in mindspeak.

I suppose nearly dying after destroying the enemy army had negated my fear of death, so I was no longer afraid of it. I was afraid of pain, instead. Afraid of the pain from losing those I loved.

Jae was gone. It seemed so long ago that happened, when less than a year had passed.

"What are you thinking?" Kerok asked.

"About Jae." I turned my head so he wouldn't see the sudden tears in my eyes. I'd lost a staunch friend that day, and there was no bringing her back. The enemy was now moving toward us again, and more friends could fall in ensuing battles.

If they had another plane and another bomb—that thought made me shiver. *What if they had more than one?*

I'd mindspoken that thought to Kerok. "What? More than one of what?" he asked aloud.

"More than one big bomb, and more than one plane, this time?" I turned toward him again.

"That is my fear as well." He dropped his eyes to stare at his nearly-empty plate. "We could all die, if that's true."

"Perhaps we should break with tradition and go looking for them now, before they arrive at the border and set up camp."

"I don't know," Kerok hedged.

"I understand your father's stance on this, I do. But we're no longer dealing with things as we did in the past, Kerok."

"I know. I hesitate to send any part of the army out looking for them, in case we're attacked. They may be hoping to divide our resources, to make us more vulnerable."

"Then I'll take Cole and his people, if they're willing."

"Sherra," he frowned deeply.

"We'll discuss this later," I said, standing. "I have training to do, but I'd like a shower first."

* * *

Kerok

"I'm not sure how to deal with this," I told Hunter.

"You're not dealing with it," Hunter stated baldly.

"What are you saying?" I demanded.

"We've been without a King since Drenn died."

"Father is still alive," I hissed, angry immediately.

"And unable to perform his duties. You should be acting in his stead in all things, yet you are not. Things are floating along as they always have because your father is still alive, but he is unable to discharge the duties of his office. The best thing you've done as Crown Prince was done as an apology to Sherra, when you declared an outlawed book to be safe for trainees to use. Admit it—you wouldn't put up with inaction as Commander of the Army. Why should you do the opposite as Crown Prince?"

Chapter 15

"You've been thinking about this for a while, haven't you?" A part of me knew he was right, but I still felt angry about my shortcomings being handed to me so bluntly.

"The Council should have been disbanded already, in favor of looking for better representation for the villagers. We've had almost a year, Thorn, and so many things could have been accomplished."

"Why are you saying this to me now?" I asked.

"Because the enemy army is approaching, and we're doing nothing to stop them."

"Not you, too." I drew a breath and closed my eyes. My hands, resting on my desk, clenched into fists.

"Who else told you this?" Hunter asked.

I blinked my eyes open and studied him as he stood before me. "Sherra. She suggested taking Cole's troops to look for them, because I wasn't cooperating. I don't want to divide the troops, in case you're wondering."

"Then let Sherra take hers out—you're not comfortable adding them to the army anyway."

"You're trying to make me feel more guilt than I already do?"

"You don't dislike the idea of sending Cole and his people out to search for the enemy army; you worry about Sherra going with them." Hunter's insight was an uncomfortable reality I was forced to acknowledge.

"Nothing good was ever accomplished by hiding from the truth," Hunter added.

"Fuck."

"Agreed."

Chapter 16

Sherra

Cole brought eighty-seven with him; fifty-three men and thirty-four women. They were busy settling belongings into barracks while I spoke with Cole in the Camp Commander's office. The small space held two desks and still contained Kage's and Weren's records and personal things.

"They understand that things may be strained at first," Cole informed me.

"I wish that weren't so, but Az-ca has fought against Ny-nes for so long," I admitted.

"We know this. What Prince Thorn should understand is that we have also fought against Ny-nes all our lives—against the damage caused by their neglect, disgust and mistreatment. Those things are a part of us and will always be."

"I'm not sure they recognize that completely," I conceded. "The warriors, especially, have seen escorts and fellow warriors die—too many times to count. Trust is an issue, as you can imagine."

"Kyri says we were all one people long ago," Cole shook his head. "Something caused a rift among our ancestors, and the End-War came. I don't know more than that."

"Are you saying we could be related?"

"It's possible," he smiled.

"That sounds nice," I said. "I don't have any living relatives, to my knowledge."

"With me, it is the same. Lives are cut short in Ny-nes—from poisoned air, water, sometimes food. Those born with power might live longer there, but they're killed young, so who can say? My years have been extended, thanks to Kyri's invitation."

"I can say the same—if I hadn't gone to her after the enemy's bomb exploded, I'd be dead," I agreed. "She and Pottles saved my life."

"Pottles?"

"The name Doret went by, when she lived in my village and oversaw my upbringing. I learned so many things from her."

"I feel the same way about Kyri. She saw that I was cared for and raised properly—and given love along with my lessons. I am most grateful for the ability to read, actually. Most are not taught in Ny-nes. Only those who are better off and in the good graces of the Sovereign Leader receive an education."

He spoke the title of Sovereign Leader with disgust. "Did you ever see him?" I asked. "Or Ruarke, before you left Ny-nes?"

Chapter 16

"Ruarke, yes. Kaakos, I did not."

"Is that his name? Kaakos?"

"It is the name he calls himself. I don't know if it is his real name or not."

"And now they're sending an army to destroy us," I slumped in my seat. "I really want to hunt them now, and destroy their weapons before they come within firing range of Az-ca."

"It would be good to know when they plan to arrive," Cole said. "The trucks they use are solar powered, and can only travel part of a night on a day's battery charge from the sun, because it takes so much power to carry the weapons, supplies and troops. We could gauge distances, if we knew their plans a little better."

"That's an interesting thought. Do you know anything about the roads they travel to get here?"

"They are forced to weave their way around mountains and across waterways between here and their major cities in Ny-nes. Kyri has some maps in her home; I've seen them. Their biggest obstacle, of course, is the Inner Sea, which was once a wide river that divided the continent. They have limited access to cross their vehicles—only a few ferries are large enough to carry that load, and then it is only one or two trucks at a time."

"We took more than ten vehicles from them while I was in training camp," I said. "That must have been a blow, to lose so many of them to us."

"I'm sure it was, but it was only a fraction of what they had, I'm sure." Cole's mouth tightened at the thought of the enemy's might.

They had vehicles and weapons—we had flesh, blood and power. "How many years has it been, Cole, that Ny-nes and Az-ca have been at war?"

"Kyri says Ny-nes wasn't aware of Az-ca's continued existence until nearly a century after the End-War. Once they discovered that some of their original enemy survived, they renewed the war, and made plans to attack Az-ca. This was when they learned that in the years following the End-War, Az-ca had found another way to defend itself. Ny-nes thought Az-ca had nothing to combat their machines and bombs, and that the war would end with the first battle. It did not, as you know. That's when they began calling you demons, witches and other hated creatures. They cannot accept that once we were all the same; we merely believed differently."

"So. Beliefs are their excuse for killing and torturing." I felt weary, now.

"And for killing your people, too, never forget that," Cole grumbled. "Also for attempting to kill me and all those who came with me today. We have waited long to stand against them, and we are now old enough and strong enough to do so."

"If things went as you'd like, how would you want this to turn out?" I asked.

"Hmmph. That Kaakos, Ruarke and those who believe in them would fall. That someone would come to teach the people a better way—that the lies they've been told and have believed all along are just that—lies."

"It may take time to do that," I pointed out. "A long time."

Chapter 16

"I know. Please allow me some small hope that the people who have been led astray will have a chance for something better."

"How many of them want something better?"

"I don't know. They are afraid to speak of those things, and it has been more than fifty years since I was among them. There may be no hope left in them. Nothing left worth saving."

I didn't say it, but that future felt so dark and bleak I wanted to shiver. How many, even in the best of circumstances, would continue to see the people of Az-ca as something evil? How long would it take to eradicate those ideas?

Once those ideas were released, was there any way to call them back? Ever?

"I didn't mean to make you feel hopeless, too," Cole reached out to pat my hand. We'd never touched, before.

Just that brief connection made me want to scream in pain, the memories that coursed through him were so horrible.

He was willing to give his life to protect others—others who'd never suffered as tragically as he had.

He'd been seven, and the adults in his life had turned against him. His body bore the scars of his pain—castration was the first thing they'd done to him, and then torture had followed.

You want to hunt them as much as I do, don't you? I sent to him.

Yes. Perhaps more than you do.

I have an idea, I told him. *Let me see if I can reach Adahi. After that, we may go our own way in this.*

We follow you, Cole dipped his head.

Rose and Thorn

* * *

Kyri

"I dislike the thought of your return to Ny-nes. You know why," Adahi's deep voice rumbled.

"I'll take Sherra with me and employ her technique. I can be assured of passing the border with her power assisting me."

"She has already agreed to take Cole's people to hunt the approaching army," Adahi pointed out. "Perhaps it is time to give her the truths you've hidden."

"No." That answer came quickly and firmly from my lips.

"What if the Prince declares her a deserter?"

"He won't," I huffed. "He loves her too much."

"He also knows the laws, Kyri. Don't let your anger affect your divinations."

I hadn't bothered with divination in this matter and he likely knew that. Adahi couldn't help me in this, for obvious reasons. He'd gotten me out of Ny-nes once before, at great cost to himself. He could never do that again.

My fault, a small voice informed me.

I'd had three centuries to consider the mistakes I'd made, and to work on ways not only to correct them, but to better myself so I wouldn't fail again.

Ruarke—he was the stinging insect atop the maddened bull, in my opinion. Doret would argue, because she felt about him the same way I felt about Kaakos. I wanted to laugh at the name he'd given himself. If it hadn't been for me, he'd never have had knowledge of the word to begin with.

272

Chapter 16

At least Sherra had pulled away half of Thorn's Book from Ruarke's greedy hands. The most dangerous spells were in the last half of the book anyway.

That's what you're telling yourself, the small voice taunted.

"You have to ask yourself what Kaakos is willing to do to destroy you and Az-ca," Adahi pointed out after my protracted silence.

"You know he'll sacrifice anyone except himself," I said.

"I do. I merely wanted to know if you understood that."

"Adahi, I am far too old for riddles or tests," I snapped.

"Age has nothing to do with it," he replied. "You should know that too." He disappeared before I could reply.

* * *

King's Palace
Kerok

"Spin your shield to make a tube."

Sherra made things look so easy. I wanted to grumble about that but kept the words behind my teeth. Cole, aggravatingly enough, was far ahead of Hunter and me.

"I've been making shields for a long time," he shrugged at me. "Sherra says you've only been doing it for a year or so."

I hated to admit it, but Cole was well-spoken, intelligent and likeable. That irritated me for reasons I couldn't explain.

Sherra said he was sixty years old—very close to my own age. Like me, he looked half that, due to his power.

Cole laughed aloud when the fat log he'd aimed at splintered; his tubed blast had gone right through it with a resounding thunk.

Kerok? Let me touch your hands to show you how to do this, Sherra sent mindspeak.

"Touch Hunter, too," I grumbled.

"All right. Give me your hands—both of you."

Hunter was much more willing than I was. Cole stood by while Sherra took our hands and gave us images—images that would enable us to accomplish what Cole had already done so easily.

Sherra sensed my irritability, but said nothing. When Adahi arrived to watch, my growing anger and frustration threatened to spill into audible sentences.

Your jealousy has no foundation, Adahi informed me. *Sherra will love no other, have no fear.* Adahi stood on the sidelines, his hood down and arms crossed over his chest. *As for Cole,* he continued, *his genitalia were removed as part of his torture as a child. It is a common practice among the barbarians to mutilate their victims.*

My breath stopped, as if I'd been punched in the gut and couldn't breathe for a moment. *That's horrible,* I managed to say after several moments passed.

Imagine your whole life spent that way, Adahi's mouth tightened and he looked away. *The barbarians ensure that their victims will never have children, in case they do manage to escape, somehow. There is nothing gentle about Ruarke, Kaakos or any of their closest followers, as you may imagine.*

Why do they do this? Can they hate us this much?

They do it because it pleases them, and yes, they hate anyone who has anything to do with Az-ca.

Their beliefs dictate this? This confused me; how someone might hate anyone they'd never met, on the strength of the tales others told.

Someday, Prince Thorn, perhaps we will discuss these things, along with the End-War and why it came about.

Chapter 16

Hate and fear are two sides of the same coin, you see, and when the goods to be bought are violence and lies to further your agenda, then you not only sow the seeds of destruction, you ensure that your followers stay loyal, out of fear or fanaticism. Either of those things, to our enemy, is acceptable.

"I've never put a face on the enemy before," I spoke aloud to Adahi. "Now I'm seeing more sides of it than I ever imagined."

"At least one small side is allied with you," Cole turned toward me. "Another small part of those in Ny-nes may be too afraid to speak against the norm. The rest are in total acceptance of the regime Kaakos and those who came before him have built."

"How long has Kaakos been in power?" I asked.

"Four hundred years, more or less," Adahi shrugged. "To put that in perspective for you, he came to power roughly twenty years before your namesake, King Thorn, passed."

"Did you know him?" I asked. "King Thorn?"

"He and I were well-acquainted," Adahi said.

"Perhaps we should talk about him, sometime," I said. "Sherra, let me see if I can build a tube blast, now."

"I'll set up a new log for you," Cole offered. I waited until he set a new, thick log on the stone before me, then stepped away.

Sherra didn't coach or remind me. Carefully I formed a shield, then built it into a funnel, which elongated into a tube. Sending the tube toward the log target, I formed a small blast to launch through it.

"Now," Hunter breathed the moment I released the blast.

"Perfect," Cole shouted as the blast burned a small hole through the log without raising splinters on either side, it was so clean and well-aimed.

* * *

"I can't believe how simple and effective it is." Hunter was still marveling at the technique after we walked into the palace for a midday meal.

After being upset for the first half of the lesson, the last half had gone surprisingly well for me. "With your permission, I'd like to get all the palace warrior-guards trained in this, if possible," Hunter said. "What are we eating? I'm starved."

"Hunter," I clapped a hand on his back, "Welcome to warrior training. It takes a lot out of you."

"I'm very pleased," Cole told Sherra as they walked behind Hunter and me. "I would never have imagined it possible. This is so effective at eliminating a single target, rather than launching a fireblast, which can kill many at once."

He was right. This was quite useful, especially if the enemy chose to hide behind hostages, as they'd done recently.

So far, I'd seen nothing alien or unsettling about Cole, other than Adahi's description of Cole's torture and status. Adahi had left us when we stopped our session, telling me he would return later. I wondered if he had other things to teach me in private.

Barth appeared around a corner, striding toward us. By the look on his face, he had news.

Bad news.

My thoughts went immediately to my father.

Chapter 16

"Weren sent a messenger," Barth handed a sealed note to me. "We have a problem."

* * *

Sherra

"Caral and Misten are in Secondary Camp's lockup. They are involved in a forbidden relationship, and several have come forward, revealing knowledge of this. Several troops and officers signed an affidavit, verifying that Misten and Caral are together, as cannot be, because of that stupid, unfair, one-sided law."

Pottles frowned as I explained the trouble. Cole and I—somehow, we knew we had to search for the enemy army now. As for the affidavit, I didn't know whether those who signed it had actual proof.

I knew it to be true, however. If Barth did his divination, he'd find the truth, too. I couldn't leave Az-ca when my friends' lives were in jeopardy. It was bad enough that I'd be leaving Az-ca without Kerok's knowledge or permission; he was the Crown Prince, in addition to being the head of Az-ca's army.

"I thought Weren would be better than that," Pottles snapped as she strode toward the window in her suite. Her window didn't overlook the garden; its view was of peaked mountains in the distance, outside the domes of the King's City. She gazed toward the peaks, but I wondered if she actually saw them.

"What if they remove their power?" I whispered to Pottles' back.

"Hmmph. If Thorn follows the law, they're marked for that and death afterward. You know what they'll find if divination is done; I can see it in your face."

I hunched my shoulders. This couldn't be. Not now.

Not ever.

Cole, I sent mindspeak. *Meet with me later. Please.*

I am at your command, Cole's reply came immediately.

* * *

Mountain Camp
Ruarke

Merrin was more useful than I'd given him credit for. All I had to do was a simple divination on him and I'd gotten all sorts of information I could use.

I still had my spies, and they were more than capable of spreading information. I'd attempted to take Caral and Wend before.

There were other methods available to destroy Caral. Granted I wouldn't get credit for it, but it would happen anyway, and cause a rift within Az-ca's army. I looked forward to receiving the news of two deaths, at the very least.

Others could follow, once additional information came to me. As for Wend, I hadn't seen anything useful about her in my divination of Merrin, but that could change.

I relished the idea of killing the enemy from the inside out; pitting them against one another satisfied me greatly. Then, once Kaakos' army arrived, we'd increase our attacks on Az-ca, outside and within.

* * *

King's City Training Camp
Sherra

"You have enough supplies?" I asked Cole aloud. *I plan to rescue my friends from Secondary Camp*, I silently added.

The Prince will be forced to declare you rogue and place a sentence on your head, too, Cole pointed out. "We have everything we need," he said.

Chapter 16

I know. I think it's been coming a long time, I admitted. *I had a forbidden book and learned from it when I was young. He ignored the law in that case, but this time, he won't be able to ignore what I'm planning to do now.*

"Good," I nodded at Cole.

I will come with you to Secondary Camp, he offered.

No, let me do this alone. I can get past their shields. This way, the rogue status and death sentence will fall squarely where it belongs—on my shoulders. Afterward, we'll hunt the enemy army.

Then tell me where to meet you.

I will.

You say this because you don't know if you'll survive the rescue attempt—is this correct?

Yes. I don't intend to kill anyone while doing this.

Which will place you in danger.

I hope my shields hold and nobody decides to launch fireblasts indiscriminately. Bystanders could be killed in the backwash.

Then I and my people will wait until you call for us. "We have everything we need," Cole said. *Including tents and camping supplies.*

"Let me know if anything changes," I said and walked out of the training camp commander's office.

* * *

Kerok

"Weren, did you know anything before this cropped up?" I slammed a hand on the written affidavits of several of his troops, including two officers. All of them claimed knowledge of Caral's and Misten's relationship. Whether that was true or not, I knew what Barth would find should he perform a divination on either of the women.

Rose and Thorn

Weren and I sat in my study, having a private meeting on the situation with Caral and Misten, and what was being done to keep them in the lockup at Secondary Camp.

"I suspected." He lowered his eyes. "I should have come to you shortly after I took the position of General, but I didn't. If I had, perhaps this could have been avoided."

"You knew there were still those among us that disagreed with the changes we've gone through, didn't you? Those who'd employ any excuse to disrupt everything within the army."

"Yes, Prince Thorn. I hoped things would settle down once everyone got used to the new ways, but the invitation for former washouts to join the ranks upset more of the troops than I imagined it would. A few—disagreements broke out between former instructors and their students."

"On the escort side, right?"

"Yes. The warriors sided with their escorts, as you may imagine. I do admit that I didn't realize how bad things had become."

"Weren," I closed my eyes in weariness and anger, "This isn't your fault. I doubt anyone would have handled this differently. I suspect there's something else behind this, pushing, but I'll be damned if I can prove Merrin had a hand in it. You and I know Sherra stopped Ruarke from taking Caral and Wend before. This—he's involved in this and we know it."

"Perhaps removing their power, and placing them in the King's City lockup for a few months," Weren suggested. "It will keep them alive until we can sort through this mess."

"With the enemy army on the way? They're needed, Weren. Next to Sherra, Caral is the best at shielding. Wend and a few others are right behind her. How long before

Chapter 16

Merrin devises a way to destroy Wend and the others? All because of the fucking laws."

"I believe you're giving Merrin more credit than he's due for being sharp enough to devise those plans," Weren observed. "Ruarke has his hands in this, if I'm not mistaken. Merrin may be a source of information, but the deviousness? That belongs to the enemy."

"You're right," I admitted, blinking at Weren. "They're destroying us from the inside, now, and when their army arrives, we'll be attacked from all sides."

"What does your rose say about this?" Weren asked.

"Hmmph. She won't even talk to me. These are her closest friends, Weren. What do you expect her to say?"

* * *

Secondary Camp

Armon

Levi sat beneath a tree outside our cabin, shielding himself from view with a mirror shield Caral taught him how to make. He was grieving already, for Misten and Caral.

It was one thing to lose an escort in battle. This—this was untenable. According to the law, they'd be put to death. With the current mood running through half the army, if Thorn refused to follow the letter of the law, a mutiny could erupt.

Levi and I knew the accusers. They'd found a way to get back at those of us supporting the new ways. Even if the accusers had no actual proof, I knew, as did Levi, that Caral and Misten would be proven guilty of disobeying the laws once a divination was performed.

If nothing else, their power would be removed and they'd become outcasts.

The law was wrong.

I'd known that for a long time. Suddenly, I felt weary. Fighting battles for Az-ca's preservation no longer held interest. I was tired and sick to death of all of it—because of stupid laws.

At first, I'd considered contacting Sherra, but held back. Somehow, Merrin's information on Caral and Misten had been used against them. There was past information on Sherra that could be used against her, too, involving a forbidden book. She'd broken that law, and Kerok hadn't made acceptance of the book retroactive. That old law could trap her, too; I had no doubt about that.

Merrin was still destroying the army, in every way he could. What he couldn't destroy, his new-found allies would annihilate when they arrived.

I jumped and nearly shouted my terror when Adahi walked into the cabin without bothering to open a door. "I have a solution, Colonel. Take it or leave it," he said.

* * *

King's City
Sherra

Armon and Levi are waiting to assist you when you arrive to release your friends. They will also join you in your and Cole's efforts to find the enemy army, Adahi informed me in mindspeak. *Go now to release Misten and Caral. If you do not, their power will be removed upon General Weren's return, and they will be transported to the King's City lockup, on the Crown Prince's orders.*

Then I need to send Cole and his people away when I leave, I felt the beginnings of panic—things were happening far too fast for me to think coherently.

282

Chapter 16

Then send them to the northern edge of the bomb crater at the border, Adahi suggested. *You can meet them there after you collect your friends from Secondary Camp.*

All right.

I'd gone to the suite I'd selected after my disagreement with Kerok. He hadn't sent mindspeak or bothered to contact me about any of this, once the initial announcement was made that Caral and Misten were in lockup.

Snatching clothing and stuffing it into a travel duffle, I struggled to gather thoughts which had flown in every direction at Adahi's sudden contact.

Armon and Levi. They'd be marked for death, too, once Kerok discovered their duplicity.

Rogue. A term that had frightened me all my life.

Things had changed in the past year. Kerok could declare me rogue all he wanted. My heart squeezed at the thought of never seeing him again, but my feelings were unimportant at the moment.

Lives mattered, now.

I'm coming, I sent to Armon.

We know, he replied. *We're ready.*

* * *

Doret

"Gather your things—quickly," I told my charges. "We're going back to Kyri's City tonight."

I'd gotten the warning from Adahi—that once Sherra disappeared, Thorn would tear the palace apart and interrogate anyone close to her.

I wasn't willing to answer questions he should bloody well be able to sort for himself. Besides, I had no idea where Sherra planned to go and didn't want to ask.

I also didn't want to contact Kyri, mostly because I didn't want to be privy to her plans, either. That knowledge could upset me more than what was currently happening with Sherra's friends.

"Yes, that's good enough," I waved a hand at Kyal and Laren. "Come now, we must hurry."

* * *

Secondary Camp
Sherra

It was one thing for me to get inside the shields around the camp. It was another to get several other people out.

I stood outside the walls, where the outermost shield lay. Wend had placed this one; Caral and Misten had been forced to remove theirs. The one I'd placed around Secondary Camp wasn't a concern for me—I could walk through it anytime without difficulty.

Wend's shield I could also walk through, because I knew her power well. I wondered if any of the others would or could present a challenge. For now, that was an unknown.

If I formed a tube, and made it large enough to walk through, then sent it under the wall—that would eliminate the problem of more shields. That method had definite possibilities, and could get the others out, too—if I left it in place long enough to do so.

Yes. That could work.

* * *

King's City
Kerok

Weren didn't want to remove Caral's and Misten's power. I understood that. I also understood his reluctance to return to Secondary Camp for that very reason. That's why I consented when he'd asked if he could have dinner with his wife before leaving the King's City.

That left me alone inside my study, where I turned King Thorn's diary over and over on my desk, contemplating how much I hated my position at the moment.

My study door opened and Adahi walked in to sit on a guest chair. Dark eyes considered me carefully. His hood was down, his long, dark hair falling in a braid over his shoulders.

"It's interesting that you should be handling that book right now," Adahi finally spoke.

"Why's that?"

"Because what I have to tell you concerns him—and Ruarke."

"What about those two? How are they connected?" I had no idea what Adahi meant, and I didn't welcome his presence—I'd wanted this time alone to think on current events and how to handle things with Sherra.

A slow smile spread across Adahi's features. "You said the proper word," he chuckled. "Connected."

"All right, now you're becoming an annoyance," I growled.

"Do you recall the conversation you and I had weeks ago, when we spoke about King Thorn's Book on divination?"

"I do. So?"

"What did I tell you?"

"That Merrin had Thorn's Book, and it was dangerous. That because Merrin had royal blood, he could use it. That Thorn had left out a word in his spell, which would prevent anyone but me using it," my words faltered.

"You and Kyri were worried about the book falling into Ruarke's hands," I spoke my growing fear aloud.

Rose and Thorn

* * *

Mountain Camp
Ruarke

It had come to me finally—the full spell I'd performed against Caral and Wend, before I'd been interrupted.

This time, I'd use it for another purpose. I could either pull someone to me, or bend their will to my own. I wanted to laugh at how perfect it was.

* * *

Secondary Camp
Sherra

I'm coming, I informed Armon. *I had to build a tunnel, but it's a way for us to get out*, I added.

Then hurry, he said. *Things are turning strange.*

Strange?

Get here, Armon shouted his mindspeak, just as a fireblast detonated inside the walls.

Chapter 17

Secondary Camp
Armon
With Weren absent, Caral's and Misten's accusers decided to act on their own to enforce the laws. How that happened I had no idea, as I'd have called them too cowardly to do anything of the sort before.

They'd gathered enough courage to do this, though, and I wondered about outside influences.

They thought the way clear, too, when Levi and I hid behind a mirror shield outside the lockup, where we waited for Sherra's arrival.

That's how the fireblast they launched at the wooden building bounced off our combined shields and landed in an empty spot between the lockup and the mess hall. I sent mindspeak to Sherra, begging her to come quickly.

Rose and Thorn

Another fireblast was leveled against our shield; Levi grunted at the force of its impact.

Sherra walked inside our shield, then, as if it were as thin and fragile as a soap bubble. "We have to hurry," she said. "Tie off your shields and come with me."

With a nod, Levi tied his off first and disengaged, then I did the same. Sherra *stepped* us inside the lockup, where Caral, Misten and *Derissa* huddled, with shields held about them for protection. *How had Derissa gotten in?*

"Let's go," Sherra said, offering her hands to lift Caral and Derissa to their feet. Levi was already helping Misten to stand.

"Where are we going?" Caral asked.

"Rogue," Sherra replied before *stepping* us out of the lockup.

* * *

King's City
Kerok

I'd risen to my feet and turned my back on Adahi. I hadn't spoken my fears aloud—I was desperately attempting to sort them. Adahi and Kyri had both been terrified of Thorn's Book falling into Ruarke's hands.

Because he had power, I reminded myself.

They'd said he was far more talented and dangerous than Merrin could ever be. But, if Ruarke was of the enemy, why would he be able to use the book? He wasn't of King Thorn's royal blood—*couldn't be.*

"And he arrives at the obvious. Finally," Adahi rumbled.

"That anyone with power can use the book?" I whirled to face Adahi.

"And it's the wrong conclusion," Adahi tossed up a hand. "I should have known better than to trust your logic."

"If only those with royal blood can use the book, does that mean those royals in Ny-nes can use it too—if they have power?"

"There is no royal blood born in Ny-nes, and never has been. Only power is born there, of the mundane and supernatural varieties." Adahi sounded impatient with me, now.

I went still. "This is impossible," I snapped. I wanted to shout, but that would send guards and anyone else within hearing distance running toward my study.

"No. It is not. Tell me who Ruarke really is. If Doret were still here, she could tell you easily who he is and was."

"Where is Doret?" I demanded. "I saw her earlier."

"I warned her that you'd be angry about what I came to tell you, so she gathered the children and transported them back to Kyri's City. They are safe, there. Ask yourself, dear Prince, why Doret simulated her kidnapping and death three centuries ago."

"I don't know why," I did shout, this time. "All the records are destroyed or murky around that time."

"What happened then that you do recall?"

"That's when it was decided that a Crown Prince couldn't serve as Commander of the Army—because a Crown Prince died at the hands of his escort."

"Do you recall that Crown Prince's name?"

"Wulf. Crown Prince Wulf. My father is named after him," I retorted.

"Oh, the irony," Adahi snorted. "What was his full name? You all have extended lists of names, do you not?"

"I don't know his full name." I couldn't help glowering at Adahi as I made that reluctant admission.

"Then I'll enlighten you—for future reference, you understand. His full name goes thus; Wulf Tadson Ruarke Rex. Now do you get it? Doret wasn't the first to simulate a death, you know. Ruarke killed her sister, Daria. Doret still wants revenge for that terrible act. Now, it is time for me to go—I have other things to attend to, and Sherra and her friends are all safely away."

I sank onto my chair, feeling completely numb. Not only had a Crown Prince of Az-ca deserted his country, he'd aligned himself with the enemy, and now tortured and killed his own countrymen.

"Sherra?" Adahi's words finally penetrated my brain. "What have you done with her? Where is she?"

"She, in her own words, has gone rogue," Adahi replied. "She has rescued her friends at Secondary Camp, and not a moment too soon, I may add, because some of your troops were manipulated by the very Ruarke we have discussed tonight, and those troops attempted to kill Caral and Misten by destroying the lockup. Sherra is gone and may not return to you." He laughed at my shock and outrage.

"I will kill you for distracting me while this happened," I formed a funnel with my shield, then built it into a tube. The fireblast was forced through it before I fully considered what I was doing.

The chair Adahi sat on now bore a cleanly-burned hole in it. Adahi hadn't disappeared and remained whole before me, albeit somewhat transparent. He even appeared to be amused by my actions, if that were possible.

"There's something else you should know," Adahi said as he rose from his seat. "You can't kill what is already dead, my dear Prince."

Chapter 17

When he walked *through* the door rather than opening it, I realized how accurately we'd name him when we'd called him the phantom.

"What's wrong?" Hunter burst into my study, with Barth right behind him.

"Get Weren. We're needed at Secondary Camp," I barked.

* * *

Marc and Wend had taken the attackers into custody and waited for our arrival, but Sherra had taken the prisoners and was long gone. Armon, Levi and Derissa had voluntarily gone with her.

That served to make my anger sharper as I glared at the prisoners inside Wend's shields. It had taken hers and several others to hold them, but these warriors knew better than to launch blasts while contained within those bubble shields.

"You couldn't wait for the King's justice?" I shouted at cowering warriors.

Barth had come with me, leaving Hunter at the palace. One heir needed to be present, there, especially in light of recent actions—Adahi's and Ruarke's.

Not to mention those who stood before me, trapped inside a bubble shield. For all I knew, they could still be under Ruarke's influence. Their power would be removed before I left Secondary Camp; their fate could be decided later, when I had time to cool off and consider all options.

I was forced to admit how angry I was at Sherra, Armon and Levi, too—for deserting the army.

And me.

Fuck.

"Barth, remove their power and send them to the lockup in the King's City," I waved a hand. "They can keep Garkus company until I decide what to do with them."

* * *

Bomb Crater, Northside
Sherra

Cole's people were used to this. They'd built a fire, put up tents and handed out provisions they'd carried away with them.

Caral and Misten sat near the campfire, arms wrapped around one another as Derissa leaned in against Caral.

Derissa had carried a meal to Caral and Misten in the lockup, hoping to convince them to escape, if a way could be found. A way to escape had caught up with all three, while they'd attempted to protect themselves from an unexpected attack.

"Cole," I said, "Armon and Levi have years of experience commanding troops. I'm the newcomer. I'd feel much safer placing lives in their hands," I said. The topic had turned to our small army, and how we'd begin our search for the much larger force coming from Ny-nes.

"If we wait for them to cross the land bridge," Armon said, "They're already too close."

"Wherever they set up, it'll have to be close enough to get those flying machines to the army or the King's City— those two things have to be their main targets," Levi said.

"I agree," Cole nodded at Levi. "For now, Az-ca's army is at Secondary Camp, and all of it is in one place, making it a vulnerable target. Once they eliminate that, they can safely cross the border and get close enough to attack the King's City."

Chapter 17

"We've given up any influence we may have on moving the army elsewhere," Armon gruffed. "Even if we send mindspeak, they won't listen."

"Do you think that's true?" Cole's eyes narrowed to slits as he gazed at Armon. "Will they not listen, or do you worry that they'll be obstinate in the face of good sense?"

"I think it's the latter," Armon nodded after a moment's reflection.

"Thorn may be unwilling to listen to advice from anyone at this point," Adahi walked out of the shadows to join us. He dropped to the ground across from me, the image of his dark eyes flickering in the firelight between us.

What did you say to him? I sent mindspeak.

The truth, which we can discuss at a later time, Adahi replied. *In a day or two, when he works through recent events, he may become more approachable. Unfortunately, by that time, the enemy army may be upon us, and it will be far too late for him to act in any rational sense.*

That means we have to do something, doesn't it?

Yes. And quickly.

"So. The timing of this was well-planned, wasn't it?" I spoke to Adahi aloud. "That Ruarke would cause problems within Az-ca's army, hoping to direct the attention to that, rather than Ny-nes' encroaching troops and machinery."

"I believe that to be truth," Adahi dipped his head in acknowledgement.

"We need a battle plan now, don't we, if we are to stop them from reaching the land bridge?" Armon said. "I will entertain any and all ideas," he added.

"Sleep on it tonight," Adahi suggested. "In the morning, make your plans and do it quickly. Time is short."

"What about Ruarke?" Cole asked.

"Hmmph," Adahi huffed. "Should we be successful in destroying their army, that whelp will run back to Kaakos. He values his own skin, you see, and when he learns that rogues from Az-ca are actively hunting him on Ny-nes' soil, he'll move to protect himself."

"How will he learn that rogues are hunting him?" Caral spoke for the first time.

"He has mindspeech," Adahi chuckled. "As do I. I intend to tell him."

* * *

King's City
Kerok

The day couldn't get any worse—until it did.

Hunter called me back from Secondary Camp. The physicians were at my father's bedside when I arrived. I'd spoken to Father earlier in the day, but things had changed drastically since then.

He'd fallen unconscious, and his breathing was labored. I found it more than difficult to watch someone who'd been so strong and active when he was younger, fall ill and waste away like this. With every struggling breath my father drew, I wished to ease that for him and felt powerless to do so.

"I am here, Father," I gripped his hand in mine and wept.

* * *

Bomb Crater, Northside
Sherra

I sat, cross-legged, inside Caral and Misten's tent. At least here, they could be together openly. There wasn't anyone in our camp who would accuse them of breaking a law. In fact, several of Cole's people were together, male and male, female and female.

294

Yes, they'd been mutilated young, but that didn't prevent them from loving someone, whether sex could be a part of that or not.

"I feel so guilty," Misten wiped tears away. "I couldn't hold back any longer, and Caral didn't stop me."

"There really wasn't a good reason to do that," I attempted to reassure her. "The law isn't just and we all know that."

"We can't ever go back," Misten whispered.

"You'll be welcome in Cole's village, or Kyri's City," I soothed. "It's not Az-ca, but you'll find that in many ways, it's much better."

You've cut yourself off from Kerok, Caral informed me in mindspeak. She'd hit the subject head-on that I was desperately trying to avoid.

That is my choice to make, not something for you to feel guilty about, I told her. I didn't add that I felt guilty enough for both of us, for deserting him without a word.

"Look, we need rest if we're going to find a way to deflect the enemy army tomorrow morning," I said, rising to my feet. "Try to get some sleep, all right?" I walked out of their tent, focused on finding my own, when Hunter's mindspeak came.

King Wulf is dying, he informed me. *Thorn is at his bedside. As yet, no warrant has been issued for your arrest.*

You think he'd let me walk back in after what I've done? I demanded.

He needs you now. Tomorrow can take care of itself.

Then he can issue a warrant tomorrow—or whenever he gets to it, I responded. *Tell him I'll come unless he doesn't want that.*

I'll tell him.

Rose and Thorn

He says come, Hunter's next message came quickly. *He guarantees no harm will come to you.*

Thank you. I'll be there in a moment.

Step *into the King's chamber; neither Thorn nor I want the guards to see your arrival.*

All right.

I waited until I was inside my tent before *stepping* to the King's palace.

* * *

King's Palace
Kerok

Hunter brought Sherra to me—I refused to leave Father's bedside. Silently she sat next to me, on a chair Barth had brought from Father's sitting room. Without a word, she gripped my hand in hers.

That wasn't enough for me. I pulled her toward me, until she was on the same chair as I, half-sitting on my lap as I wrapped arms about her.

This wasn't the time for apologies, accusations, or anything else except my father and his final hours.

* * *

Sherra

The King passed three hours after my arrival. I spent the rest of the night with Kerok as he made arrangements for a royal funeral and asked Hunter to have a place prepared for the body in the catacombs, not far from Drenn's resting place.

"The catacombs are extensive, have multiple levels and were originally built as a bomb shelter," Adahi appeared beside me as Kerok spoke to messengers outside his suite. Those messengers would carry the news throughout Az-ca, regarding the King's death and Kerok's elevation to that title.

296

Chapter 17

"A bomb shelter?" Adahi's words found their way into my numbed brain.

"Yes. There was a well-founded fear that they'd collapse if a bomb landed directly atop them. These domes were built above the catacombs before that determination was made," he added.

"So, they'd fall—like a crushed honeycomb?" I blinked at Adahi.

"Something like that."

"Huh."

"Sunrise will come soon—here and at the camp," he reminded me.

"And we need a plan to thwart the enemy." I rubbed a hand over my eyes to relieve blurry vision. "I need tea," I sighed. "To wake up."

"Ask Hunter to lace it with the marching draught—he has access."

"I suppose that's a good idea."

"For now, it's the only idea," Adahi warned.

Kerok aimed an angry glower at Adahi when he found him standing beside me. A servant rushed in, breaking up a tense moment as he set a tray of tea down and raced out again.

"He did not see us," Adahi nodded to me. "Drink—the tea contains the draught."

"You asked Hunter?" I frowned at Adahi.

"I did. Drink—we must return to the camp. The enemy is closer than we think."

"What in the bloody hells are you talking about," Kerok sputtered.

"You should drink, too," Adahi motioned toward the cups and teapot. "It will be a very long day, my dear King."

Rose and Thorn

* * *

Levi and I were awake; we joined Cole at the campfire outside his tent where someone had already served him tea and a small meal. I found it was Derissa, who nodded to both of us and went back to the cooking tent to fill plates for us, too.

"King Wulf is dead," Cole sighed as he lifted his cup to drink. "Sherra went back for a time under a temporary truce, I believe, to comfort Prince Thorn. He is now King. She and Adahi are on their way back."

"Has she been awake all night?" Levi asked.

"Yes."

"Don't worry, I've had a dose of marching draught," Sherra held up a fragile teacup as she *stepped* into camp. Adahi was right behind her.

Still, she looked weary and sad to me. I refrained from pointing out that obvious fact. We needed her, fresh and alert, to determine how to defeat the enemy with our small army of less than one hundred.

Caral and Misten arrived, both looking as if they'd had a troubled night, too. That was to be expected—they'd be declared rogue soon if they weren't already.

"Join us—we have plans to make," Cole invited.

Sherra sat beside Cole, who nodded to her; Caral and Misten sat together beside Levi. Adahi took his place next to Sherra. "Does anyone have anything to start?" I asked.

"I have a question," Sherra said.

"Ask," I gestured toward her.

"How important is the land bridge? Do we need it for anything?"

Chapter 17

* * *

Kyri's City
Doret

"Whatever they're planning, it will keep Ruarke and Kaakos occupied long enough for me to make the attempt," Kyri tied her duffle before pulling it from her bed and dropping it to the floor. "If I pass through Kaakos' barrier on the southwestern side, through the marshes, he won't ever know."

"Kyri, you can't count on that," I hissed. "You know what happened last time. He wants you dead, and tortured long and painfully before you die."

"Someone has to destroy him. You know why it has to be me," Kyri snapped. "Let me go, Doret. If I fail, then your warning is well-given and I ignore it at my peril."

"What if it doesn't have to be you? Convince Sherra to go. If anyone can," I stopped talking when Kyri cast a dark look at me.

"Adahi warns against it. Besides, she didn't start this mess. You know that. I have to try. Once Sherra showed me how to get past a divination shield, the way opened to get past Kaakos' boundary."

"What do I tell the people?" I flung out a hand. "When you don't return? Will we even know if you are captured or killed?"

"I don't intend for either of those things to happen."

"Nobody intends it, but it still happens," I argued.

"Ruarke is outside the boundary, leaving Kaakos alone to face me. There is an opportunity here, and I must take it."

"He can return to Ny-nes quickly—you know that," I said. "I have never seen you act so rashly, Kyri."

"Then hope for my success," she said. "I'm going."

Rose and Thorn

I sagged against a wall as she hefted the duffle over a shoulder and walked out of her bedroom toward the front door. She'd be at the tiled rose in no time, and *stepping* to the designated place outside Kaakos' boundary a blink after that.

* * *

Bomb Crater, Northside
Sherra
The land bridge was less than twenty miles from where we stood. It was narrower now than it had ever been, thanks to the earthquakes precipitated by the same bomb that formed the crater south of us.

The same bomb that nearly killed me, I reminded myself. They could be bringing more than one, this time.

Armon had frowned skeptically at me when I outlined my plans for what to do after we destroyed the land bridge.

The enemy would have to find a way around it, traveling backward toward the edges of the poisoned lands. That could take several days, and we needed that time to set our trap. It would take all ninety-four of us, working quickly, once the location of the trap was pinpointed.

I hoped the marching draught had a long-lasting effect—I was going to need the stamina to see this through.

"Caral, will you and Misten place a mirror shield over the camp?" Armon asked, drawing me away from my thoughts. "We may move it after the land bridge is destroyed, but we'll consider that after we finish that task."

"It's done," Caral told him moments later. She stood tall and strong in the early morning, with our tents serving as a frame for the crater's edge in the distance. She felt the loss of her home and country, though; I could feel the sadness in her.

Chapter 17

Caral, I sent mindspeak. *We'll get back there, I swear it.*

I don't share your faith, she replied. *I've been outcast all my life. This has been my worst fear all along.*

"Stop beating yourself." I strode toward her and wrapped my arms about her. She was taller than I, but her head drooped onto my shoulder. Usually, she was the strong one. This time, she needed the support.

"All will be well," Cole came to stand beside us. "Come now; we have much work to do."

* * *

Ny-nes, Southern Border
Kyri

Things had changed since I'd been here last. *That was almost a century ago,* I reminded myself. I hadn't had the courage to attempt another journey through Kaakos' barrier, then. I knew he'd receive the warning of my return, so I'd watched for a day before leaving, feeling the defeat that he'd handed me more than ever.

This time, I had a way to get past his barrier. Pulling the small coin from my pocket, I studied it carefully.

This coin was ancient, and its face was all but worn away. It came from before the End-War, and was a lucky survivor, if you could call it that.

Once, it bore words in addition to its value. Hardly anyone living would know what those words or value were, now.

I knew, because I'd studied those things. This coin had belonged to the one calling himself Kaakos, before he took that name and cast away his old one.

This coin would get me through his barrier safely, without his knowledge. For now, I could only wait until things changed for his army, which now approached Az-ca. Around me lay the spongy marshlands, where once solid ground held homes and businesses.

Before the End-War.

Inside the barrier, even the fishing shacks that dotted the landscape before were gone. No structures remained as far as I could see, and brackish water surrounded small hills as if they were islands.

Had the fish disappeared, too? They'd carried poison from the End-War within their bodies, but some fish and people had adapted to it. Many others died, eating poisoned fish and foods because they would starve otherwise.

Either way, death was the end result.

Forming a bubble shield, I sat upon it and made myself comfortable. Sherra's small army would provide a distraction soon, and I'd make my move then.

* * *

Ny-nes' Army Camp
Ruarke

Merrin and his small band blinked in surprise as we walked toward the commander's tent. The army would be crossing the land bridge later today, and we would be riding with them.

All around us lay the tents of other commanders, with regular troops standing guard outside. They knew me and let me pass, while my clerics and Merrin's band followed in my wake.

All the guards dipped their heads in reverence at my passing—as they should. They believed I carried the god with me, as well as his power. It suited me very well to be seen this way—as a much-feared representative of their deity.

Perhaps one day they'd learn that *I* was their deity.

Chapter 17

I was the one to be feared.

Laughter bubbled up inside me; I quelled it as High Commander Finn and General Venge exited Finn's tent to greet me, bowing in reverence, just as the others did.

* * *

Land Bridge
Sherra

I'd never seen the land bridge before. On the western edge, far below the cliff that formed that side of the land bridge, lay the sea. I could hear it booming against the rocky sides of the bridge far below.

Eastward lay an enormous canyon, that I could barely make out in the distance. Sunlight shone red against its walls.

"At the bottom of that canyon, a river runs," Cole informed me. "It carries seawater inland, now. Once, the land extended far west of here. The End-War destroyed much of it; more has been worn away since then. Past the canyon, far to our east, lie the poisoned lands. It could take weeks for the enemy to work their way around that large hole in the ground and come at us from another side."

Cole knew his geography, and for that I was very grateful.

"I think we need to change our plans," I said.

"What?" Cole and Armon turned and spoke in unison.

"I think," I said, working to clear the fog of no sleep out of my brain, "That this is an opportunity we can't afford to lose. The enemy wants to cross here. I say we let them cross."

* * *

King's City
Kerok

Rose and Thorn

Commander? Armon's mindspeak was tentative. *Careful.*

Armon, what in the blasted hells were you thinking? I laid into him.

I was thinking the fucking laws need to be fucking changed, he snapped back.

All right, I conceded. He'd never lashed out like this.

He'd never gone rogue before, either, I reminded myself. *Why are you contacting me?* I asked.

To tell you that Sherra placed me in charge of this rogue army, and that we're about to attempt to destroy the enemy convoy. They're close, Thorn. Very close. They'll be crossing the land bridge later today.

Fucking hells, I sent. *What do you want me to do about it?*

Tell Weren. I suggest that you have the army waiting for them if they manage to get across the land bridge. If that happens, then we've failed and it'll be your turn to fight them back.

What are you planning? I demanded.

I can't tell you that, because it will reveal our location. We're rogues, remember? You'll be forced to apprehend us.

Fuck that, I sent. *I'll inform Weren.*

Do it through Wend—Weren's main source of mindspoken messages is currently running amok. Armon's flash of humor came through in his sending.

Armon? I sent.

What is it, Commander?

Thank you.

You're welcome. I grieve for your father, and I'm sorry for the pain his death brings to you; I know you loved him dearly. I have to go; if we don't get started now, the trap won't be finished in time.

The King's blessings be upon you, I said. We stand or fall together.

As it has always been.

Chapter 18

Army Convoy
Ruarke

Traveling over rough ground inside a vehicle wasn't my preferred method of travel. The truck creaked and groaned with every dip or rocky place we were forced to drive across.

Looking out the back end of a truck at passing scenery held no interest for me, either, which forced me to tamp down my impatience at how slowly we were approaching our goal.

"What are those tall plants? They look like trees," Niles asked Merrin.

"Cactus," one of Merrin's warriors answered. Merrin wore a frown, as if he were thinking. I wanted to laugh—his thinking generally got him in trouble.

Soon enough, he'd be of no use to me and the torture would begin. He didn't think anyone here could remove his power.

He had much to learn.

"We'll be across the bridge and into enemy territory in three hours," I said. "There, we'll set up camp and build a runway to send the planes out."

"It will bring us great pleasure to see the King's City die," Niles grinned.

"What?" Merrin lurched to his feet. "The King's City is mine. It was promised to *me*."

"Little man," Niles hissed, "There was never anything promised to you."

Niles should have kept his mouth shut; Merrin *stepped* away before we could stop him. Because I was angry enough as it was, I blasted Niles to ash without a second thought.

I should have held back on that impulse; Merrin's three sets of warriors and escorts disappeared as well, leaving only former Council members to face my wrath.

* * *

Secondary Camp
Wend

Marc and I had been elevated so quickly, I was still attempting to deal with the changes. Marc was now Weren's Second-In-Command, while I was the new mindspeaking liaison between the General and King Thorn.

When the message came from the King, I almost didn't believe it. Nevertheless, I passed the information to Weren, and now the entire camp was in a rush of preparations. Weren wanted us on the southern edge of the bomb crater by midday, and we were struggling to make that happen.

Chapter 18

I still wanted to call the new King by the old name I knew—or Commander, even—when neither of those titles were correct. *General Weren says the army will be in place by midday*, I sent to King Thorn.

Keep me apprised of the situation, he replied smoothly.

Of course, my King.

Thank you, Wend.

You're welcome, Commander.

* * *

Land Bridge

Armon

Cole understood quickly what Sherra wanted to do, so he and his people gathered about her, to lend her strength to accomplish the feat.

She'd said Adahi had given her the idea earlier, but didn't explain further than that. As for Adahi, he'd disappeared without a word, just as he usually did.

Sherra suspected there was something more to Adahi, just as I did. She may have arrived at his truth faster than I had, however.

"She's building a tunnel, like the one she built beneath the wall at Secondary Camp," Levi brought a mug of fresh tea that Derissa made for us.

"Is she planning on hiding inside it?" I turned to Levi.

"I don't know, love," Levi sighed. "I haven't figured this out, yet."

It was the first time he'd felt comfortable calling me an endearment in public. "This is going to ruin your tough-warrior persona, you know," I told him, before turning back to watch Sherra and her group work.

"Bullshit," Levi laughed.

"And there's the man I know and love," I sipped my tea.

Rose and Thorn

"I had no idea she could spin a tube, then widen it out and strengthen it the farther away from her it goes," Levi said. He didn't bother hiding the smile in his voice. "All those people are either in contact with her or one another," he added. "We should have considered things like this long ago."

"You think this will work?" I asked.

"I have no idea. I'm still in awe of the skills these people have."

"Thorn is organizing his army on the southern end of the bomb crater—in case the enemy gets past us," I admitted.

"You contacted him?"

"I did. He was less than pleased at first."

"He came around?"

"He did."

"Good." Levi visibly relaxed.

"We've worked with him a long time. I think he remembered that after a few seconds."

Colonel Armon? Wend's mindspeak interrupted my conversation with Levi.

Wend? I'm surprised to hear from you, I replied.

We ah, have a situation, she reported. *Merrin, two other rogues and their escorts just showed up outside our walls. We were ready to step to the south end of the bomb crater when they arrived. Merrin is screaming something about traitors and the enemy, but we can't understand what he's saying. He can't get past our shields, either, so there's no way to get close enough to hear him better.*

"By the first warrior," I cursed. "Levi, I think we're needed elsewhere. Let me tell Sherra where we're going," I began.

Chapter 18

"I will accompany you," Adahi appeared beside us. "Come—time is short. In minutes, you'll begin to hear the rumble of the first vehicles approaching. Perhaps Merrin will make himself useful after all."

I gripped Levi's sleeve as Adahi *stepped* us to Secondary Camp.

* * *

Secondary Camp
Wend

"I can see he's upset about something," Marc said as he and I stood outside the gate, watching Merrin and four followers from a distance.

Levi, Armon and the one called Adahi appeared near Merrin then, startling the other warriors and their escorts. The warrior who fired a blast against Levi's shield dropped where he stood and didn't move again.

Adahi lowered his arm; I hadn't seen him raise it to begin with, it happened so quickly.

"Let's go," Marc gripped my hand and pulled me toward the outer shield protecting the camp. I ran to keep up with his swift strides.

* * *

Armon

"What the fuck are you talking about?" I shouted at Merrin, who, on his knees, begged us for the third time to listen to him.

"His brain is addled by that foul drug," Adahi turned toward me.

"Does anybody know anything?" I shouted at Merrin, the remaining warrior and both escorts.

"We just came from the enemy convoy," one of the escorts stepped forward timidly. "After Ruarke said they're going to destroy the King's City. Merrin—they promised the King's City to him. Said he'd be King there."

"They lied, as is their habit," Adahi growled. "Tell me, if you know," he continued. "How long is the enemy's convoy?"

"Really long," the other escort answered. "There are three long trucks hauling planes at the back."

"Longer than half a mile?" I demanded.

"I think so," the escort whimpered.

"Bloody hells," Levi cursed. He knew, as did I, that the land bridge was little more than a half-mile long.

"What's going on?" Marc and Wend arrived at the outside edge of the shield covering Secondary Camp.

"Tell Weren he needs to get the army to the rendezvous point now," I barked. "We'll have to let some of the enemy convoy through after all, and that means he'll have a fight on his hands the minute we spring our trap."

Wend and Marc exchanged glances before *stepping* back inside the camp's walls.

"What do we do with these?" I gestured toward Merrin and the others.

"Let me deal with them," Adahi offered. "Take your news back to Sherra and Cole. Their plans must change quickly to accommodate the new information."

* * *

King's City
Kerok

"Your father's body has been moved to the receiving chamber, to lie in state," Hunter sat on a guest chair. "You won't believe the weeping and wailing coming from the Council, none of whom have bothered to visit Wulf in the past few months. I can't wait to hear the excuses," Hunter snorted.

Chapter 18

"You sound tired. You should have taken a marching draught, too," I pointed out.

"I hate that stuff," he waved away the suggestion. "I have trouble sleeping for days afterward."

"I hoped I'd find you together," Adahi announced as he appeared, flinging four people onto the floor beside Hunter's chair.

I was on my feet immediately, as was Hunter, but I shouldn't have worried. The phantom had already removed their power; I imagine he waited to see what I wished to do with Merrin, the murderous traitor, and three of his followers.

"The city belongs to me," Merrin said, his words and tone soaked in belligerence.

"You idiot, you placed it in danger," Adahi growled.

"Thorn?" Merrin turned toward me. "Tell him. I'm the heir."

"Merrin?" Hunter knelt so they'd be at eye level with one another.

"What, Uncle Hunter?" Merrin blinked at him.

"This." Hunter punched Merrin square in the face, rendering him unconscious.

"Couldn't have done a better job myself," Adahi said.

"These will be delivered to the lockup," I said as the escorts cowered and the warrior blanched.

"Prince Thorn, I was coerced," the warrior began.

"That's King Thorn to you, you pathetic bunghole," Hunter hissed. "Guards," he shouted. "Bring cuffs and come quickly."

There is a concern, Adahi informed me while Hunter waited for the guards to arrive. *You should consider leaving the city.*

"What concern?" I spoke aloud.

Adahi didn't bother replying in kind—he showed me his visions instead.

* * *

Land Bridge
Sherra

"Never say things can't get worse," Cole advised. "Someone will take it as a challenge."

Caral and Misten, after hearing that the enemy convoy could be longer than the land bridge, had covered themselves in a mirror shield and left to scout the situation. They were back quickly.

"It's three times as long," Caral reported after dropping the shield about them. "The trucks carrying the planes are at the end, as Levi said. We assume the vehicles ahead of those are the ones carrying the bombs. Those trucks are closed and show no signs of carrying troops."

"That means we must allow the bulk of the troops with their normal ration of bombs through," Cole grumbled.

"The army is prepared to meet them at the southern edge of the bomb crater," Armon said. "I just received mindspeak from Wend."

"That gives Ruarke ample time to get away," I pointed out. "Which he will do; he won't stay around to see what we have planned for the others."

"Will he *step* back to Ny-nes?" Caral asked.

"I don't know," Cole shook his head. "I've attempted to contact Kyri, but she isn't responding."

"What about Pottles?" I asked.

"I'll send a message," Cole agreed.

"We have to hurry," Caral said. "I can hear the trucks coming, now."

Chapter 18

She was right—I could hear them, too.

"Caral, mirror shield," I snapped. "Misten, add your power to hers."

"On it," Caral said.

We stood at the southwestern edge of the land bridge, and in moments, the first trucks would appear and begin to cross.

We had to wait until the trucks carrying the planes and bombs came along. "Move back and to the sides," Armon shouted. "Go now. Do not engage the enemy, do you hear? Az-ca's army is waiting for them."

Sherra? Caral said as I remained where I was.

I have a plan—just for me, I told her before forming a mirrored bubble shield about myself. I could send bubble shields into the air and hold them there. I was about to see if I could include myself in that equation.

* * *

Armon

Sherra? She'd disappeared and I had no idea where she was.

I'm fine, I'm adjusting things to deal with the wind.

The wind where?

On the west side of the land bridge.

You are not *on the land bridge,* I snapped in mindspeak.

No, I'm in a mirrored bubble shield, hanging in the air over the water so I can watch the convoy. I want to release the trap at the right moment, and this location will give me the best view of it. I'll relay information as they pass by, if that will help.

Anything will help, but bloody hells, Sherra, I cursed.

Rose and Thorn

So far, things are going all right—for my first time at this. They're about to cross; I can see the lead trucks.

I can see them, too, I retorted. *From a safe place south and west. On. The. Ground.*

Armon, be careful, all right?

Me? You're saying this to me, while you're hanging in a bubble shield in midair? I'm overcome by the irony.

Armon, I see rockets—between vehicles carrying troops. These are far bigger than those I've seen before, Sherra reported. I could detect the fear rising in her mental voice. *So many troop vehicles—they're crossing three and four abreast,* she added. *Armon, it looks like they've emptied Ny-nes.*

I see it, I said before sending hasty mindspeak to Wend and Thorn.

* * *

King's City
Kerok
Don't give them enough time or space to set up their launchers, I shouted mentally at Wend. *Tell Weren to move the army forward—to the northern edge of the bomb crater.*

He's moving the troops now, Wend sounded breathless. *I'm instructing the escorts to construct a mirror shield—those who can,* she added.

Good. We don't want them to know we're anywhere except Secondary Camp. Make sure everyone is hidden.

We're working on it, Commander.

"Hunter," I shouted aloud.

"Here," he almost ran into my study.

"You're in charge. I'm going to the front," I began pulling my formal clothing off so I could dress in an old uniform.

316

Chapter 18

"But the law," Hunter protested.

"Says that the Crown Prince cannot serve as Commander of the Army. It says nothing about the King participating in a battle."

"But," Hunter objected.

"Hunter, you'll make a good King, if it comes to that. I'll be back." I *stepped* to my suite; surely one of my old uniforms was lying about somewhere.

* * *

Sherra

Caral, Az-ca's army is on the northern edge of the bomb crater. Is Derissa safe?

Some of Cole's people got her away, Caral replied. *I'm not sure where—they just said she was safe.*

All right.

What are you seeing? she asked.

Too many troops, weapons and vehicles.

Sherra? Wend's voice interrupted the conversation.

Wend?

We've emptied Secondary Camp. All the former washouts, trainees, everybody is here, she said. *Tell me how to keep them alive.*

Put them together, I said. *Let them build shields together, to protect themselves and the ones firing blasts. For those who can do neither, then set them up to provide energy. Make sure they know what their limit is and to disengage when the limit is reached.*

I will—we taught them that; Caral, Misten and I.

Good work. Just remember, we'll be on the back side of the enemy after they cross the bridge; I think Cole has something planned for this end of things.

Rose and Thorn

We've set up mirror shields, so they won't realize we're here, she added.

Perfect, I said. *Let them scramble when they can't see their enemy to fire their missiles and bombs.*

I told General Weren where you are, Wend said after a moment. *He says they'll have to adjust the distances on their fireblasts so they won't hit Cole's people.*

I'll advise Armon and Cole, I said. *They need to ensure they're shielded well enough in case of a misfire.*

Sherra? Wend suddenly sounded unsure of herself.

What is it? I asked. Her tone worried me.

The King is here—to fight with us, she informed me.

* * *

Armon

I struggled to hide my surprise when King Thorn informed me he was with Weren and the army on the north rim of the bomb crater.

We're on the southwestern side of the land bridge, I reported when he asked for our location. *We'll move in behind the enemy, once Sherra springs her trap.*

Where is she?

I was afraid he'd ask that question.

She's ah, floating in a bubble shield on the western side of the land bridge, so she can gauge the proper time to release the trap.

I waited several seconds before receiving a reply from Thorn. *Over the water, she's hanging? In a bubble shield?*

I believe it's a mirrored bubble shield, but yes—that's how I understood it. Sir, I believe she loves you very much, I added.

Right. I look forward to seeing her when this is over.

With your permission, I'll wait to pass on that message.

Chapter 18

Understood and agreed.

Commander? I'd already fallen into old habits, calling him by an old title. *I can see the trucks carrying the planes*, I said. *They're approaching the bridge, now.*

The troops are ready; let me know when the enemy is in the proper position.

I suspect they'll begin their preparations the moment the trap is sprung.

* * *

Ruarke

My remaining clerics groveled if I looked at them. I'd held off burning former Council members to death inside the vehicle—the hole I'd blown into the side when I'd done away with Niles left an ugly gap in the canvas. The ragged edges of the remaining fabric flapped in the wind with annoying regularity and wore on my nerves.

We'd already passed over the land bridge; I could still see it behind us in the distance, as the vehicles pulling the planes and carrying the massive bombs began their crossing.

Soon enough, the enemy would be destroyed and I would dance on the remains of the King's City.

Wait.

It hit me, then—hard. The premonition. How had I not felt it before? Fear crawled up my spine and I shouted for the driver to stop as the land bridge collapsed behind us with a terrible roar, dropping bombs and planes toward the sea below.

The driver pulled over, but only when the first fireblast exploded at the head of the convoy, nearly a mile ahead of us.

There was no mistaking that sound, however, and I cursed before realization dawned. I *stepped* away before anyone could attempt to stop me.

Rose and Thorn

* * *

Sherra

The tunnels I'd built beneath the land bridge had mimicked a honeycomb, much like the one Adahi described in the catacombs beneath the King's City.

Once I collapsed all the shields I'd built to hold the tunnels in place, the bridge fell, beautifully and in slow motion, taking planes and bombs with it, until they fell with a scream of twisting metal into the sea.

The land bridge was gone, and in the distance, I could hear the boom-boom of fireblasts targeting the head of the enemy convoy.

I needed to get myself back to land and do what I could to help.

Except Adahi appeared from nowhere inside my bubble shield, floating there as if he were nothing more than air.

Perhaps he was.

"I need you, and the King's City needs you," he said quickly. "But, to be at your most effective, you must be unconscious." The blow that hit my face had power behind it, if not physical flesh. I discovered later that it didn't matter which it was—I was rendered unconscious immediately.

* * *

Kerok

We'd done damage before the first bombs and rockets were fired in our direction, but these weapons were more powerful than any I'd seen before. I became worried immediately that shields wouldn't hold.

Sherra? I sent mindspeak.

I received no answer and that terrified me.

Armon?

Commander?

320

Chapter 18

Have you heard from Sherra?

No, Commander. I haven't seen her either, although the land bridge collapsed, just as expected. The vehicles carrying the planes and their bombs are now in the sea.

Have Sherra contact me if you hear from her.

I will.

I didn't tell him that fear froze my heart. If she were alive, she should have answered.

Fuck. I fired another blast, determined to make the enemy pay.

* * *

Ny-nes

Kyri

The time had come. I knew that both armies were now engaged on Az-ca's border. Kaakos would be sending his divination tendrils in that direction, to find the roots of this early attack.

His attention would be diverted. Taking the coin from my pocket, I began my spell to breach his barrier.

* * *

King's City

Ruarke

Where was the fucking city? I knew better than anyone just where it was, and had *stepped* to a place outside the outer northern dome. I'd been here recently, in fact; it couldn't have been moved or destroyed in that length of time.

Something had prevented me from stepping farther in than that, this time and last, but I couldn't determine what it was. Kaakos' mindspeak rattled inside my head while I studied my surroundings, demanding to know what had gone wrong and why I hadn't received a premonition as I usually did, before the land bridge was attacked. *There's no way for the army to get out again, except through the poisoned lands*, he railed at me.

I ignored his mindspeak as I considered the problem before me.

The domes of the King's City—all of them—had disappeared. Only desert, cactus and heat waves had greeted me upon my arrival.

No matter. I knew what lay beneath those domes, and I'd known for a very long time how fragile and vulnerable the catacombs made the domes overhead.

All I had to do was send a few blasts into the ground and they'd collapse—*just like the land bridge had collapsed.*

Someone else had worked against me in this—someone powerful. Could it be Adahi?

He's dead, I reminded myself. Kaakos assured me the body was still in Ny-nes. *Was it the one who'd shown me Adahi's face?* It took power to replicate features like that.

What the fuck are you doing? Where are you? Kaakos screamed in my mind.

I'm about to destroy the King's City, I replied calmly.

Oh. Carry on, then.

The first fireblast would be the strongest, I decided, and began to build it. A single figure walked out of the heat shimmer, then.

A woman.

Dark hair. Tall. Slender. Dressed in a dark uniform. She held up a hand. The fireball fizzled in my hands and died.

I built another, only to watch it die, too.

She came closer. I could see the fire in her eyes. The anger in her expression. No—it was fury.

Chapter 18

Putting up a shield, I waited for her approach. No woman was going to threaten me. No woman had been born who was stronger than I, and I'd show her my strength the moment she came close enough.

Her screams would please me before she died.

"Good afternoon, Wulf Tadson Ruarke Rex," she hissed.

"So you know," I shrugged off her knowledge. "You won't live long enough to tell anyone else."

"You think so?"

"Who are you?" I demanded while setting up additional layers of shielding and strengthening them.

"You can call me the Black Rose."

"An escort? That's laughable," I crowed.

"I have never been an escort," she said. "I was always more than that. Delude yourself if you want, but before you go, I have a message for the one who holds your leash."

"Nobody holds my leash," I hissed and began forming another fireblast.

"He's listening through you right now—haven't you figured that out, yet? You're pathetic," she dismissed me with a wave of her hand.

What's the message? Kaakos' mindspeak made me shiver.

How had I not known? How?

"Kaakos, the dreamwalker is coming," the woman announced. "That one will see you dead."

"The dreamwalker is already dead," I couldn't keep Kaakos' words from spilling out of my mouth. "His body lies in my palace, rotting away."

Beads of sweat dripped inside my collar, landing on bare skin as I fought to take control of myself.

I couldn't. Kaakos held me, like a hare in a trap.

"You see now what he can do to you?" The woman spoke again.

"See what *I* can do to you," Kaakos' words screamed from my mouth.

Chapter 19

Adahi

I held myself invisible until the last, but remained close enough to do what needed to be done. Ruarke's shields would never have held Kaakos' power back.

Mine, combined with Sherra's?

That became a far different story. Kaakos released his blast through Ruarke, aimed directly for Sherra's dreamwalker.

The blast ended at the inside of our combined shields, and the resulting explosion and fireball was so fierce and intense that Ruarke didn't have time to scream or whimper as he was reduced to ash.

Before I could stop her, however, Sherra's dreamwalker disappeared. I had no idea where she went, because I *stepped* back to the bubble shield that held her body. It now floated on the sea, far away from land. The current carried it farther away with every passing moment.

I transported the bubble shield to the King's City, but Sherra remained unconscious inside it.

That worried me greatly.

There is one rule that applies to every dreamwalker, however.

Never wake them.

* * *

Battlefront

Kerok

Commander, we're about to initiate an attack from the rear, Armon informed me. We're aiming at the center of the convoy, so there'll be no stray blasts coming your way. I will warn you, however, that there's a rather large concentration of bombs and rockets in that area. Fireblasts may cause an explosion.

Wait, I said. Give me the location you're firing at.

Our target is passing the triangle outcroppings now, Armon replied.

All right. We'll focus on that location, too. Wait and fire on my command.

It will be done.

"He wants to target the same area, doesn't he?" Cole spoke beside me.

"Yes."

"A very good idea," Cole agreed. "A coordinated effort—I like it very much."

* * *

Ny-nes

Kaakos

Chapter 19

My study was destroyed, as were the two guards who'd stood outside it, after Ruarke was burned to death inside a shield I hadn't known about. There at the last, though, I'd seen the one posing as Adahi—he'd made himself visible to me. All along, it had been him, instead of the woman, who presented the larger threat.

My newest mission was to learn who this imposter was, and how dangerous he could possibly be. The reason I'd destroyed Adahi to begin with was the ill-gotten prophecy he'd spouted.

That the dreamwalker would see my death.

I'd wanted to keep him alive—to torture throughout the years, of course—until he said *that*.

It angered me so much I'd killed him for it.

I had no idea he'd been distracting me all that time, so *she* could escape. That's when I'd devised my barrier; to keep her from entering Ny-nes again. If she did, she'd die in the attempt.

My power had only grown in the face of her challenges; I hoped she understood that. If she didn't, then I'd be happy to kill her on Ny-nes' soil. She was behind the occasional disappearances of children—I had no doubt she was calling them away to train them. Her efforts were useless; their ability was nothing compared to what I'd become.

Eventually they'd die, just as Az-ca would. Yes, my army was under attack, but the weapons we'd built for this war were much more powerful than anything we'd sent against Az-ca in the past.

I cursed Ruarke again, as I realized my eyes and ears on the battlefield were nothing more than black ash outside the King's City in Az-ca.

* * *

Rose and Thorn

King's Palace
Hunter

I sat at Thorn's desk, writing, when Adahi appeared before me. Lifting my head, I blinked at him in surprise.

He always came to Thorn.

Always.

"Sherra's sleeping body is inside her suite—do not wake her," Adahi's low voice commanded.

Carefully I set down the pen I'd been using, while struggling to draw in a breath. "Thorn?" I asked.

"Is doing well for the moment," Adahi shrugged. "I came to tell you important information. As you're already writing, I determined it a good time to give you the news."

"What news?"

"Ruarke is dead. I will give you the images now," he told me. I almost cried out in surprise when the images and sounds entered my mind.

* * *

Ny-nes, Southern Boundary
Kyri

The spell was finished. All I had to do was walk through the boundary, now.

Why was I hesitating? Sudden fear made me shiver. *Was this a mistake?* Adahi thought it was, as did Doret.

Somewhere, near Az-ca's border, a battle raged between two armies. I hadn't done divination to see which might survive. I had one goal—one purpose for being where I was.

Kaakos.

Adahi had given up his human life to save mine, centuries ago. I owed him a death in return.

Clenching Kaakos' coin in my fist, I took a step forward, only to be flung back so hard I hit the ground and rolled.

Chapter 19

When I got my senses back, I found Sherra standing over me.

Except I could see the late afternoon sun shining through her.

Sherra's dreamwalker had come.

"That is your death," she hissed, pointing toward Kaakos' boundary.

"You can't stop me," I said, before rising awkwardly and brushing damp dirt off my trousers. They'd carry a stain, now, but it would blend in with the rest of Ny-nes, once I got inside the barrier.

"No, the barrier is your death," she said. "You can't get through it using what you learned from me earlier."

"Then what do I need?" I snapped at her. "I intend to kill Kaakos and Ruarke, both."

"Ruarke?" She laughed. "He's dead."

"You killed him?" My voice squeaked in an embarrassing manner.

"Adahi and I," she said.

"Then I only have one target," I said and walked toward my duffle, which lay where I'd dropped it after Sherra's dreamwalker flung me away from the barrier.

"Come back with me now; your people need you."

"I'm not going back. Not until Kaakos is dead—or I am. Doret and Cole can deal with those things."

Sherra's dreamwalker stiffened, and I knew, without a doubt, that something had happened at the battlefront.

Had I imagined her initial treatment rough as she'd flung me back? When I was flung forward, sailing through the boundary while shielded with power, I landed with a jolt that should have broken bones while Sherra's dreamwalker disappeared.

Rose and Thorn

* * *

Battlefront
The Black Rose

The bomb that destroyed the enemy army the year before, had created numerous cracks and fissures beneath the surface. Combined with Sherra's tunneling beneath the land bridge, the entire area had become unstable.

When Armon and Cole's troops targeted the center of the convoy on the northern end, while Thorn and his troops did the same from the south, a disaster was bound to occur.

At the same moment, the enemy prepared to fire a volley of powerful rockets—fifty-nine of them—at once.

The escorts' shields would never hold.

Twenty miles of land, between the land bridge and the bomb crater, was crumbling and ready to fall. The force of three massive blasts, occurring within a blink of one another, was deafening.

I heard the screams for help as bodies, vehicles, and everything else strung along a twenty-mile stretch began to collapse and slide downward. The powerful rockets aimed at Az-ca's army broke through many shields, bringing death as the ground crumbled beneath their feet.

Step away, I sent to all those still capable of doing so.

For those who didn't have that capability or the presence of mind to do so, and who didn't belong to the enemy army, time was extremely short.

I went roaring after them, struggling to fight time and collapsing earth simultaneously, as everything caved toward a hungry sea.

* * *

King's Palace
Hunter

330

Chapter 19

"I want two guards outside her door. Don't let anyone in," I ordered as we strode toward the suite Sherra chose for herself.

"They're cleaning that floor," one of the guards informed me. "Since the occupants of those suites left unexpectedly."

"Fucking hells," I snapped and *stepped* toward Sherra's suite.

* * *

Secondary Camp
Kerok

"Take a head count," I shouted at those who *stepped* onto solid ground around me. I'd never forget the feeling of the earth crumbling beneath my feet moments after we'd launched hundreds of blasts in unison, only to be hit with a volley of rockets so powerful, they destroyed many shields and those beneath them.

To the north, Armon, commanding Cole's troops, had done the same.

The ground had crumbled from the land bridge southward, and from the bomb crater northward. I struggled to get my fears under control before sending mindspeak.

Armon? Sherra? Cole? I couldn't hold back a mental shout at my attempted contact. *Armon?* I repeated.

"We're missing some—many," Marc yelled at me after doing a swift count of those who'd returned to camp.

"Where's Weren?" I shouted back, craning to see over the heads of troops gathering about me.

"I haven't seen him," someone answered from close by.

"Find him," I said. "Quickly!" *Cole? Sherra?* I continued my mental communications. So far, there were no replies.

* * *

King's Palace

Rose and Thorn

Hunter

"No," My whisper failed to travel far enough or swiftly enough to stop the maidservant's entrance into Sherra's suite. Her shriek followed quickly, when she found the suite occupied instead of empty; filled with an invisible bubble shield and a woman hanging at the center of it, unconscious. That shriek was both badly-timed and ill-advised.

The maid's scream awakened Sherra, who yelped in terror at the sudden noise. At the time, I had no idea how much misfortune that had caused—or how many deaths were attributed to her sudden waking.

I only learned later that it was many.

* * *

King's Palace
Kerok

More than a third of Az-ca's army died that day, from an attack by the enemy and the untimely actions of a hapless servant.

General Weren was among the casualties; as were so many others. Seasoned warriors and escorts died, who hadn't been prepared for the destruction of the shields over their heads or the ground falling beneath their feet. If they received Sherra's message to *step* away, it came far too late and Sherra's dreamwalker had been wakened much too soon, or she might have saved some of them.

The only consolation any of us could draw from the tragedies of that battle, were that the enemy army and its cargo of bombs, rockets and planes had also been destroyed.

I'd consider myself a fool if I believed Kaakos was done with us, however. If anything, his anger had ramped up to an unexpected level. He'd find a replacement for Ruarke—I had no misconceptions about that. Perhaps he already had a replacement hidden away, in case Ruarke managed to get himself killed.

As for the first half of Thorn's Book—Adahi brought it to me after locating Ruarke's last camp. Ruarke had woven spells about it, but Adahi managed to unravel those, somehow.

Both parts of the book, stained with Ruarke's blood when he was stabbed by Sherra's dreamwalker, were now locked away in the treasury, inside a special vault that only Hunter and I could access.

I'd received the missing dagger and coronet with the book; all those things had been found with Ruarke's other belongings.

The dagger I kept; the coronet I handed to Hunter, as was proper.

"Here are copies of the pardons," I slid a folder of papers toward General Armon. "These," I slid another folder toward him, "are the citizenship papers for Cole and his people."

"Caral and Misten asked me to extend their gratitude— for these and for changing the laws so quickly," Armon grinned and tapped the folders.

"Thank Hunter—he wrote them out while we were off fighting the enemy," I shrugged. "All I had to do was sign my name."

"How's Sherra?" Armon asked, taking on a more solemn expression.

"Worried. Regretful. Feeling guilt she shouldn't feel," I sighed.

"I hear Doret has her hands full, overseeing the training of all the younglings born with power," Armon changed the subject.

"I've been to the training camp—it feels to me as if those children have come alive for the first time in their lives."

"Has Sherra gone to help?"

"Not yet."

Neither of us spoke our worries aloud—that Sherra had been affected more deeply by recent events than anyone thought possible. I just wanted her back—the way we were before Ruarke and bloody, fucking Kaakos intervened.

Armon and I—we waited for Kaakos to make his next move; we'd destroyed his entire army this time, of that I had no doubt.

To lead another army against us, he'd have to send them far out of the way and across poisoned lands to do it. Somehow, I imagined he'd find a way past that obstacle.

Eventually.

"How is it so cool in here? It's baking outside," Armon observed. "The seawater coolers have never worked this well."

"Ah. Well. I've spent some time with Thorn's Book," I replied. "Turns out, there's a cooling spell in it. It's actually quite handy."

* * *

Ny-nes

Kaakos

My anger against Az-ca had reached new levels. If I could, I'd have blasted it apart from where I stood.

I'd have to be closer than this to do it, however.

In the meantime, I had plans to make and soldiers to recruit.

Beginning with the ones I recognized easily—through their contact with Ruarke.

Chapter 19

Hello, Merrin, I inserted into his mind. *From now on, you will follow my instructions—if you wish to have your power restored.*

I watched through his eyes as he scrambled off the cot in his jail cell while shock and terror coursed through his body.

Soon enough, a trial would be held for him, and the ruling body in the King's City would be present.

As would I; waiting inside a few well-chosen subjects before releasing my power against them.

Epilogue

Sherra

S I sat in the King's garden at the outdoor table, while bees drifted among late-summer flowers. A few had bumped into the shield I held around myself, before buzzing away.

"I owe you an apology," Adahi took the chair across from mine.

"Are you required to sit?" I asked.

"It's expected. As is consuming tea or food—or at least pretending to do so. I can still scent those things and find them pleasing, but the physical consumption is not necessary."

"What did you come to apologize for?" I didn't care about an apology—most days I felt numb and couldn't bring myself to care about anything. Neither food nor apologies made a bit of difference to what had happened recently.

"I punched you, to render you unconscious," Adahi moved uncomfortably in his chair. "It was the swiftest method to achieve the necessary result."

"I don't care," I waved a hand.

"You'd care if I did it again," he snorted.

"Maybe."

"Cole asked about you. I just came from Secondary Camp."

"How is he?" A brief stirring of interest came at the mention of Cole's name.

"He is well. He worries about you, as do the rest of your friends. Now, tell me about Kyri. Did she cross into Ny-nes safely?"

337

"I—well, the Black Rose tossed her through the barrier, after coating her with Kaakos' power."

"Where did that power come from?" Adahi's words and attention became sharper—more focused.

"I saw him—in a vision from long ago, I suppose. I didn't know who he was. The Black Rose did. She took that part of him—the malevolent part, and used it to spin a shield around Kyri. If she dies in Ny-nes, it will be from her own foolishness and not from Kaakos' boundary."

"Damnation," Adahi rubbed his face. I suppose old habits were hard to break—his dreamwalker didn't need any of those gestures.

Neither did mine, if it came to that.

"Tea, my Queen?" A servant approached with a tray. I could smell honey cakes from where I sat. My stomach rumbled a response.

"Yes. Thank you," I said as the woman set the tray on the table. "Adahi, will you join me?" I asked.

"I believe I will," he grinned and accepted a cup of tea.

The End

Sherra and Kerok's adventures will continue in *Black Rose Queen*, Book 3 in the Black Rose Sorceress series.

Names of Characters and Places Appearing in this Book:

Adahi: AKA the phantom; well acquainted with former King Thorn. Dreamwalker, who has a long history with Kyri and events in Ny-nes

Ana: North Camp Instructor, Second Cohort

Anari: 17-year-old black rose girl with mindspeaking and stepping talent

Armon: Colonel in Az-ca's army, currently serves as First advisor to Prince Commander. Chosen by Caral

Az-ca: Desert country ruled by King Wulf; always at war with barbarians from Ny-nes

Barth: King's Chief Diviner

Beckley: Warrior, chosen by Reena

Bela: Former washout

Barney: (Barna) escort trainee and former washout

Blane Grove: Former Council member and Merrin's ally

Bones of the Prophet: a drug given to those in Ny-nes' army and its clerics, to ensure their compliance

Book of the Rose (The): A book in the King's library, describing talents and duties of Black Rose escorts

Bray: Barth's secondary Diviner

Bulldog: a nickname used by Yasa, North Camp Instructor, Sixth Cohort

Calli: escort who, with her warrior, deserted the army and joined with Merrin

Caral: Fourth Cohort trainee at North Camp

Cole: a refugee from Ny-nes. Born with power, he was tortured as a child until he escaped by stepping to Kyri's City at her invitation

Colonel Kage: Training Instructor for warrior trainees in the King's City—becomes a King's assassin

Colonel Weren: Training Instructor for warrior trainees in the King's City; becomes General of the Army

Names of Characters and Places Appearing in this Book:

Commander Alden: Post Commander for Secondary Camp

Dar-den: Caral's former village

Daria: Doret's sister, killed by Ruarke

Derissa: Caral's older sister, from Dar-den

Dayl: General Linel's personal messenger

Derk Beadl: former Council member and ally of Merrin

Doret: Former Queen of Az-ca; more than 200 years old

Drenn Wulfson Meris Rex: Crown Prince of Az-ca (deceased)

East Camp: one of four training camps for black rose trainees

End-War: crippling event that changed and destroyed nearly everything on the planet

Falia: Instructor at North Camp

F'nexscot: AKA the King's City

Gale: Armon's former escort

Garkus: Drill instructor at Secondary Camp—became a King's assassin

Garth: Outpost Commander

Geb: retired warrior—now works as a traveling instructor for all trainees

General Linel: Chief Commander of the army in the Prince Commander's absence

Grae: Kerok's deceased escort

Gram Plicton: former Council member, who became Merrin's ally after Drenn's death

Harel: messenger who was burned by Merrin's warrior allies before escaping to take the news of Merrin's location to the Crown Prince (deceased)

Hari: escort abandoned by her warrior (Narris)

Harnn: Bela's warrior

Names of Characters and Places Appearing in this Book:

Hayla: black rose trainee

High Commander Finn: Supreme Commander of Ny-nes' army

Hunter Lattham: King's advisor, Uncle to Merrin, Drenn and Kerok

Jacob: Council member for Dar-den, Caral's former village

Jae: black rose trainee—Sixth Cohort, North Camp (deceased)

Kaakos: the name taken by the Sovereign Leader of the Free Nation of Ny-nes.

Kage: see Colonel Kage

Kerok: AKA Thorn Wulfson Kerok Rex, King Wulf's youngest son and Prince Commander of the army—becomes Crown Prince upon Drenn's death, and then King upon his father's death

Ketchi: the village where Cole and many other refugees from Ny-nes live. All were born with power and were sentenced to death by Ruarke

King Wulf Carlson Alexander Rex: King of Az-ca (deceased)

Kyal: 11-year-old warrior boy with mindspeaking talent

Kyri: Female Diviner—believed to be a legend or myth

Laren: 16-year-old warrior boy with mindspeaking talent

Lera: escort abandoned by her warrior

Levi: Captain, serves as Secondary Advisor to Prince Commander. Chosen by Misten

Lewus: Council member for Merthis and five other villages

Lieutenant Marc: Chosen by Wend; promoted to Captain

Lilya: North Camp Instructor, Fourth Cohort

Mari: black rose girl; Romma's daughter

Marra: Daria's chosen warrior

Marta: General Weren's wife

Names of Characters and Places Appearing in this Book:

Merrin: Nephew of Hunter and King Wulf; cousin to Drenn and Kerok (on mother's side)

Merthis: small village where Sherra was born

Miri: North Camp Instructor, Fifth Cohort

Misten: North Camp trainee, Sixth Cohort

Narris: warrior-turned-traitor who left his escort behind (Hari) before deserting army

Narvin: deserter who, with his escort Willa, chose to follow Merrin

Neka: North Camp trainee, First Cohort

Nguyen-Mei: resident of Kyri's City—caretaker for Mari, a black rose girl

Niles: cleric who became Ruarke's second-in-command upon Ward's death

Nina: North Camp Instructor, First Cohort

North Camp: One of four camps where black rose trainees are taught

Ny-nes: Land of barbarian enemies

Nyra: Levi's deceased escort

Olan: Chief Diviner for the army

Oren: Messenger for Crown Prince Thorn

Pa-sen: small village in southwestern Az-ca

Phantom: see Adahi

Pottles: Blind pot seller and friend to Sherra (see Doret)

Poul: Assassin for King Wulf (deceased)

Querl: Army deserter and Merrin's chief ally

Reena: Former washout

Reva: escort who, with her warrior, deserted the army and joined with Merrin

Romma: Resident of Dar-den, mother of Mari, a black rose girl

Names of Characters and Places Appearing in this Book:

Ruarke: Chief Cleric of Ny-nes, and Kaakos' second-in-command

Secondary Camp: Location for final escort training after warriors are chosen

Sherra: Black Rose trainee from Merthis. Bonded to Thorn Wulfson Kerok Rex; Doret considers her an adopted daughter

Tera: North Camp trainee—Sixth Cohort

The Rose Mark: a forbidden book. That decision was overturned by Crown Prince Thorn, and copies were provided to all trainees.

Thorn's Book of Advanced Divination Techniques: a forbidden book

Ura: North Camp trainee and one of the Bulldog's pets

Vale: Northernmost supply village for Az-ca's army

Varnon: village elder in Merthis

Venge*:* Top General in Kaakos' army

Veri: North Camp trainee and one of the Bulldog's pets

Ward: cleric and Ruarke's second-in-command (deceased)

Welton: Chief Physician, military post

Wend: North Camp Trainee, Sixth Cohort

Wendal: Assassin for King Wulf (deceased)

Weren: Former Colonel and warrior trainee instructor. Becomes General of the army

West Cana: area where Kyri's City is located

Willa: escort bonded to warrior Narvin. She and her warrior deserted the army to follow Merrin

Wulf Tadson Ruarke Rex: see Ruarke

Yasa: AKA Bulldog, or the Bulldog